<u>Special Thanks:</u>

To Alex and Leo and Max—Merry First Christmas, Max! я тебя люблю!

To my family—I love you!

To Stacia—Not only my editor but a best friend as well.

D1525641

SLEIGH ALL DAY

First edition. September 21, 2021.

Written by Gina LaManna.

Happy Holiday season to my readers :)

Blurb

When Detective Kate Rosetti is startled awake in the middle of the night by a phone call from her mother, she knows it's not good news. It turns out Kate's father, the notorious Angelo Rosetti, is missing. There are no witnesses and no leads, and with only a week to go before Christmas, Kate hopes to find her father before the holidays.

As Kate begins the hunt for Angelo Rosetti, she gets another case added to her plate at the precinct. A local man is gunned down in front of the neighborhood market. The fact that he was shot five times points to a story darker than that of a happily married suburban husband.

Kate dives headfirst into both cases, determined to wrap them up before the Christmas holiday. However, when too many coincidences begin to reveal themselves, Kate's worried the story is more twisted than she could ever imagine.

Chapter 1

"Kate, honey, wake up."

"I'm awake now, Mom. What is it?" I sat up in bed and squinted at the clock. "It's one thirty in the morning. Is it Jane? What happened?"

I leapt out of bed and rushed into the hallway, skidding with the effort of moving while still half asleep. I pounded Jane's door open to see if my sister was in her room.

"What's going on, Kate?" Jane flew into a seated position in bed. "If I had a gun, I'd have shot you. Why are you barging in here in the middle of the night?"

"What happened to Jane?" my mother shouted over the phone. "Something happened to Jane too?"

"Sorry," I muttered to Jane. "Go back to sleep. False alarm."

"You need a vacation," Jane snapped back at me. "For Pete's sake. I also need to start locking my door."

I closed Jane's door behind me and slunk back to my room. My heart was pounding. Usually phone calls in the night weren't good news. Especially considering that I had a career as a homicide detective, so most of the time, phone calls after midnight meant someone was dead.

"What happened to Jane?" My mom sounded worried. "Is she home?"

"Yes, fast asleep in the bed," I said. "Well, now she's awake because I stormed the door. Do you want to tell me what's going on?"

"I didn't say anything," my mother said, sounding a little defensive. "I just said, 'Hi honey, wake up.'"

"So this is just a social call in the middle of the night? You owe me a week of free coffees for this heart attack situation."

"It's your father."

"What about Dad?"

"Well, he never came home tonight."

I hesitated for a moment. It'd been over twenty years since my mother had uttered any such phrase. They hadn't lived together since before his stint in prison, which began when I was five. It took me a moment to fully process the implication of it all. Usually, I was pretty quick to connect the puzzle pieces. However, when clues involved my parents, apparently I was much slower to interpret them.

"How would you know that?" I asked cautiously. "Last I heard, the two of you weren't living together. You know, for the last few decades."

My mother cleared her throat. "He's been staying here. You know, once in a while."

"No, Mom, I don't know. No one has kept me informed of these things."

"We didn't want to get your hopes up, honey. In case things didn't work out."

"I'm an adult. It's not like this is *The Parent Trap* or something. What you guys do is your own thing now."

"Which is why we didn't tell you. We wanted to figure things out quietly, on our own, without outside pressure."

"Does Jane know?"

"Well, yes."

I made a noise in my throat.

"It's not my fault she comes around," my mother said. "She's come over for breakfast before and found your father still here. Maybe if you swung by for no reason, you'd have seen it too."

"Point taken. Let's get back to the reason you called. Dad never came back tonight, but he was supposed to?"

"I'm worried about him, Kate."

"He's not a missing person after only a few hours. There's nothing I can legally do just yet."

"I'm not asking you to file a report. You're his daughter. There's got to be something you can do on a personal level."

I didn't feel my mother's level of concern just yet. Probably because I was a hardened, cynical cop, and my mother was still a lovely, optimistic woman despite her being double my age. My mother believed people could truly change; she believed in the best in people, and she trusted others implicitly—often to a fault.

On the other hand, I found it hard to trust anyone. I didn't believe most people really changed, at least not without a lot of concentrated effort. I knew my dad was a career criminal. I had my doubts on his being in danger just because he forgot to swing by my mother's house for a night.

"Do you know where he was tonight?" I asked. "Are you sure he was even coming over to your place? Did you try his cell phone?"

"Obviously I tried all those things, Kate. I'm not an idiot. My husband was a cop, my daughter's a cop. I'm not calling you for *funsies*."

"What do you think happened?"

"I don't know. That's why I'm on the phone with you."

"Mom, take a breath. Try to help me out. I'm gathering information."

I could almost see my mother gathering herself on the other end of the phone. I could envision her sitting in the kitchen, an unsipped cup of tea in front of her, her hands clasped around the cup for warmth while she cradled the phone between her ear and her shoulder.

"It's partially just a gut feeling. I admit that," she said. "I think something's wrong. Your father said he was going out with some friends tonight. He said he was coming over after. He's always here by midnight. He knows I lock the door after that and go to bed. I don't wait up for him anymore."

The way my mother said that last line was with pride, as if she was really putting her foot down against my father. I had to smile. It was sort of adorable.

"Do you have the names of these friends?"

"They were a few of your father's old friends from prison. One guy is named Isaac, and the other is Patrick."

"Dad still hangs out with guys from prison?"

"It's a support system. You know, like AA but for criminals."

"And hanging out with other criminals was supposed to prevent him from relapsing into a life of crime? Do you see the irony here?"

"Isaac is a lovely gentleman who is eighty-five years young, as he likes to say. Patrick goes to our church. He was only in for a few years due to a bank robbery. He wasn't even armed or anything."

"Wow. What a saint."

"He got out for good behavior," my mother said stoutly. "He's a very nice man."

"Good behavior in the prison system. Put him up for beatification."

"I don't appreciate your skepticism, Kate. I'm trying to be helpful."

"Sorry. I'm not skeptical of you. Just Dad and his intentions."

"You're not being very supportive. Your father's trying very hard. It wouldn't kill you to show him a little forgiveness. He's still your dad."

I waited a beat. "He's still my father, yes. But he was your husband too. Don't forget, Mom. I was there when he went to prison. I saw what it did to you, to our family. I grew up without a dad. He left you without a partner. You'll have to excuse me if I'm a little cynical of him getting out of prison and waltzing back into our lives like nothing happened. I can't stand the idea of him hurting you all over again, not now, not when you've got your life together, the café—you've got a lot going for yourself."

There was silence on the other end as my mother fumbled with something. She sniffed. "I love you too, honey."

"Oh, Mom. Don't go getting emotional. I'm just trying to view this like I would any other case. It's how I work. I work off facts, not gut feelings. That's all."

"Okay, well, you're right. He was meeting his buddies for a drink at Gallagher's bar. Over on Selby."

"That's a place to start. Thank you," I said. "And he was usually over by midnight if he was staying the night with you?"

"Always. He was rarely out that late at all. The only exception was if he was having a night with the guys. He knows I don't tolerate comings and goings at any hour anymore. He also knows I like to have a general sense of where he's going to be."

"You believe him? That he was with those two guys?"

"Why wouldn't I?"

I cleared my throat but ignored her question. "Great. I'll check with Isaac and Patrick, then. Do you have last names?" As my mom rattled them off, I jotted them down. "Isaac Clayborn and Patrick Hamilton, got it. Has dad been acting different lately?"

"Not really," she said. "I didn't notice anything."

"What's he been doing for work?"

"I don't know. I think he's living off his savings. We haven't combined our finances yet."

"You haven't asked how he's paying for stuff? Mom, he's a criminal. This is sort of important."

"His house is paid for." My mother sounded exasperated. "He had some cash in savings. It's not like he has much in the way of expenses. He doesn't take vacations or buy new clothes. These days, he eats most of his meals at my house. His bills are practically zilch."

"He still has to have something to get by. He can't be subsisting on nothing. Unless you're trying to tell me he stashed away a huge nest egg when he went to prison and didn't give any of it to his struggling family?"

"I'm not getting into that now," my mother said. "Your father has been spending a lot of time looking for work. He's a complicated individual. Normal jobs don't hold his attention."

"Yeah, well, lots of people suck it up so they don't have to take bribes."

"Kate."

"All right. So he's unemployed," I said. "Is there anything else I should be considering? Anyone else I should be talking to?"

"Isn't that *your* job?"

"You're not giving me a lot to go on," I said. "What do you think happened? Where do you think Dad is if you had to guess?"

"I think he's in trouble," she said. "I don't know what kind of trouble. Maybe his past caught up to him. Maybe someone he arrested years ago saw him and decided to retaliate. Maybe he ran into someone he knew in prison that was holding a grudge. I don't know. There are plenty of options."

"Plenty of options, and I have practically nowhere to start. I'm not even convinced something is wrong."

"Just look into it. Maybe nothing is wrong," my mother said, sounding both doubtful and hopeful. "Obviously that's what we're hoping for. But I can't help feeling like he's in trouble, and you know us Rosettis. If someone's in trouble, we help them out. He's family. I know you still love him. And even if you doubt that fact, you know that I love him, and I know you love me. You'll do it for me, Kate."

I glanced down at the couple of notes I'd scratched out on the pad next to my bed. I could hear how conflicted my mother was by her voice. She didn't want my father to be missing because that would mean he was in danger or that something awful had happened. At the same time, I could tell a part of her almost hoped there was a reason for his silence. If there wasn't, it would just mean that my father had stood her up again, and that was all sorts of painful in a different way.

I couldn't help but think that my father better have a good explanation for where he was tonight, and not just because he'd cost me sleep but because he'd gotten my mother's hopes up. If he brought them crashing down again by making another series of poor choices, I wasn't sure she'd be able to handle it a second time around.

"I'll look into it," I promised my mom. "Don't expect answers right away. It will take me a while to follow his trail. It always does. This is normal."

"But you're the best in the business. It shouldn't take you that long."

"Mom—"

"I know, I know. I'll try to be patient."

"Thank you," I said. "I'll call you if I find out anything."

"I love you."

"Mom," I said, "if Dad calls you—for any reason at all—I need to hear about it. No matter what he might tell you."

Another beat of silence. "I understand. Thank you, honey."

When I hung up after the conversation with my mother, I set my phone on the nightstand and lay back against my pillows. I knew there was no way I'd be getting any more sleep tonight, but seeing as the bar would be closed by the time I arrived, there was nothing for me to do until morning.

I waited a few minutes, staring at the ceiling, then hauled myself out of bed to find my father.

Chapter 2

"Feel like sharing what that middle of the night heart attack was all about?"

The next morning, I found Jane in the kitchen. She had a pot of coffee brewing and was curled up at the table in her bright yellow pajamas, thumbing through a magazine.

I headed over to the coffeepot and poured myself a mug full of the hot liquid. I poured a cup for Jane, then handed it to her. "Sorry about that. I had a heart attack, too, if it makes anything better."

"I mean, not really," Jane said. "What was it about?"

"Mom called."

"Is she okay?"

"She's fine," I said. "She's worried about Dad. Did you know he was spending nights there?"

"Yeah. For a little while now. I figured you knew too. I mean, he's always there in his pajamas when I swing by in the morning. I don't have to be Detective Kate Rosetti to put those clues together."

"Huh."

"I guess you need to start eating breakfast some more." Jane frowned. "Wait a minute, what's wrong with Dad?"

"Mom said he never came home last night. She thinks he was supposed to be there. She said she tried his phone and couldn't get ahold of him."

"Did you call him?"

"I tried last night. I couldn't sleep after I talked to Mom. There was no answer. I just tried again this morning—no answer. I've been digging into the few things I could on my computer, but I haven't turned up anything. I'm going to pay a visit to the guys he was with last night to see if they know anything."

"Weird."

"What do you think?"

"Me?" Jane looked surprised. "Why do you care?"

"You obviously have a better understanding of our parents' relationship than I do. Plus, I value your opinion. I don't really know what to make of this whole thing as it's a lot to take in at once. I trust Mom, and I want to help her out, but what if Dad's just... you know, being dad."

"He's changed. I think you need to give him a little bit of a break."

"I don't know why everyone's mad at me." I raised my hands. "I'm just trying to help. Mom called me. I'm trying to look at this case objectively, like a detective—it's the only way I can hope to figure out what went wrong. Assuming that something did go wrong."

"That's what you do," Jane said, pointing a finger in my direction. "Right there. Those little quips. Did you need to say the part about assuming something went wrong? It implies you don't trust Mom and Dad."

"This is why we're not allowed to work official cases that involve our families." I shook my head. "It's too difficult. Look, if a random stranger called me to say their husband hadn't come home in the middle of the night, and then told me the same backstory that Mom and Dad have, I'd think they were panicking preemptively. I wouldn't go file a report the next morning. I'd think maybe the guy was having an affair. Maybe he was working some sort of job he didn't want his ex-wife to know about. Maybe he had a couple too many drinks with his buddies, his phone died, and he was sleeping it off on his friend's couch."

"This isn't just anyone. This is Dad and Mom."

"That's my point exactly." I expelled a breath. "I didn't say I'm not going to help. Just that I have to look into every possible scenario—the good and the bad. I can't just assume Dad hasn't done anything wrong. Especially with his track record."

"Fine. I just think you should give him the benefit of the doubt. He was finally getting back together with Mom. They were happy. Our family was almost whole again. He wouldn't risk that."

"Again."

"What?"

"Risk it again," I said. "Because he already risked it once."

"That was a long time ago. It's different now."

"I hope so," I said. "For Mom's sake. Well, I've got to get to the office."

"It's Saturday."

"I realize that, but since I'm not reporting this as an official case yet, I've got to do a little work on my own time. Plus, I've got that stupid party tonight. Are you going?"

"You mean Mindy's bachelorette party?"

"That's what I said."

Jane gave a small smile. "I can see you're really looking forward to it."

"She didn't invite me to her engagement party. I'm sure Gem's just forced her to include me on the guest list. It's a pity invite, so I feel stupid going."

"It is not a pity invite."

"Is too. And I wouldn't go except that Gem reached out asking about it. I'd feel guilty making this an issue, so I'm going to just show up, put in some face time, and head home."

"Have you seen Gem lately?"

"I've run into him a couple of times over the last few months, but we haven't talked much. Why?"

"Just curious how he's handling the whole wedding thing." Jane bit her lip. "Never mind."

"Never mind what?" I asked, looking at the calendar Jane had taped to the fridge. "He's getting married in a week. It's just about Christmas."

"Never mind," Jane said again.

"You're lying."

"Wes isn't sure Gem is handling the wedding situation very well."

"What makes him say that?"

"It's nothing Gem's said directly." Jane looked down as if she knew she shouldn't be saying anything but couldn't quite help it. "But Wes and Alastair have been best friends for a long time. Wes can read him like a book."

I raised my hands. "I'm staying out of it. Last time I got involved, it made everyone mad. I already have one personal case to deal with. I'll leave it at that."

"Good plan," Jane said. "I'll see you tonight, then?"

I grabbed my things and waved goodbye to Jane, promising to see her later. On the way out, I hesitated, then turned and called to my sister as she poured a second cup of coffee.

"Have you noticed anything off with Dad lately?" I asked. "Was he being secretive? Disappearing for long periods of time? Hanging out with anyone odd?"

Jane shook her head. "No. I'm telling you with absolute certainty that he wouldn't have done anything to jeopardize our family. Not this time."

I left Jane in the kitchen, shrugged into my winter jacket, and pushed open the front door to my house. December in Minnesota was about the time I started cursing myself for not having the foresight to buy a house with an attached garage. Or a car with a remote starter. Or a condo in Palm Springs.

As I eased down the slippery front steps, mentally reminding myself to put some salt down when I got home from work, an image of Alastair Gem shoveling my sidewalk popped into my head. It was an unwelcome image, not one I'd intended to conjure up as I headed to the precinct, but it still made me smile. It was one of the first times I'd wondered what else I didn't know about this mystery billionaire who kept showing up in my life.

I climbed into my car and started it up, cranking the heat and giving my hands a few minutes to unfreeze so I could grasp the steering wheel. Now that man was getting married in a week to my enemy. Okay, Mindy Hartlett wasn't my enemy, but she had been a defense lawyer for some of the worst criminals this town had ever seen. She'd gotten rich by helping mobsters and the like win court cases on dumb technicalities, while I had dedicated my life to making sure my cases were tied up so neat, people like her couldn't unravel them and let killers and criminals go free.

But she made Gem happy, and at one point, I'd even thought Mindy and I had buried the hatchet between us. Though I'd never been engaged or married, I was aware of the term bridezilla, and according to Gem, Mindy had been affected by this sort of wedding-inspired virus. I only hoped for his sake that after the wedding, she returned to her regular self.

As I drove to the office, I called Russo.

"Good morning, sunshine," I said. "Enjoying a lazy Saturday morning?"

"I got home at three a.m. from the office," Jack Russo said sleepily into the phone. "I'm trying to wrap up this case, so I can make it for the wedding without having open files hanging over my head."

"Don't tell me you're having second thoughts about flying in this week. I don't think I can handle an Alastair Gem wedding without you by my side."

"You say that like there's going to be more than one."

I laughed. "Just get here, okay?"

"I wouldn't miss it. It's been almost two months since I've seen you."

"I know. I'm sorry I had to reschedule our last visit."

"You can't plan murder. I had to work that weekend anyway."

"We're a mess, aren't we?"

"I wouldn't want to be a mess with anyone else," Russo said. "What are you up to today?"

"I'm headed to the office."

"New case?"

"Sort of. Not officially."

"Okay, I'm awake and intrigued."

I told Russo about the middle of the night phone call from my mother. By the time I finished the story and had answered Russo's preliminary questions, I'd arrived at the precinct. I hung up with Jack, then glanced next door to the Seventh Street Café, the coffee shop my mother owned, and noticed her presence was missing. Through the windows, I could see Elizabeth working the front counter by herself. A ping of concern shot through me.

My mother's business was everything to her. It was her baby, her love, her passion. After my father had been hauled off to prison, my mother had been practically bereft. The one thing that had pulled her back from the ledge was a purpose: the purpose to provide for her two young daughters. The café had provided that and more. If she was avoiding going to the place she loved, a place that was practically home to her, she was even more worried about my father than I'd given her credit for.

I climbed out of the car and made my way into the office. I put on the coffeepot since I'd barely touched my first cup at home. The office was mostly empty. A few cops filtered in and out to check on things, file some paperwork, putz around on their computers. Nobody said a word to me.

I was surprised when I felt a presence behind me. A hovering, lingering presence I'd grown to recognize over the last few months. As I spun around, I knew who was there before I laid eyes on the newest member of the team.

"Chloe," I said with a curious half smile, "are you aware it's Saturday?"

Chloe was dressed in a pink tracksuit. Her hair was pulled into a ponytail, and she looked like she was ready for a day of shopping at the mall. Not a day at the precinct.

"I'm aware," she said, gesturing down at her clothes. "That's why I'm in my funsies outfit. What about you?"

"I'm just finishing up a few things."

"If this is about the paperwork from the Harding file, I sent that off to the chief last night."

"I know; I saw it," I said. "Great work. Thanks for doing that. This is actually more of a personal thing."

"Ooh, say no more," she said, easing into her seat and snapping a piece of bubblegum that matched her outfit. "An off-the-record case? My favorite kind."

I stared at her until she got the point.

"Right, Rule Number Twenty: Don't chomp gum in your ear." Chloe sat in the swivel chair at her desk, pausing to spit her gum into the trash. "Sorry."

"It's actually a bit of a personal thing."

"All the more reason you need a hand," Chloe said, not getting the picture. "It's hard to be objective when you have a personal case."

"When I say personal, I mean private."

"I'm a great confidant," Chloe argued. "Plus, I know how to keep my mouth shut."

"Unless you're chewing gum."

Chloe laughed. "Yes, my mother says the same thing. Anyway, are you sure I can't help you?"

"Trust me, it's fine. I'm not sure anything's wrong yet."

"You can't tell me these tidbits and not give me a little more," Chloe said. "How about I ride along with you?"

"What makes you think I'm going anywhere?"

"You've got your keys in your hand. You always do that thing where you flick your keys around when you're getting ready to go somewhere."

I sighed. "Chloe..."

"It's Saturday. Technically you're off the clock. I'm off the clock. Let's call it a girls' day."

"Girls' days are when you go to the mall."

"Or interview people," Chloe said. "Who is first up on our agenda?"

I got the impression that Chloe wasn't about to make things easy for me. I sighed. After the surprise I'd gotten a few months back when I'd found Chloe waiting behind my desk, my opinion of her had gradually morphed and changed. Despite her colorful tracksuits and dangling earrings and gum-chomping habit, she was a hard worker.

She never complained about staying late at the office or coming in early. She was smart and capable, and she had a way with people that sometimes even I didn't. I'd been forced to come to terms with the fact that she was a good addition to the team. I was even starting to like her, which was a surprise to everyone in the office, myself included.

"Come on," I said. "I'll explain in the car."

Chapter 3

Once we were situated in my car, I gave Chloe the same rundown I'd given Russo barely an hour before.

"Let me guess, we're off to visit your father's old prison buddies from the bar," Chloe said. "Do they know we're coming?"

I shook my head. "I wanted to catch them off guard. I'm planning on playing the part of the worried daughter, not the part where I'm a homicide detective."

"Are you telling them you're a cop?" Chloe asked. "Should I keep quiet about it?"

I glanced over at her. "I don't think anyone's going to be mistaking you for a cop today. Maybe Elle Woods, but not a cop."

"Hey, Elle Woods made for a fine lawyer."

"I'm not saying it's not a good movie."

"You like *Legally Blonde*?" Chloe swiveled her head to face me. "You surprise me every day, boss. I thought you'd throw that DVD in the trash sight unseen."

"An underdog woman shows up all the stuck-up males in her life?" I gave Chloe a small smile. "You underestimate me, Officer Marks."

Chloe grinned. "Fair point. Maybe you do have an inner Elle Woods. If you wanted me to take you shopping after—"

"Hold your horses. I don't relate to the movie that much. I'm not going to be bending and snapping anytime soon."

Still smiling, Chloe glanced out the window. We drove in silence for a few more minutes before she spoke again.

"What do you really think?" she asked. "Do you think your dad messed up and is hiding out from your mom?"

"I'm not sure. I'm trying to look at it objectively. You sound like my sister. And my mom."

"They don't think he did anything wrong?"

"No. They think he's reformed."

"You don't think so?"

"I don't need you judging me too," I said. "I get that enough from my family. Trust me."

"Hey, I understand about messed up families," Chloe said quietly. "I'm not judging you. That's why I'm asking. What do you think?"

I glanced over at Chloe, curious as to the details she'd hinted at but hadn't revealed. Maybe that was why I'd started to like her. I'd realized, belatedly, that there were a lot more layers to Chloe Marks than I'd assumed off the bat. I wondered what other secrets she was hiding, but I respected her enough not to ask.

"Honestly, I don't completely trust my dad when it comes to the law," I said. "I do think he loves my mother. I think he wants to be part of our lives again. He just has a different definition of right and wrong than I do."

"He thinks the end result can justify the means?"

I glanced over at her. "Something like that."

"The opposite of you."

I shrugged.

"You catch bad guys for a living," she said. "People who clearly broke the rules. There's not always a lot of wiggle room when it comes to the law."

"I'm learning there's a little wiggle room."

"But not much." Chloe said it like a statement. "I'm not judging. I think it's noble."

"Noble? What's that supposed to mean? You're a cop too."

"Yeah, but it's complicated."

"My dad was in prison for being a corrupt cop. How much more complicated does it get?"

"People like you don't understand."

"What do you mean, 'people like you'?"

"I'm sorry." Chloe flushed. "I think the tracksuit is getting to me. I haven't had coffee yet this morning, and I'm in Saturday mode. It's not appropriate for me to be saying these things aloud. You're my boss."

"I like you because you're honest. Don't ruin it."

Chloe shifted in her seat. "I just mean that people like you. Let me put it this way. You're like the hero of any movie."

"I'm the least likely person to be the hero of anything. But if I were, it would be a heroine, not a hero."

"I just mean you're the person in every book or movie who has a moral compass made of gold. It never wavers, not even for a second, in the face of evil. It's admirable. I'd honestly be jealous of you if I wasn't so in awe of you."

"You know I don't like brownnosing."

"I'm wearing a pink tracksuit. I'm not trying to suck up to you this morning, trust me." Chloe cleared her throat. "It's just that people like you are rare. I'm not sure if you were just born with a perfect sense of right and wrong or if you've developed it over time."

"I'd argue it's pretty simple. My dad didn't follow the rules and it ruined our family. I didn't want to follow in his footsteps."

"Maybe, though, I'd argue there are way more people who come from complicated home situations who turn out to have issues themselves."

"Oh, I have issues."

"Sure, but not the kind I'm talking about," Chloe said. "Just take it for the compliment it is, boss."

"How is it a compliment if you say *people like me* don't understand?"

"Because you don't give in to temptation. You'd arrest your own father if you found out he deserved it. Most of us aren't wired to be that good, that pure of a person."

I parked outside of Isaac Clayborn's house. I sensed the conversation with Chloe was winding to a close, and I wasn't sure how I felt about it. Everything she'd said had sounded like a compliment. When I looked into her eyes, I could tell she genuinely meant it that way. So why was I having such a hard time accepting it as a positive thing?

We made our way to the front door, and I noted I wasn't the only one in a quieter, more contemplative mood than when we'd gotten into the car. I wondered how Chloe's life could possibly be complicated. A young, high-achieving cop who snapped bubble gum and wore cotton-candy-colored clothes. What could possibly have gone wrong in her life?

My musings were cut short as I knocked on the door to the house and transferred my thoughts to business mode. Missing father or not, there was only one way I knew how to solve problems and that was to be objective and focused.

"Two beautiful women delivered to my doorstep on a Saturday morning?" An elderly man with a shock of white hair and kind eyes smiled. "Have I died and gone to heaven?"

Chloe gave a sugary-sweet laugh. "You're too cute."

"You're Isaac Clayborn?" I asked. "I'm Detective Rosetti, and this is my partner Officer Marks."

"I should've known this situation was too good to be true." Isaac winked at Chloe. "Then again, I've always found women with a badge to be attractive."

I continued, undeterred. "Can we ask you a few questions?"

"Rosetti, you said?" The man's eyes lost a bit of their sparkle as he turned to me. "You must be Angelo Rosetti's daughter."

"Yes, that's me. You can call me Kate. I'm not actually here on official police business. I wanted to ask you a few questions about my dad."

"I have a rule not to speak to the police on an empty stomach." Isaac shuffled out of his house. "I'm headed next door for my Saturday morning eggs Benedict. Susie will be cooking it up right now, and I'd hate for it to get cold. You're welcome to join me."

Isaac slipped between Chloe and I and hobbled down the front steps. For an eighty-five-year-old man, he was a rather spry individual. There was a faded, somewhat sagging tattoo visible on his lower wrist. He wore only a sweatshirt and jeans despite the freezing Christmas week temperatures.

"Here, let me take your arm," Chloe said, giving me a confused side-eye glance as she helped Isaac get his footing. "It's slippery out here."

"Beautiful and kind?" Isaac looked at Chloe. "You're a real angel."

I shuffled behind the pair as they made their way down the slippery walk. Isaac's house was in the Selby neighborhood of St. Paul. Tucked away from the fancy homes off Summit, Isaac's place was a modest single-story house with a pipsqueak of a yard that could probably be mowed in about four minutes flat. Across the street from his place was a new coffee shop. Next to his house was an old restaurant. Both were decked out in twinkling Christmas lights.

As we neared the restaurant next door, I glanced at the name above it and was surprised to recognize it. The place was called Gallagher's, and according to my mother, it was the bar where my father had come last night.

I pulled open the door to the diner-esque business and waited while Isaac greeted what felt like every single patron and staff member in the joint. It took a good eight minutes for us to get to our seats because apparently he had to inquire about everyone's daughter, mother, husband, or son on the way to his usual seat near the back.

"It's like family here," Isaac said, sliding into a booth near the bar. "I've been coming around since I learned to walk. When I made my first couple of bucks from the paper route, I spent that money on a stack of pancakes right in this very booth."

"That's amazing," Chloe said. "Have you always lived in the house next door?"

"Bought it from my parents when they moved to a nursing home. They bought it when they were first married before I was ever around."

"Impressive," I said. "You've been in this area a long time."

"Longer than even your father." Isaac eyed me knowingly. "It's changed a lot since my childhood. I'm sure you've seen the same thing happening since you were a little tyke."

"It has changed," I admitted, "It's still changing."

"Sure is," Isaac said. "Can I buy the two of you ladies coffee?"

"I'm fine," I said, and Chloe agreed. "We are actually just hoping to discuss—"

Isaac raised a hand. "I told you, not on an empty stomach. I'm a downright cranky old man when I'm hungry."

"If this is you cranky, then you're the nicest cranky man I've ever seen," Chloe said. "Where do I find someone like you who's my age?"

"A nice young woman like you, still unattached?" Isaac shook his head. "A crying shame. What's wrong with men these days?"

Chloe blushed. "Actually, that's not true. There is someone. He's an FBI agent."

"Handsome?"

"Very," Chloe said.

"Kind?"

"Very kind."

Isaac seemed to consider this, as if his opinion on the subject really mattered. "Well, I admit I'm jealous of your suitor, but I'm happy you have a good one."

Fortunately, their banter was interrupted by a woman I could only assume was Susie. She had tall hair, wide hips, and a colorful apron that fluttered around as she moved. She looked like she'd been around since about the days of Isaac's paper route too.

"How much is Isaac paying the two of you ladies for your company?" Susie winked at me and Chloe. "Blink twice if he's holding you hostage."

Isaac cackled and elbowed Susie playfully. "Don't be jealous now, honey."

"Who, me?" Susie dropped a plate on the table. "Here's your eggs Benedict. What can I get for the ladies?"

"Nothing," I said. "We're just here to keep Isaac company."

"Bring 'em both coffees," Isaac said. "They haven't had the pleasure of trying your coffee, yet, Suze. It's a crime."

Susie patted the table. "Enjoy, folks. You ladies should know you've made Isaac's day. He'll be bragging about this breakfast for a week. Usually he's in here with a couple of old gents just like himself."

Before I could ask exactly what she meant, Susie had sashayed back to the bar. I gave Isaac a few minutes to sip his coffee and tuck into his breakfast. Another server dropped off a couple of cups of coffee for Chloe and me, and I was surprised to find how perfectly delicious it tasted. This was my third try at coffee for the morning, and it was a pleasure to actually drink a cup before it went cold.

"Can we talk now?" I asked. I wanted to direct us toward business before Chloe could start another conversation about her boyfriend. "Were you here with my dad last night?"

"Sure was," Isaac said. "I see him a couple of times a month. This place is a diner most of the day, but after dinner, they dim the lights and serve beer. It's all above board. They've got their liquor license."

"I'm not here to bust the place," I said. "I'm not here to get anyone in trouble. I'm just trying to find my father."

Isaac chewed slowly. "Find him implies he's missing."

"Yep. Any idea where he might've gotten to after you met him last night?"

"No clue, but I hope you find him."

It felt almost like he was dismissing us with that statement. I glanced at Chloe, not happy with how the conversation was going. Isaac seemed completely disinterested in my father's whereabouts.

"Look, I understand you probably don't like talking to cops," Chloe blurted. "You've been in prison, right?"

Isaac looked at her curiously. "It was a while ago."

"I just mean that people who have had trouble with the law tend to get uneasy around the police." Chloe crossed her arms and leaned back in her seat. Dryly, she added, "Ask me how I know."

"A nice thing like you couldn't have been in trouble with the police," Isaac argued. "Plus, you're a cop yourself. I have to say, you don't look like a cop. No offense, but it's easier to talk to you than it is to talk to Rosetti here."

"But my dad's your friend," I said. "I'm his daughter. I'm just looking for him."

"You've got doubt in your eyes. You think he did something."

"I do not," I said, but a twinge of guilt plucked at my gut. "I'm just trying to look at this like I would any other case. I have to be objective if I want to uncover the truth about my father."

"What about family? Blood running thicker than water and all of that?"

"Look, I'm—"

"It's complicated," Chloe said, interrupting me with an apology in her eye. "Detective Rosetti is just nervous because it's her father missing. I'd be the same way if it were one of my parents. Is there anything you can tell us about last night? Was Mr. Rosetti acting strangely? Did he seem like he had somewhere to be?"

Isaac gave a small laugh. He seemed to do better focusing on Chloe. I decided to sit back and see how this situation played out. Maybe Chloe was right, and I was a little too close to the case. Or maybe my mother was right, and I wasn't loyal enough to my own family.

"That man's always got somewhere to be lately." At Chloe's prompting, Isaac continued. "I mean, he's been making amends with his wife. Ex-wife, I should say. She keeps him on a somewhat tight leash. Not that I blame her. It's good for people like us. Me and Angelo—we do well with rules."

"If that were true," I said, "don't you think you'd have avoided prison?"

Isaac ignored me. "Usually Angelo takes off around ten thirty, maybe eleven. Like I said, he wants to get home to the missus. He once got home at twelve oh five, and she locked him out. She's feisty, that one. But they love each other. It's adorable. Since then, he's never missed that midnight curfew once."

"Last night?" Chloe asked. "Was it the same routine with him leaving around ten thirty?"

"Same thing," Isaac confirmed. "I'll even bet that Susie might have his bill still. That'd say what time he clocked out. If I had to guess, though, it was around ten forty. He always asks for the bill at ten thirty on the dot. Some nights he lingers later than others. Yesterday, he just paid and left."

"Did he say where he was going?" Chloe asked. "Did you just assume he was going home?"

"I assumed he was going straight home. I can't remember if he actually said it or not. Where else would he be going?"

"That's what we're trying to figure out," Chloe said. "Can you tell us a little bit about your relationship with Mr. Rosetti? How you met him, how long you've known him, that sort of thing?"

"I met him in prison. I've been out almost five years now. We met up on the outside once we were both released. We're similar, he and I; we understand one another. Neither of us wanted to relapse. Meeting, talking with someone who gets me, helps keep us on the straight and narrow."

I found it a tiny bit humorous the fact that this eighty-five-year-old man who could barely shuffle down the sidewalk without a helping hand was worried about returning to prison. Chloe, however, nodded with grave understanding.

"Was it just the two of you who met regularly?"

"And Patrick," Isaac said. "I didn't know Patrick on the inside but Angelo did. He introduced us after Patrick was released. Patrick's a good guy, younger than both me and Angelo. He's got a wife and kids and the biggest reason of any of us not to go back. His kids are still little."

"What were you in for?" Chloe asked. "Sorry if that's personal. It's just me being curious. No judgment."

"Bank robbery. Not armed," Isaac said. "I was the best in the business. Never hurt anyone, though. I promise you that."

"And Patrick?"

"Same thing," Isaac said. "We bonded right away over our shared interests."

I cleared my throat. "So you know them pretty well, then. Did you ever get the impression my father might have—as you put it—been tempted to relapse?"

"No. He didn't relapse." Isaac shook his head. "Absolutely not a chance that's what happened."

"What makes you so sure? How can you be so convinced? It's not like he'd tell you if he was flipping to the dark side."

"He might," Isaac said. "But it's more than that. Your dad's an honest guy."

"Well, he was a known crooked cop."

"Are you sure you know every detail? Do you know the reasons behind it?" Isaac stared at me. "I'm not going to go into any more detail as that's Angelo's story to tell. I'm just saying your father isn't a bad man. He had a lot of time to think while he was in prison, watching his girls grow up from the outside. It hurt him, changed him, and he learned."

I glanced down at my cup of coffee.

"He's got a second chance right now with your mother," Isaac said, "and he wouldn't do a thing in the world to jeopardize that. Add on the relationships he's started repairing with you and Jane, and your father would die before risking his freedom for a few bucks."

"By that same logic, that would mean he should have gone home," I said, more to myself than anyone else. "If he really was concerned with upsetting my mom, then he wouldn't have risked randomly disappearing on her."

"Bingo," Isaac said. "Hence the reason your mother's worried. She knows Angelo's heart. She knows it's with her. If your father didn't go home, it wasn't a voluntary detour."

"Do you know anyone who might've wanted to hurt my father?" I asked. "Or any reason at all someone might have taken him against his will?"

Isaac shook his head. "I'm telling you that your father was on the straight and narrow."

"He might have been at one point, but he's still a Rosetti," I said. "He's got ties to the Bellini family. He still plays cards with some of his old friends. He knows things. He's in circles that I've only heard whispers about."

"You're a Rosetti as much as he is," Isaac shot back. "Does that mean you're associated with all those circles too?"

"Has he been acting differently lately?" Chloe asked. "Missed any meetings, been cagey as he talked with you guys?"

"Not that I can recall."

"Thanks for the information," I said. "We should probably talk to Patrick while it's still early."

"It's nice that you three have each other," Chloe said, sliding out of the booth. "We'll find Mr. Rosetti."

"I know you will," Isaac said, sounding completely unconcerned. "If Kate here is anything like her father, then she's the best in the business."

On the way out, I stopped by the front register, caught Susie, and paid for our coffees as well as Isaac's meal. Then we headed outside and returned to my car. Once we climbed in, I programmed the GPS coordinates for Patrick Hamilton's house before turning to face Chloe.

"That, back there." I nodded toward Gallagher's. "What was that?"

"I'm sorry," she said. "I shouldn't have interrupted you. I know it's your father's case and all, but—"

"No, I mean..." I hesitated. "What I'm trying to say is thank you."

Chloe looked surprised. "For what?"

"You have a way with people that I don't have. I don't think Isaac would've said half as much if you hadn't been there."

"You have plenty of other skills that I don't have. Plus, I'm pretty sure it was just the pink tracksuit and the little bit of cleavage I've got going that warmed him up to me."

"Gross."

Chloe laughed. "I use my God-given gifts."

I shook my head good-naturedly as I pulled away from the curb. "By the way, what'd you mean when you said you understood about being in trouble with the police?"

Chloe shrugged. "Just, you know, saying stuff to relate to the guy."

"You were making it up?"

"Sure."

But every one of my detective alarm bells were ringing. It seemed I'd stumbled on the little fact that I might have misjudged Chloe for the bubbly young woman she appeared to be. The more I learned about her, the more I was discovering I'd been wrong. I wasn't often wrong when reading people. She was an anomaly, and in some odd way, she was an anomaly that I was starting to like having by my side.

"You up for one more visit?" I asked. "I'd like to speak with this Patrick guy before we call it a day."

"You're going to call it a day?"

"I have some stupid party to go to tonight," I said. "I don't even have a good dress to wear for it."

She sucked in a breath. "Holy smokes. This is Mindy's bachelorette party, isn't it?"

"How do you know?"

"I'm trying to be a detective," Chloe said. Then she looked sheepish. "Okay, I read it on your friend Lassie's blog. She's detailing every event of the wedding. How exciting you get to be there."

"Yeah, well, it's not like you don't have fun plans this week. Honestly, a quiet visit with your boyfriend sounds more relaxing than a billionaire's wedding."

"Yeah," Chloe murmured, then she shook her head. "But just think of the *food*."

Chapter 4

The door to Patrick's home opened on the second knock. It caught me a little off guard to find his wife standing there instead of him. She looked to be at most a few years older than me. Dressed in leggings and a loose sweater, she looked peppy and fresh-faced as she greeted us with a big smile.

"Good morning. Can I help you?"

I returned her smile. "I was hoping to speak with Patrick."

"Are you..." She hesitated, then frowned. "Did he do something?"

"No, not at all," I said. "It's about my father. It seems he's disappeared, and I know Patrick was friends with him."

"You're Isaac's daughters?" She looked between us. "Oh, you're the Rosetti girls."

"I am," I said. "I'm Angelo's daughter. This is my friend Chloe Marks."

"Come on in. Patrick's just finishing up breakfast with the girls."

Chloe and I entered the house behind Patrick's wife. It was such a normal house, in such a normal suburb, with such a normal Saturday morning feel. The smell of bacon and coffee and eggs wafted through the house. We were led into a living room that was mostly neat and tidy, with a few toys scattered on the floor and one overturned couch cushion.

Patrick's wife quickly righted the cushion, then flipped off the cartoons that were rolling in the background. "I'll grab him for you. Please, make yourselves at home. Can I get you something to drink?"

I thanked her and declined. She set off toward what I presumed was the kitchen. Lively chatter was coming from behind a wall, a heated debate about which Pokémon was the most powerful. I couldn't help but smile with nostalgia at the scene.

At the door, however, Patrick's wife turned around. "Whatever you think he did, he didn't do it."

"My father?" I asked, confused.

"No, Patrick." She gave me a careful smile. "Patrick was fortunate. He got a reduced sentence and was out early for good behavior. He really did learn his lesson. There's no way he'd do anything to jeopardize his family life. He has two young girls who are counting on him, and Patrick would never, ever let them down. Not for a second time."

"Ma'am, I don't think he did anything," I said. "I'm just trying to find my own father."

She gave a single nod, but she didn't seem entirely convinced. I was willing to bet she knew we were cops even though I'd refrained from introducing myself with a badge. People like her, people like me, people like my mother and Chloe—we could almost always tell a cop from a mile away.

Patrick appeared a few minutes later. He was wearing the remnants of a pleasant smile that told me he'd been enjoying breakfast and conversation with his daughters. It hit me then that these moments were the ones I'd missed. The little conversations over Saturday morning breakfasts. The heated discussions over cartoons. The mundane moments that turned out to be the best moments of all.

I remembered flashes of times like these from before my father went to prison. I hadn't thought about them much in years because it was too much of a reminder of what could have been. There was no sense imagining what if.

"Good morning," Patrick said. "Can I help you ladies with something? Miranda said you had some questions for me."

"Hi, Patrick." I rose from my seat. "I'm Kate Rosetti. This is my friend Chloe Marks. I'm looking for my father."

"Angelo."

"Yes," I said. "I'm sorry to barge in here on a Saturday morning, but my father never made it to my mother's house last night, and she's worried. I promised her I'd check things out."

"You're a cop," he said definitively. "Is this an official investigation?"

I took a deep breath. "No, not yet. I don't technically have enough to declare him missing."

"Plus, you might be taken off the case if you were to put things on record."

Patrick obviously had a decent understanding of the system. "I'm just asking around. I'm trying to figure out if there was any foul play involved, or if my father might have had an alternative agenda."

"Nope," Patrick said. "If Angelo didn't make it home, it wasn't his choice."

"How can you be sure?"

The conversation was already feeling like an echo of the one we'd just finished with Isaac.

"He's on the straight and narrow. Trust me." Patrick's eyes flicked toward the kitchen where a burst of laughter had erupted. "That's how we bonded."

"You mean, in prison."

Patrick rubbed at his forehead. "Yes. In prison. He has two daughters and so do I."

"I'm a grown-up. You still have little girls."

"He only wanted to help me. He told me his story because he saw the similarities between us. Every decision that man makes is laced with the regret of missing out on life with his girls. You can say my situation hit home for him, and he took pity on me. Took me under his wing."

On a hunch, I asked, "Do you know what he does for money?"

"Huh?"

"For work. He's been out for a while now, and I don't know of any sort of job he's been holding down lately. Do you? How's he paying his bills?"

"I don't know. I guess he never mentioned it."

"Isn't that weird? He just magically had enough money to survive?"

"People like us..." Patrick looked concerned and stopped speaking. "Forget it."

"Sir, we're here off the record," Chloe said. "I don't want to take a father away from his girls. You seem like a nice guy. It sounds like Mr. Rosetti has helped you. If that's true, please help us now. This is not going to come back to haunt you, I promise. It's personal. There's a reason Kate didn't introduce herself using her badge."

It was odd to hear Chloe call me by my first name. It was usually Detective Rosetti or boss or something similar. But it fit this time. I knew what she was doing, and it was smart. I was learning to back off in situations like this, situations that Chloe seemed better able to navigate than me, and it seemed to be working. Patrick was softening like gum before my eyes.

He steepled his hands, glanced at Chloe, and nodded. "He has been like a guardian angel. He hooked me up with the lawyer that got me out early."

"Then what were you going to say?" I asked. "Please, I just want to find out the truth about my dad."

He nodded. "People like us, me and Isaac and your father, if we're smart, we make sure our families are taken care of. In our previous, uh, lines of work, we each made a nice sum of cash."

"You stashed some money, hypothetically, that the police never found."

"Hypothetically," Patrick confirmed. "Let's just say I've got a talent for investing. I assume your father and Isaac are the same way. That they took the same precautions I did."

"If that were true, then my dad might have a hidden nest egg of sorts he could live off?"

"It's one possibility," Patrick said cagily.

"Do you work?"

"I do. I went back to school while I was on the inside. I'm working as a personal trainer right now at the gym down the street."

"And Isaac?"

"He's eighty-five years old," Patrick said. "He's got enough money for two more lifetimes. I don't think he works. Then again, I guess you could call what he does at Gallagher's a job. It's practically a career the way he keeps up with everyone there. He's trying to get Susie to go on a date with him, has been trying for the last fifty years. Before and after he got out of prison."

I sat back at a loss of what to ask. A Christmas tree sparkled next to the fireplace. Presents were already stacked beneath it. The home was warm and inviting. It felt wrong to be here, asking these sorts of questions so close to the holidays.

"Look, I hope you find Angelo, but I don't know what happened to him," Patrick said. "Do you have any guesses?"

"You met with him last night?" I asked. "Were you at Gallagher's with my father and Isaac?"

"Yes. We meet a couple of times a month on average. It helps to get together with people who understand."

"What time did my father leave the diner last night?"

"Before eleven, for sure," Patrick said. "He always asks for the tab at ten thirty. Some days he lingers longer, but yesterday he seemed more anxious to get home. To his wife, I mean."

"Ex-wife," I said. "Still making amends."

"Ah, right."

His story matched with Isaac's. "Are there any names you can give us?" I asked. "Anything Angelo might have mentioned lately that could give you an inkling he'd stumbled across something he shouldn't have?"

There was the slightest hesitation in Patrick's voice as he contemplated his next words. I leaned forward, resting my elbows on my knees, and watched him. The way he glanced at me, he knew I'd sensed the hesitation.

"I don't know anything for sure," he said finally, "but Angelo didn't completely cut ties."

"With whom?"

"Some people from his past," Patrick said. "He encouraged me to do it. Isaac had mostly done it. But Angelo had some friends and family he was resistant to give up. I think some of them are still involved in certain...things."

"Any names?"

"He never told us names. He wouldn't have wanted us to get into trouble."

"How do you know, then?"

"He'd mention getting together with some buddies but never gave specifics on it. Both me and Isaac had told him several times he needed to let them go. But Angelo was adamant that he could handle it."

"Handle what?"

"You know, the exposure to that lifestyle," Patrick said. "Angelo thought he could handle the temptation. That he was so firm on his straight and narrow path that it didn't matter who he hung out with."

"But you both thought it was a bad idea."

"He's the one who encouraged me to completely avoid anyone from my past," Patrick said. "I've done that and don't regret it. Trust me, I have every incentive in the world to not screw up again." He gave a nod toward the voices again. "I wouldn't do anything to sacrifice my life with my family.

But people like us, me and Angelo and Isaac, the pull can be strong. It can be hard to say no to a job if the right people are asking. It's better to avoid the situation from the start."

"Do you think it's possible Angelo caved?"

Patrick shook his head. "I really don't."

"Then why are you telling me this?"

"Because you asked." Patrick sat back in his seat. "And because he's in close proximity to people who might've gotten him mixed up. Just because your father is a straight shooter doesn't mean he didn't hear something or see something that got him in trouble. That's the cost of hanging out with people like your father's friends. People like my old friends. Even the innocents get swept up sometimes."

"You're sure you don't have any names? Places?"

Patrick shook his head. "I'm sorry, but he never said. I'm sure it was his way of protecting us."

"Thanks for your time," I said. "We won't keep you any longer."

"Hey, I hope you find him. Sincerely," Patrick said. "He's a good guy. I wouldn't be where I am today without him. If you need anything else, let me know."

I nodded my thanks, then followed Chloe out of the house. We headed back to the car and climbed inside.

"To the mall?" Chloe asked.

I glanced at her quizzically. "I'm looking for my father."

"You said yourself you needed a dress for tonight."

"I don't do the mall."

"I do the mall," Chloe said. "You just come with me. C'mon. In and out in an hour."

I sighed, then turned the car on. "Chloe, I don't think—"

My phone rang, interrupting us. I answered it to find Jimmy on the other end of the line.

"You know that grocery store co-op thing with the fancy breakfast burritos?" Jimmy asked. He didn't wait for me to confirm. "We've got a body outside. I'll see you there."

"Why were we called?" I asked. "Why weren't the local cops called?"

Jimmy sniffed. "Why don't you get here and see for yourself?"

I glanced over at Chloe. "Sorry, the mall's going to have to wait."

"Can I come with you?"

"You sure you want to?"

"Of course," Chloe said. "I'm not the one who's going to end up at a billionaire's party without a dress."

Chapter 5

Chloe and I arrived on the scene some fifteen minutes later. We were back from suburbia in a neighborhood I was familiar with. I parked in the small lot outside of a co-op type grocery store with lots of signs boasting organic and fair trade and locally grown products. I shopped there as regularly as I shopped at any grocery store which, admittedly, wasn't all that often. Jimmy, however, stopped here weekly for the made-fresh breakfast burritos and coffee on his way to work.

"I'm sorry we didn't find out more about your dad," Chloe said as we climbed out of the car. "I guess, on a positive note, both guys seemed really sure that your father's disappearance wasn't voluntary."

"That's a good thing?" I raised my eyebrows at her. "At least if he ran away, I wouldn't have an off-the-books case to work, and we'd know he was safe."

"I guess. But he's a good guy. Doesn't that make you feel better?"

"I'll feel better once I prove that for sure. Once I find him."

I could tell Chloe wanted to comment on the fact that I needed proof of my father's converted nature, but I didn't want to dwell on that. We had a real, dead body before us, and I turned my attention to the case.

"Well, if you want help looking into his friends," Chloe said. "Or, you know, in picking out a dress for the wedding. Just let me know."

"When do you leave for DC again?"

"Tuesday."

"Right," I said. "Let's just see what we're dealing with today, and we'll go from there."

Chloe confirmed with a nod of her head. A more somber silence settled over us as we made our way around to the front of the building. As we turned the corner onto a tree-lined street coated in a layer of ice, I began to see Jimmy's point. It wasn't difficult to understand why the TC Task Force had been called.

The front of the building had been sprayed with bullets. A body lay in a pool of blood before the grocery store. Most of the windows along the street facing the side of the building had been shattered. Melinda and a few members from her team were already there. A few of them were digging bullets out from the boulevard or the walls. Melinda was kneeling over the body and starting her examination.

"Yikes," I said. "Whoever wanted this guy dead wasn't taking any chances on missing."

We headed over to where Jimmy was waiting for us. We checked in at the scene, then took another moment to survey the destruction before us. I was almost afraid to ask my first question.

"Did anyone get hurt?" I asked. "I mean, aside from the guy on the ground."

Jimmy shook his head. "Thank God, no. I don't know how; it's some sort of miracle. There're always people coming and going along this sidewalk. Moms, strollers... You name it. This could've been a real catastrophe."

The grocery shop was located right off West Seventh. It was a family-oriented neighborhood. Lots of pedestrians,

lots of folks walking to the store daily to grab their fresh pro-
duce and bread. How the killer had managed to isolate a single victim in this spray of bullets was, as Jimmy said, nothing
short of a miracle.

"Looks like our victim had already gone into the store," I
said, nodding toward the bag of groceries on the ground next
to him. A baguette poked out of the top along with the green
tops from a bunch of carrots. "They caught him on the way
out?"

"Yep. Guy's got his ID on him. Name is Charles Marlo."

"Anything on him yet?"

Jimmy shook his head. "Everyone's just getting here.
Melinda only beat you by a couple minutes." Jimmy did a
double take at Chloe, as if he was just noticing her standing
next to me. "How'd you get here?"

"She was with me," I said quickly. "We ran into each other at the office."

"You were at the office when I called?"

"No, it's complicated," I said. "I'm looking for my dad."

"Huh?"

"I'll tell you later. Let's go touch base with Melinda."

We approached Melinda, who was busy with her initial
assessment. She had gloves on and barely looked up as we
reached her side. She started speaking without taking her
eyes off the victim.

"Forty-two-year-old man," she said. "First glance tells me
he was hit by a minimum of five bullets. I won't know the fa-
tal shot until I get him to the lab."

"I think we can pretty well assume cause of death," I said.
"Were there any eyewitnesses?"

"None that we've found so far."

"Who called it in?"

"Someone in a car driving by," Melinda said. "There's a McDonald's down the street. A family went through the drive-through and were headed home. They stumbled across the scene as they drove past."

"What do you make of it?" I asked. "Any first impressions?"

"That someone definitely wanted him dead," Melinda said.

"Why the overkill?" I asked. "No pun intended. All I'm saying is that something like this really causes a scene, which is what got us called into the office on a Saturday in the first place. If the killer had used a single bullet, the case would've been patched through to the local cops."

"Maybe the shooter wanted to make a statement?" Jimmy mused. "He was going for style points? Who knows. I'm assuming it was a drive-by. Maybe the killer didn't want to risk coming into close contact with the victim."

"There would've probably been two people if that's true," I said. "Someone driving and someone shooting."

"There's a lot of assuming and theories going on here," Melinda said. "How about you guys let me do my job, and I'll do my best to get you more information? In the meantime, you can find out who this guy is and go from there since we have an easy ID today."

The situation was so unusual, especially in this part of town, that it was hard not to leap to different scenarios in which a shooting like this would make sense. It wasn't that St. Paul was crime free, but senseless drive-by shootings—especially of this caliber in this neighborhood—were quite rare.

"She's right," I said. "Who wants to head back to the office and start digging into Charles Marlo's history?"

Jimmy looked longingly through the shattered window. "I don't suppose they'll be getting a lot of foot traffic in there today. I'd probably be doing my duty as a Good Samaritan to go in there and take the rest of the burritos off their hands, right?"

"Burritos?" Chloe asked. "I haven't eaten anything yet, and I don't work well when hungry."

"I'll get it to go," Jimmy said. "Why don't you guys talk to the clerk and see if she saw anything while I take care of our meal?"

As Jimmy picked up a sackful of burritos, Chloe and I spent another half an hour poring over the crime scene. A chat with the frightened clerk inside the store told us that Charles had indeed already been inside the building earlier that morning. Apparently, he was a local who frequented the market several times a week.

"I work every Saturday morning," a woman named Lila told me, "and I see him religiously around this time. It's sort of funny. He always buys the same things. He comes in here about a minute after the fresh pot of coffee is brewed around eleven. It's like he knows when we brew the fresh coffee and times his visits accordingly."

"He always buys the same things?"

"Pretty much," she said. "I can't remember everything exactly, but it's the same general stuff. The basics. Potatoes, veggies, bread, milk. Some deli meat, a fresh cup of coffee, some yogurt. A pint of ice cream."

"Seems like you know him well."

"I've been working here for six years. He's been coming here for almost that entire time."

"Did you ever talk to him about personal things?" I asked. "I mean, just normal, daily conversation while he waited in line?"

"Not really. Some people just give off the vibe they're not chatty. He was one of them," Lila said. "He wasn't rude. I guess you'd say he was efficient. Polite and all, but our conversations never went beyond a random comment about the weather or whatever."

"Did he ever come in here with anyone else?"

"I never saw him with anyone. He'd sort of come in here, make his way through the store in the same pattern he always did, and then check out. Never got any creep vibes from him or anything. Just that he liked to mind his own business."

"By the way, how did he pay?"

"Always cash."

"Thanks," I said. "I appreciate it."

"That's weird," Chloe said as we turned away from the clerk. "I keep one ten-dollar bill in my car for emergencies. But I wouldn't really dream of carrying cash around in this day and age."

"It could signal something, but it might not," I said. "He was approaching middle age. It sounds like he liked to keep to the same patterns. Maybe he wasn't a fan of change and just thought paying cash was easier."

"I guess," Chloe said, "or he could be one of those people on that Dave Ramsey budget. Don't they pay with cash?"

"I have no clue," I said. "What's a budget?"

Chloe grinned. "I guess if you have no vices, like shoes, you don't have to worry about overspending."

"I have plenty of vices."

"Like what?"

"Coffee."

"Yeah, and your mom owns the coffee shop you frequent," she said. "Let me guess, even your house is paid off."

"Okay, okay, enough with the psychology lesson. Let's focus on Charles."

We met up with Jimmy and returned outside. I took another look at the body. Sure enough, I saw many of the items Lila had mentioned splayed on the sidewalk. Melting ice cream, a package of deli meat, a roll-away potato that'd made its way halfway down the block from the force of his fall.

"Anything?" I asked Melinda.

She shook her head. "We haven't found much in the way of particulates or physical evidence. We're checking the street for tire marks signaling any sort of abrupt stopping left by the vehicle, but so far we've come up empty." Melinda sat back on her heels. "Other than that, I'll confirm time of death and cause of death, and we'll see what ballistics has to say when they're finished on their end. The rest of the questions will probably have to be answered via old-fashioned detective work."

"It's almost like that's my job," I said with a faint smile. "We're going to head back, but give us a call if you find anything else."

As Chloe and I made our way back to my car, I glanced at the clock and calculated I had just a couple of hours left in my Saturday afternoon before I needed to take off and head to the bachelorette party.

When I woke up this morning, I'd thought the worst part of my day would be facing a bridezilla on too many shots of tequila. Since then, I'd gotten suckered into investigating my missing father and taking on a case of a next-to-impossible-to-solve drive-by shooting.

"So much for taking the weekend off, huh?" Chloe said as she read my mind. "Hey, boss, I can postpone my trip this week if you want."

"Don't be ridiculous." I pulled my car door open. "It's Christmas. Go, spend it with Agent Brody, and have a great time."

"But—"

"You're not canceling your trip."

"You'd do it," she said. "If the situation were reversed, you'd cancel your trip."

"Yeah, well it's my dad who's missing, not yours."

"I'm just saying."

"Do you want to go out to DC?"

"Yes," Chloe said. "Of course. I miss my big, handsome fed. It's been a few weeks since we've seen each other. I'm sure you know how that goes."

"Go, Chloe. I promise, you won't be missing anything here. It's nothing Jimmy and I can't handle."

Chapter 6

An hour later, the precinct was as quiet as when we'd first arrived. Aside from our drive-by-shooting case, it had been a quiet Saturday in the Twin Cities, and most of the detectives were taking the weekend off. The only difference from earlier this morning was the faint smell of greasy burritos from the bag Jimmy had dumped on the table in the center of the room.

Chloe, Jimmy, and I each sat quietly at our computers, sifting through any information we could find on Charles Marlo. Asha had dragged herself into the office as well, back early from a day skiing at Afton Alps, to assist on the case. So far, nobody had turned up anything that might suggest why Charles Marlo had been the target of such a vicious shooting.

"I've confirmed his address from the driver's license," Asha said, appearing before my desk. "He lived in an apartment a few blocks away from the co-op. He's rented it out for the last eight years. Before that, he was living in Atlanta."

"Georgia?"

"That would be the one," she said. "I lose his trail there."

"What do you mean you lose his trail?"

"I mean, I'll find it eventually." Asha sounded annoyed, and I was betting she wasn't thrilled about giving up a day of skiing to sit behind her desk. "I'm just giving you what I've got so far. He was single, not married. I also can't find any family to notify."

"Either he lives a lonely life, or there's something funny happening here."

"It better be something funny to call me off the slopes. I'm going to get back to it, and with any luck, I'll be able to hit an afternoon run. Are you going to check out his place?"

I glanced over at Jimmy. "You want to go?"

Jimmy was already grabbing his keys. Chloe looked torn between staying to assist Asha and wanting to come with us. I put her out of her misery and instructed her to stay back and help Asha with the technology side of things. Chloe had already proven she had a knack for it.

"If you don't watch out," Jimmy said as we left the building, "Chloe's going to quit as your assistant and go join Asha."

"I wouldn't blame her." I flipped my keys around. "Asha's easier to work with than me."

"I'm not sure that's true. Asha scares me."

"She scares me too, but for some reason, she and Chloe seem to click. It's like Chloe's brain works in the same way hers does."

"What about you and Chloe? Do you click?"

I thought back to yet another eye-opening morning with Chloe. It was barely midafternoon, and already, the search for my father seemed to have taken place years ago. I hated to admit it, but my father's missing status had gotten pushed to the back of my mind by our newest case. In my defense, a body riddled with bullets outside of my local grocery store was pretty distracting.

"She can be helpful."

"That's pretty much a five-star recommendation coming from you," Jimmy said. "I'd hate to hear what you say about me when I'm not around. Chloe's faster than me; she's definitely prettier than me; she's nicer than me. Frankly, I'm surprised you haven't given me the boot yet."

"All in good time, grasshopper."

Jimmy opened the door to his car and slid behind the steering wheel. I joined him on the other side, and we made the drive to the address listed for Charles Marlo. His apartment complex blended into the buildings around it. There was a simple buzz-in code on the front door, but apparently it was our lucky day because someone held the door open for us on the way in, letting us bypass the security panel.

Jimmy and I made our way to the receptionist. A woman in her thirties sat behind the desk. She wore bright pink lipstick and had long, black hair. I introduced myself and Jimmy, showed her my badge, and a quick conversation later, she'd volunteered to let us in Charles's apartment.

"He's dead?" she said. "I can't believe it. Then again, it's not like I know him at all."

"Do you know most of the people who live here?" I asked the woman who'd identified herself as Cindy. "Do you work a regular schedule here?"

"Yeah. I work nights at a bar down the street. I get a discount on rent if I sit at the front desk and watch Netflix during the day. It's easy enough to do. I work three days a week, which is regular enough to see most people who live here coming and going at some point."

"Did you ever see Charles coming in or out?"

"Maybe, like, once?" she said. "I mean, either the guy's a vampire and is coming and going at odd hours, or he's a complete recluse."

"That's odd."

"Right? I mean, how did the guy get his food? He'd need groceries delivered or something, and he never had any deliveries. I mean, not a single one. Okay, I take that back. A courier once delivered something here for him, and the only reason I remember that is because I thought it was so quaint." She brushed a strand of black hair away from her face. "I mean, what are we living in, ancient Rome? Who uses couriers anymore?"

"Did this courier package arrive a long time ago or fairly recently?"

"It had to have been a few months back now."

"Did you give it to him in person?"

"Nah. It didn't come until the end of my shift. I passed it off to the building manager, a guy named Ricardo, and I assume he passed it along. The next time I worked, there were no outstanding packages for me to get to residents, so it'd gone to someone."

"Do you remember who it was from? Either the name on the label or the courier service who delivered it?"

"Now that you mention it, I don't think the courier gave a name, and I don't even think he was wearing a uniform. The actual package was wrapped in parchment and tied with string. It really looked cute. Sorry, I don't really remember more about it. I get so many packages through here that even if I peep at the names on the front, I don't remember them all."

"I understand. I can never remember what I ate for breakfast."

"This is it." She unlocked the door. "You guys are legit cops, right?"

I pulled out my badge for a second time. That seemed to help set her at ease.

"So it's okay that I'm letting you in here? Because I'm not sure how that all works. I'm not, like, invading his privacy, am I?"

"Charles is dead," I said. "And it's imperative we get as much information out of his apartment as soon as possible. If you don't cooperate, we'll just call your boss, get a warrant, and be back shortly. But we'll be a lot less happy about it."

"I mean, if the guy's dead, he can hardly object." Cindy pushed the door open. "If my boss asks about this, make sure he knows I was only trying to do my job."

Jimmy gave her an assured nod. "You're cooperating on a very important police investigation. Your help is much appreciated, and we will be happy to vouch for you."

Seemingly satisfied, Cindy gestured for us to head inside. "How long do you guys need?"

"About half an hour," I said. "We can let you know on the way out when we're done, so you can lock up."

"Sounds good. I'm not supposed to abandon my post."

As Cindy returned to the front desk, I turned my attention to the apartment before us. I felt my lips part in surprise.

"Yeah," Jimmy said quietly, "about that. I don't think we're going to need a half an hour."

The apartment registered to Charles Marlo was, in a word, threadbare. Even that was generous. His personal space looked like a furnished motel room that had recently been cleaned top to bottom by hotel staff. There wasn't a single photograph anywhere. Not a single item hung from the walls. No decorations whatsoever.

While the lack of decorations might not have been that strange for a single male, there were certain things that should theoretically be in any apartment that was being actively lived in. A coat in the coat closet or a pair of shoes or slippers by the door. There wasn't so much as a key bowl in the entryway.

"Why do I get the feeling that this place has been completely cleaned out?" I asked. "I mean, *completely* cleaned out?"

"Except I wouldn't use the word clean." Jimmy ran a finger pointedly over a counter that separated an open kitchen from the living room. "My wife would have a heart attack if there was ever a layer of dirt this thick in our living room."

I began poking around in the kitchen. The drawers were mostly empty. The cupboards held a pathetic smattering of cups and mugs that were equally as dusty as the countertop. I opened the fridge and found it bare. Not the sort of "I've been out of town" bare, where there was a bottle of expired milk and a few packets of ketchup on the shelf, but completely empty. Spotless, not even a ring from an old water bottle.

"It's almost like he was never here." I made my way to the bedroom and poked my head inside. There was a plain bed with equally plain sheets made up perfectly.

I stepped farther inside the bedroom and found that the simple dresser set and nightstands were all empty. When I tried to turn a light on, the bulb sparked and went out. I made my way to the bathroom. Not a tube of toothpaste or a toothbrush in sight. Not a streak on the sink from someone washing their hands and dripping water onto the countertop.

When I returned to the kitchen, I found Jimmy sitting on the edge of an unused couch, a mystified look on his face.

"It doesn't add up," I said. "I mean, even if there was some bizarre explanation for this empty apartment, it doesn't make sense with his grocery-buying habits. A guy who buys whole potatoes and bunches of carrots? The dude would need a vegetable peeler at least and probably a pan to roast them on."

"That's what you're taking away from all this?" Jimmy gave me a funny look.

"I'm just saying, we have it confirmed that the guy walked to the grocery store and walked back a couple of times a week. The stuff he bought is stuff he needed to cook. So where was he going with it? Who was he bringing it to if not here? He died suddenly, unexpectedly, so his living space should show some semblance of disarray. He expected to come home."

"I agree with you."

"Could the guy have another place in the area?" I asked. "Why keep paying the rent on two places?"

"I'm guessing he didn't want to be found," Jimmy said. "This is the place that's been registered to Charles Marlo for, what, years? That's a long time to pay rent on an apartment where you don't even stop to brush your teeth. The only reason I can think of for someone keeping a secret apartment like this is if he was meeting someone here."

"Like having an affair?"

"Something of that sort of clandestine nature. But this place doesn't exactly scream romance. Not to mention, wouldn't there be a bottle of wine or something? I don't get the impression this is some secret lover's den."

"Me neither. I don't know what to make of it yet."

"Agreed. Should we get going? Maybe we can complain to Asha about it, and she can pull another miracle out of that computer screen of hers to give us an idea of what might be happening here."

"It's bothering me because of how strange this all is." I took one more spin around the place and came to the same conclusion. "This guy was carrying a wallet that contained identification to a guy named Charles Marlo. Charles Marlo existed; he had a history, an address. It's a full identity. Not just a fake ID. Asha admitted there was something a little funny about it, but I figured that was just because his history trailed off before Atlanta. I thought maybe he'd been in foster care or something, and she would just have to work a little harder to track down his early past."

"There's no doubt the guy was trying to hide something," Jimmy said. "You don't carry fake ID to a fake life if you're a regular Joe Schmo going about your business. Why the fake ID? The fake life?"

"Protecting someone? Maybe Melinda will be able to find something on the autopsy. Maybe his DNA will turn up a match in the system that's different than his assumed identity."

"You ready to go?" .

"Give me a few more minutes," I said, still frustrated that none of this was making sense. "I want to take one last look around."

Jimmy began poking through the kitchen while I returned to the bedroom. I thumbed through the drawers again, peeked in the closet. Then I returned to the bathroom and checked all the usual hiding places, just in case. Nothing.

But something wasn't sitting right in my brain. Something I'd seen was niggling in the back of my head. I retraced my steps one more time and figured out what was bothering me, when I pulled open the closet.

"Jimmy, come here."

Jimmy lumbered into the bedroom.

I pointed to what I found. "See anything weird about this?"

Jimmy peered around me to look inside. He frowned. Then he took another look, and finally, he did a double take. "That's a false back on the closet."

I knocked against it, and sure enough, a hollow sound echoed around us. I wouldn't have noticed it except that the closet had seemed exceptionally shallow to me. A glance at it, and I'd wondered how anyone was supposed to fit any clothes in there. After taking a step back, I'd realized that the rear wall of the closet was a good foot closer to me than the rest of the walls around it.

I fumbled against the false back for a minute, and eventually found the latch to release it. Jimmy pulled up the flashlight on his phone and shined it over my shoulder as I pulled out a panel to expose Charles Marlos's secret hiding place. I ducked my head lower and swept away cobwebs from the little-used hidey-hole. A moment later, I pulled my head back out.

"Well, I guess I know why the guy kept this place."

Jimmy beckoned me to step aside. He stuck his head in and immediately pulled it out, his eyes wide as saucers. He cursed under his breath.

"That's a lot of cash," he said. "I've got half a mind to start loading up a few duffel bags and retire tomorrow."

I glared at him.

"Right. Sorry. Bad joke, considering present company." He winked at me.

I shook my head but wasn't offended. Only Jimmy could get away with teasing me about my dad and his rickety track record with illegal money shoved into duffel bags.

"That's not all." I pulled out a pair of gloves and snapped them over my fingers. Gingerly, I reached back in the compartment and pulled out the first of several guns. When I returned my gaze to Jimmy, I shrugged. "I think it's fair to say that Charles Marlo wasn't exactly who he claimed to be."

"I agree," Jimmy said. "But where in the world was he taking those carrots?"

Chapter 7

An hour later, Jimmy and I were back at the precinct. We'd dispatched a team to Charles Marlo's apartment with a proper warrant to collect the money and guns. The team would also be scouring the place for DNA and fingerprints, but I doubted they'd find anything of use.

Chloe and Asha had their heads bent together at the computer when I finally made it over to check on them. I told both women about the find at the empty apartment and asked what they made of it.

"You're not going to like this, babe," Asha said, looking at me. "But we are running into a brick wall on this Charles Marlo guy."

"What sort of brick wall?"

Asha stepped back from her computer. "I can follow this guy back to Atlanta pretty easily. After that, things turn pretty vague. From what I can tell, this Charles Marlo guy supposedly grew up in Florida. His parents are dead, and he has no living relatives. Legend has it that he attained a high school diploma, then went on to work as a mechanic. No college degree."

"Okay, so Charles Marlo isn't a fake identity?"

Asha shook her head. "On the contrary. I don't think Charles Marlo ever existed before Atlanta."

"I rarely see you so annoyed. Or so stumped."

"Correct." Asha ran a hand through her hair. "The only time I'm ever blocked this hard is when I'm dealing with one thing."

I expelled a harsh breath. "Witness protection."

Asha nodded.

"Crap," I said. "Any chance you'll be able to get into his official file?"

"You'll have better luck talking to your pal Russo and trying to get him to pull a few strings," Asha said. "I'm good, but these guys have an army of people working with them. They dedicate their careers to making people vanish successfully. They're *really* good."

I sighed. "Well, this does give us more of a motive, then."

"How do you figure?" Chloe asked.

"If he was in witness protection, it was because he was in danger and the government was willing to protect him. He might have been involved with the mob and flipped, or he could've testified in a big drug trial, or any number of things."

"So you think this might be revenge," Chloe said. "I suppose that makes sense if someone was able to discover his real identity. It could explain the brutal nature of the killing—a murderer who'd been mad for a long, long time."

"From what I can tell, he's been protected for about fifteen years, give or take," Asha said. "Chloe and I have already started looking into huge cases and trials during that time, but honestly, it's a crapshoot and probably a waste of time. We'd have to get extremely lucky to randomly guess what he was a part of back then."

"I understand," I said. "Don't spend too much time on it. With Charles Marlo being dead, we should be able to get a peek into his official file. It's not like someone can expose him all over again."

Chloe cleared her throat. "Detective, can I talk to you for a moment?"

"Uh, sure."

I followed Chloe as she walked stiffly out of the room and into the hallway. She made her way to the conference room, pushed the door open, and let me enter first. We took seats next to each other at the table.

"What is it?" I asked Chloe. "Everything okay?"

"I was wondering if you might have considered the fact that this might be related to the, um, other thing."

"The other thing?"

"I mean, from this morning..." Chloe was obviously very hesitant to say exactly what was on her mind. "Your dad's disappearance."

"You mean the shooting of Charles Marlo?" I gave her a mystified look. "How would that be connected?"

"I'm not trying to imply anything. I'm simply looking at the timing of things, and you've told me time and time again that coincidences don't exist."

"Okay."

"Your dad vanishes one night out of the blue, and the next day, someone who may or may not be related to the mob is shot dead?"

My shoulders stiffened. "Are you saying you think my father was the shooter? You think he sprayed bullets on a pedestrian-laden sidewalk?"

"No one else got hurt. Maybe this Charles Marlo guy was a major snitch. Maybe he killed someone. Maybe the killer thought they were doing the world a favor getting rid of him."

"My father is not a killer," I said. "He's a crooked cop, sure, but murdering an innocent person is a step too far, even for my father. I thought you were the one who was telling me that I should believe my family and believe my dad had changed and all that psychobabble."

"People like him, they have a code of honor," Chloe insisted. "Like I was saying, maybe Charles Marlo wasn't as innocent as you think."

"That still doesn't justify murdering him."

"What if Charles was a killer for the mob? What if he killed someone close to your father back in the day, then when he was caught, he squealed like a pig?" Chloe's eyes lit up with intensity as she explained her theory. "I can imagine how it'd be difficult to watch a person like that be allowed to live a normal life while your father—and others—were thrown in prison for much lesser crimes."

"We don't know that Charles killed anyone," I said. "This is all complete speculation. He could've been some sort of informant or something."

"I agree, but don't you think the timing is strange?"

"What are you suggesting? That my father randomly took off in the middle of the night and then murdered someone the next day? Why would he have left the night before?"

"I haven't figured it out completely. I'm just throwing a few theories out there that might be worth considering. I think we need to acknowledge the fact that it might be possible your father caught wind of Charles Marlo's real identity and took action on it."

"Caught wind of it?"

"It was implied that your father still has his ear to the ground in some of his old circles when we talked to Patrick and Isaac. Even if your father wasn't planning on doing anything to break the law, don't you think there could be a unique situation where he heard about this guy in town and found it impossible not to act?"

I didn't answer. The theory was so wild I couldn't quite get a grasp on it.

"Maybe it wasn't even completely your father's fault," she said. "You guessed yourself that there was more than one person involved. Maybe your father was the driver and someone else was the shooter."

"You say that like it makes things sound better."

"I'm just saying—"

"Thanks, Chloe." I stood. "You've said plenty."

"I'm sorry, Kate. I just—"

"It's Detective Rosetti," I corrected her as I made my way to the door. "I'd appreciate you staying out of my personal business."

"But if your father is linked to the case, then it's not personal anymore."

"It's *not* linked," I said. "My father's not even technically missing, remember? I confided in you about that off the record."

"But if he was at all involved—"

"If we find out my father might have been involved, then you should know I'd be the first to arrest him." I stalked out of the room, pulling the door shut hard behind me.

I headed into the office and quickly said goodbye to Jimmy. He'd been chatting with Asha, getting caught up on the witness protection issue.

"I'll call Russo," I said. "I'll see if he can pull any strings. In the meantime, I've got a bachelorette party to get to."

"I thought you were dreading going."

"Yeah, well, we're stuck here, aren't we?" I sounded snappish even to my own ears. "Sorry, it's been a long day. I'll see you all tomorrow. Call me if anything turns up."

Then I made my way out of the building and down to my car. As I drove toward home to shove myself into a too-tight dress, I let my mind wander to the conversation with Chloe in the interview room.

I didn't want to admit it, but I was having a hard time deciding if the reason I'd been so upset at her theory about a connection between Charles Marlo and my father was because it was outlandish... or because I'd already wondered the very same thing.

***

"I can ask around for you," Russo said, "but I can't promise much. The witness protection team is notoriously tight lipped."

"But the guy is dead," I said. "Nobody's going to come after him a second time."

"It's a matter of principle. They've got rules coming out the wazoo over there," Jack said. "It's not like I can just give them a call, sweet talk them with my manly charms, and they'll open their files for me."

I grinned in the mirror and adjusted the stupid red dress that I was planning to wear to Mindy's bachelorette party. "If it's any solace, your manly charms work on me."

"Hold that thought for a few more days. I can't wait to see you."

"Ugh. Me too. What a day. It feels like a week crammed into twelve hours, and it's not even over."

"Surely a bachelorette party can't be that much of a drag. Have a glass of wine or two. Maybe it'll loosen you up a little and give you a break from everything on your plate," Jack suggested. "Maybe it's just what the doctor ordered."

"I can guarantee you this is not any prescription I'm interested in taking."

"Try to have some fun. What are you guys doing?"

"I don't know. The event is being held at one of Gem's clubs. Drinking? Dancing? I haven't been to a bachelorette party in years, and even then, it was for my cousin Louisa who was six months pregnant at the time, so it wasn't exactly a wild party."

Jack laughed. "Any progress on your father's situation?"

"Not unless you count me getting ticked off at the intern because she implied my father might be involved with the shooting."

"Ouch. You haven't called Chloe 'the intern' in weeks."

"Well, I'm mad. She was the one all morning talking about stuff like family loyalty, and how I should believe the best in my dad, and how he might have really changed. Then she goes and suggests he might have murdered this guy."

"Had the thought crossed your mind before she said it?"

"Maybe. Which makes me even more mad."

Jack made a sympathetic sound in his throat. "I'm sorry, Kate. No word from your father?"

"None. I talked to my mother right before I called you, and she's convinced he's dead. She's losing her mind with worry."

"You didn't tell her your theory, did you?"

"About him reverting to a life of crime? No. I'm not that stupid."

"I wasn't implying you were stupid. Just honest."

"Even I knew better than to suggest that theory to my mom. Anyway, I need to finish getting ready. I just wanted to hear your voice."

"I love you. Have some fun tonight."

I disconnected, then made my way downstairs. The house was empty. Jane had texted she'd be going straight to the party from her boyfriend's house. For a while now, Jane had been talking about moving out and getting her own place. Over the last couple of months, though, she'd slowly stopped talking about it, and I hadn't asked.

I'd actually grown used to her living with me. The house was quiet when she wasn't around. But secretly, I knew I had nothing to do with the reason she'd stopped apartment hunting. She was simply waiting for Wes to ask her to move in with him instead of getting her own lease.

Everyone around me was getting married and moving on with their lives. Gem, Mindy, my sister, Wes... Even Chloe and Agent Brody were getting all hot and heavy in their budding relationship. Chloe had seen Agent Brody more in the last three months than I'd seen Russo in the last six. Asha had been quietly dating someone on the side even though she didn't talk much about it. And judging by the way Lassie had suddenly disappeared off the face of the earth for the last two months, she probably had a new guy on her arm too. Which left me wondering if I'd ever feel ready to take the next step with Russo.

Chapter 8

I drove to the Minneapolis club owned by Alastair Gem and left my car with the complimentary valet. I was ushered straight inside and upstairs to the VIP section, which was completely shut down for the bachelorette party.

I made my way inside of the roped-off area once my name had been cleared by security and my ID checked. The whole situation gave me the eerie feeling of arriving at a crime scene to check in. There were lots of flashing lights; none of the public was allowed to get close to the action, and people inside hung together in close-knit groups. All that was missing was a dead body.

The second I got inside, I wished I'd found a reason to stay home. No part of me wanted to be here, surrounded by Mindy's lawyer pals and a slew of her other rich friends. The dresses the women were wearing were gorgeous and elegant and very obviously expensive. There were no inappropriate-shaped lollipops or goofy-colored Jell-O shots at this bachelorette party. Instead, there was caviar and top-shelf champagne. If these women were going to have a wild night, it was going to be because they'd had too much Dom Pérignon to drink—not because they'd broken out the Jose Cuervo.

I hung back for a moment to get my bearings. Mindy was easy to spot. She had a tiara on her head that was sparkly enough to make me wonder if the diamonds on it were real. She wore a midi-length, white dress with fluttery sleeves and plenty of cleavage, and she looked absolutely stunning.

Jane, however, was nowhere to be seen. Which was unfortunate since she was the only person I had a hope of knowing here. It wasn't like I could wander up to a group of these women and bond over our commonalities. They probably talked about things like their newest vacation home or their latest trip to the Italian countryside. They probably wouldn't react kindly if I started talking about time of death calculations and tox-screen results.

My heart leapt out of my chest as I felt a hand on my shoulder. I spun around and found my sister had crept up behind me. I'd missed her approach because of the overbearing music thrumming along in the background.

"You hunt hardened criminals for a living," Jane said with a grin, "but you flinch at a bachelorette party when someone comes up to say hello?"

"I'd argue this sort of party is far more terrifying than a crime scene."

Jane laughed, but it was cut short as she looked into my eyes. "Any news about Dad?"

"Nothing concrete. You know I'd have called you if I heard anything."

"Are you at least convinced he's officially missing?"

"I'm getting there."

"Getting there?" Jane crooked an eyebrow. "You're not telling me something."

"It's just that I've got another case at the moment, and I have to wonder if Dad's disappearance is somehow related to this new development."

"What do you mean? You think Dad was involved in some sort of crime?"

"It's not some sort of crime. It's a murder."

"Dad would never murder an innocent person. Ever. He might shoot at someone if he were a cop, and the criminal was fleeing or something, but as a civilian? Not a chance."

"What if the victim wasn't innocent?"

"Kate, don't be ridiculous. Dad's not some vigilante hunter. He's just trying to get his life back on track. There's no way he'd be running around shooting people. He knows that would jeopardize his chances of ever being a real part of our family again.

"It's a leap, but I have to explore every possibility," I admitted. "I wouldn't have even thought about it if the timing wasn't so close. If Dad was involved, it could explain why he might have disappeared."

"I don't buy it. You haven't seen him and Mom together lately. I could tell that Mom was dreaming of marriage all over again. A ring on her finger, wedding vows exchanged, the whole thing. They were serious."

"That's all Mom, though," I said. "Dad already had that once and gave it up."

"He had his reasons. Just because you can't forgive him doesn't mean he wasn't trying to do the right thing for our family."

"He broke the law."

"This isn't about twenty years ago," Jane said. "This is about right now. Dad has changed. He's a new person. He's been through prison; he's lost his family, and he's starting to get them back again. Dad's not a killer. He was taken against his will. Save yourself some time and just trust me."

"If only my job worked like that."

"C'mon, let's let this go for now," she said. "I know you'll probably only stick around here for twenty minutes. You might as well try to have some fun while it lasts. At least get a glass of the champagne. It's good stuff."

I waited as Jane swooped over to a nearby server circling the room and swiped a glass off his tray. She handed me one, and before I could argue, she clinked her glass in a cheers. I took a sip, thinking the liquid confidence could only help as I prepared to face the bride and give her my happiest wishes.

No sooner had Jane and I finished our first glass of champagne did that moment come. Jane had ducked away to scrounge up a refill for us when I felt a presence behind my left shoulder. I spun around to find Mindy standing before me.

Her eyes were a little glazy and unfocused. Her tiara tipped a little to one side. Someone had draped a sash over her body that read Bride-to-Be. It was the only cheap thing at the party. She gave me a smile.

"I'm glad you could make it." Mindy gave a little wobble on her high heels.

"Thanks for the invitation," I said. "I didn't want to interrupt earlier when I saw you talking to a few other women, but I did want to pass along my happiest wishes. You and Gem make an incredible couple."

"Yeah, thanks."

Mindy didn't sound entirely convinced. I saw her eyes flick over her shoulder. "Wanna get out of here for a minute?"

"Excuse me?"

I sure wanted to get away from the dim lights and thrumming music, but this was Mindy's party. It didn't seem exactly appropriate for me to ditch out in the middle of it, let alone the future bride.

"Just for a minute." Mindy looped an arm through mine and dragged me through the crowd toward the back of the room. "I know a place."

Mindy was clearly on a mission, and I was powerless to stop her. I caught Jane's quizzical gaze as I was ushered out of the room and raised my shoulders helplessly back at her. Just before we passed through the back door of the VIP section, Mindy grabbed an entire bottle of champagne from a passing server. The man frowned and made an effort to stop her, but Mindy just raised a hand.

"I'm the bride," she said. "I paid for this."

Mindy grabbed a thick fur coat that I presumed was hers, from the back of a chair, then led me outside through a narrow fire escape. By the time she finally stopped moving, I realized we were on the very top of the building.

The roof of Gem's club was flat and easy to navigate, and the part to which Mindy led me was a smaller, raised platform offset from the rest. There was hardly any snow on the ground, making it easy to weave our way to her seating spot of choice. She climbed up, plopped herself down, and inadvertently dusted a spec of dirt from her white dress. We were protected from the wind in our little nook, and to my surprise, the cold wasn't as bad as I'd expected it to be.

She patted the ground next to her. Then she took a swig from the champagne bottle and handed it my way.

"I drove," I said. "I already had a glass. I should hold off."

Mindy just stared at me. "You drove yourself to a bachelorette party? That's sad."

"Sad?"

"You weren't planning to have too much to drink? To take a shot from between someone's boobs? To dance on a table?"

"The invitation didn't exactly cover that stuff. I had an inkling this was sort of a classier affair than most bachelorette parties."

Mindy gave a huge eye roll. "Probably would've been more fun if it was the other kind."

"You're not enjoying your party?"

"The best part is the champagne and the excuse to drink too much of it," she said. "None of these people are my real friends. There are some work colleagues floating around downstairs, one or two obligatory family invites—I mean, you're here. It's not like we're best buds."

I wrinkled my nose. "I'm sorry? I thought I had an invitation—"

"Sorry," Mindy said with a sigh. "I shouldn't have said that. I started drinking early and didn't have anything to eat."

"How about I get you a hot dog or something?"

"A hot dog." Mindy started laughing, and she continued to laugh until it reached almost hysterical levels. She wiped a tear from the corner of her eye. "I haven't eaten an ounce of fat in almost three months."

"That sounds unhealthy."

"It's a superlative," Mindy said. "I'm allowed some avocado. No cheese, very little dairy, forget about sweetener in my coffee."

"Who makes these rules about what you're allowed to eat?"

"My nutritionist. I've got to fit into my wedding dress."

"If my nutritionist told me not to put milk in my coffee, I'd probably pull out my gun and shoot her. I'd voluntarily turn in my badge."

Mindy burst out laughing. A genuine laugh this time, not the crazed version she'd let out a few minutes before. "You're funny. It's weird, as much as I dislike you, I also really like you."

"You're very honest tonight."

"I probably won't remember it tomorrow, so I should apologize now." Mindy didn't sound sorry at all. "It's the alcohol."

"I'm not surprised it hit you so hard. It sounds like you've been starved for months."

"Damn wedding."

"If this is what it takes to get married, I'm never going to be able to do it," I confessed. "That sounds ridiculous."

"Some people don't do it like this," Mindy said. "But when you marry Alastair Gem, you've got to do it right, you know? The blogs already speculate that I'm pregnant. I don't need a little pooch from eating too many hamburgers to ignite the rumors."

"Why do you care about what anyone else thinks? Your wedding should be about you and Gem. The rest is no one else's business."

"You're so logical."

It seemed like the words could be a compliment, but Mindy's tone didn't sound like she thought so. She said it as if my being logical was exasperating to her. I debated apologizing again, but I couldn't for the life of me figure out what to apologize for this time.

"Can I ask you a question?" I asked. "Why don't you like me? I thought we were fine. I mean, after that case where you were kidnapped, we hung out together at Wes's cabin. The next thing I know, I'm causing problems just by being at your engagement party."

"It's not your fault. I just don't really like you."

"Is it because I'm a cop?"

"It doesn't help," Mindy said. "But I can get over that."

"Then what is it?"

"It's you and Alastair." She glanced over at me. "You hold a place in his life that I will never hold."

"What, a detective who has investigated him for murder?"

"Honestly, I don't know what it is. In some ways, I get it. I really do. I like you, even though I shouldn't. We work on almost opposite sides of the law. You have a history with my fiancé. In no world should we be friends, yet here I am, sitting on the roof of my bachelorette party relieved to be talking to you."

"Okay."

"You're honest," she continued. "You're unapologetically you. You said it yourself. You'd never diet before a wedding."

"Because I'd be hungry," I said, thinking that was a pretty obvious reason not to diet. "I'm cranky when I'm hungry. Plus, I can't concentrate on my work if I'm starved. My job, much like yours, isn't the type where I can afford lapses in judgment. It would actually be dangerous for me to diet."

"You don't change yourself for anyone. That's a rare quality."

"Do you?" I asked. "Why would you? I mean, you can only change so much anyway. The rest is just pretending. If it's pretend, then eventually it will fade away, and people will see the truth. Why delay it? I'd rather have you not like me right off the bat than think you like me, and then later, when you see the real me, decide you don't like me."

"Because you're pretty and smart and confident," Mindy said. "There's not all that much to dislike."

"I beg to disagree, but still. You could say the same thing about yourself."

"Sure, I'm confident in my work. I'm attractive enough because I pay people to make my skin smooth and my forehead unwrinkled and my abs flat. Yeah, I'm smart when it comes to my work."

I leaned closer to her and studied her forehead. We'd been passing the champagne between us during our whole conversation, and I was beginning to feel the fuzzy aftereffects of it. "You get Botox? Doesn't that hurt?"

Mindy laughed again. "Beauty is pain."

I took another big gulp. "Another reason I never had many female friends. I just don't get it."

"Do you still have feelings for him?"

I just about choked on the bubbly. "Do you mean Gem?"

"I thought that'd be obvious."

"No. Not at all. Not romantically," I said. "I'm wholeheartedly dating Russo. I can barely handle one man. There's no room for another guy in my life, trust me. Even so, I chose to be with Jack, I continue to be with Jack, and I don't see that changing. I love him."

"It's interesting."

"Which part?"

"You could've dated Gem. Everyone knows he wanted to pursue you. Even I could see the way he looked at you. Yet you opted to date the FBI agent who lives across the country and makes squat compared to Alastair."

"I don't make a habit of dating people based on their bank balances."

"Obviously."

"Contrary to what you think, it's not like it was a logical choice. It's a relationship. It's love. I felt a bond with Russo that I wanted to explore, and I've never had any regrets."

"I don't know. Seems like it'd be hard not to wonder about what it would've been like if you'd picked Gem."

Mindy passed me the champagne, and we both took a few sips. The stars were growing more and more twinkly above me by the minute. Sometimes it looked like Mindy had three eyes if she moved really fast.

"I don't dwell on the past," I said. "I think regrets are useless."

"That's admirable, but I don't believe you."

"You're not in my head," I said. "How could you know?"

"Just a theory. I can read people. I put together defenses for bad people for a living. I know what you're doing."

"Tell me, then."

"You went with the safe option out of the two men."

"How is Russo the safe option?" I asked. "You already said it. He lives across the country. Our jobs make it almost impossible to be together."

"Exactly," Mindy said as if that explained everything. "You chose the person with whom it would be difficult to move forward. You could see the writing on the wall. This relationship would probably come to an end based on sheer logistics. You're logical, and you knew that."

"That's not at all true. We have options."

"Gem was the unreasonable choice for you," Mindy said. "You come from different lifestyles. He's rich; you're not. He's a businessman; you're a cop. But you both live in the same city. You knew he really liked you. It was too dangerous for you to choose Gem because you knew there was a pos-sibility that the relationship might be that one-in-a-million love story that never ends, and that scared you."

"Mindy, that's ridiculous. He wouldn't be marrying you if he had feelings for me."

"Maybe. Maybe he just came to terms with the fact that you didn't choose him, so he had to look for a second option. It sucks to take second place, especially when you're talking about marriage."

I grabbed Mindy's shoulders. "Listen to me. It's in your head. I don't think about Gem like that. Yes, I'm friends with him, and I care about him in a friendly way, but that's it."

"That might be how you feel, but what about him?"

I waited until Mindy looked into my eyes. Even though we were both bubbly with the effects of the champagne, I could feel a connection happen as our gazes met. "As a friend to Gem, I say with confidence that he is a good man. He wouldn't get married for the wrong reasons. If he proposed to you, it's because he could see a future with you. Because he loves *you*. If he still had romantic feelings toward me, he wouldn't do that to you."

Mindy stared at me for a long moment. Then she sniffed. "I know you're right," she said quietly. "The thing is, I'm not sure if I'm ready to get married."

I sat back, letting my hands drop from her shoulders. That was a bombshell if I'd ever heard one.

"No offense, but I sort of assumed you were the one instigating the marriage," I said. "I thought, if anything, you wanted it more than Gem."

"I did. I do. I mean, I always thought I did," Mindy said. "I'm thirty-eight. I was thinking about what a family would look like. If we wanted kids, I didn't want to wait much longer. I wanted the option to get pregnant."

"What changed?"

"Nothing changed," Mindy said. "I've never really seen myself as a family woman. In the back of my mind, I always felt like I'd just 'get there' when I was ready to settle down. You know? There's so much pressure to do it all. I have the career already. People say I should be looking for fulfillment beyond my job."

"Who is *people*?"

"I don't know. Society. But the truth is, I enjoy my job," Mindy said. "I like taking a month off and blowing a bunch of money to stay in fancy hotels across Europe. I like being on my own schedule and doing my own thing. I couldn't do all of that with kids."

"You could do some of it."

"Not in the same way. Kids change things," Mindy said. "Sure, I could do all that if I hired a nanny—Lord knows Gem can afford a fleet of nannies—but then why have kids at all if I don't actually want them?"

I took a deep breath. Then another sip of champagne. This was not where I'd seen the night going. I was already past the point of ever being able to drive myself anywhere tonight, so I decided to go big or go home. And since I wasn't going home, I was going big.

"You can still get married and not have kids," I said. "You and Gem could do those things together."

"I like my freedom," Mindy said unapologetically. "It's not that Gem's controlling. He's not at all. Almost annoyingly not. It's just the thought of committing to one person forever, even someone as incredible as Gem, that spooks me. He's got it all. He's handsome; he's kind; he's got money; he's fantastic in bed." Mindy looked over at me. "I mean, seriously, the best I've ever had."

I blinked. "Right, er, well, congrats. I wouldn't know. So would you say you're feeling claustrophobic?"

"I guess that would be one way to say it."

"Do you know what I think you need?"

She looked at me. "An intervention? Because I'm seriously crazy questioning my decision to marry the most perfect man of all time?"

"A hot dog."

She laughed. "Well, that too."

"Come on," I said. "I think it's pretty urgent we get some sustenance in your stomach."

Chapter 9

Fortunately, the party was located in downtown Minneapolis which meant nightlife went on around here whether it was winter or Christmas or any other time of year. We found a food truck parked outside a strip of bars and clubs and hopped in line. I ordered us two loaded hot dogs and handed one to Mindy. We turned away from the truck and began strolling down the sidewalk with our hauls.

I was glad I'd opted for reasonable walking shoes to go with my dress, a pair of cute, low-heeled boots. Mindy, on the other hand, seemed to be plowing through the light swirls of snow in her high heels without a second thought.

"How do you do it?" I asked, still feeling giddy from my champagne consumption. "How do you manage walking around in those shoes on a night like tonight? It's cold out. And those look miserable."

"I've worn heels for the last twenty years of my life. You learn to ignore the pain." She shrugged. "Actually, when it's cold, my feet sort of go numb, and I don't feel it until the blisters start the next day."

"That sounds completely miserable."

"The champagne helps me forget too."

"Why not just wear regular shoes?"

"Beauty is pain," she reiterated. Then she paused on the sidewalk, closed her eyes, and took a big bite of her hot dog. She moaned like it was the best thing in the world. Then she shook her head at me. "I take it back. I don't need to be beautiful anymore if it means I can't have a hot dog."

"That's what I'm saying," I agreed as we continued walking in the general direction back to Gem's club. "Why would you ever give up the really good things in life for something that makes you miserable?"

Mindy seemed completely oblivious to me and my ramblings. She was too busy groaning with pleasure over the hot dog as she stomped down the sidewalk in her heels.

"What would you want to do," I asked, "if you could do anything you wanted in the whole wide world?"

"Assuming I didn't marry Alastair?"

"I'm talking about an alternate reality," I said. "A place where you wouldn't have to make that choice. If you knew you were going to be single for the rest of your life, what would be next for you?"

"I would probably take a sabbatical from my job for a year. I love my job and am completely fulfilled by it, but that doesn't mean I wouldn't want a break to see some of the world."

"I understand," I said even though I didn't totally. I enjoyed my work and had no real desire for a break. Mostly because I had no clue what I'd do with my life without work in it. Maybe that meant I had a bigger problem than I wanted to admit.

"I'd go down to the Caribbean and snorkel for a while. Maybe meet a few friends that would only be friends so long as I was there. I'd eat all the good, local food I could get my hands on. Then when I got bored, I'd go rent a room in some vineyard in Italy. From there, I think I'd do the South of France, or even better, the French countryside."

"That sounds pretty dreamy."

"At some point, I'd get bored and come home to my job," she said. "I'd keep working, doing my thing, and eventually, I'd do it all over again. Except I'd start in Tahiti, work my way over to Australia, and maybe spend some time in Japan."

"You like to travel?"

"Travel, yes. But not the week-long vacations I do right now. I'd like to really stay someplace long enough to immerse myself in the culture. Not forever, but for a moment in time. An experience I can really hold on to and take back with me."

"I've never liked short vacations much. I never really understood the point. There's so much stress with traveling and packing and figuring out what you're going to do when you're there, it's practically hard to enjoy it."

"Detective Rosetti, I hate to sound negative, but when you talk like that, you don't sound very fun."

I finished off my hot dog. "I don't consider myself particularly fun."

"I don't think that's fair to you. You are fun, just in a different way. Plus, you're interesting, which is better than being fun in my opinion."

"Thanks?"

"Anyway, none of that's going to happen. I shouldn't even be thinking about it," Mindy said, taking another bite of her hot dog. "My wedding is in less than a week. Alastair is an amazing man."

"Do you have doubts he's the right one for you? A person can be amazing, but not amazing for you."

"Are you trying to convince me not to get married?"

"No, I'm just trying to figure out why the two of you are getting married if you're both having doubts." I stilled, knowing that was the wrong thing to say as soon as the words were out of my mouth. "Sorry, that wasn't exactly what I meant."

"Alastair's having doubts?"

"Not doubts," I said. "I wouldn't know if he is, anyway. I haven't spoken to him about the wedding in a long time. I'm just referring to the fact that he wanted to push the date back, and now you're questioning whether you actually want to go through with it at all."

"It's just cold feet. It happens to everyone. It's a normal part of getting married."

"I'm sorry. I've never been married or engaged, so I don't claim to understand. Plus, I had a lot of champagne, and I'm not even making sense to myself. Ignore me."

"I can't ignore you because you make more sense than anyone I've talked to in a long time."

We made it back to the front of Gem's club. Mindy looked up toward the roof. I detected a brief moment of longing as if she wanted to return to our private hideaway.

"I should go inside," she said, almost like she was trying to convince herself that was the right option. "It's my party."

"I'll go with you," I said. "It's not like I can drive anyway."

Mindy and I returned to the party. The second we reached the VIP section, we drifted apart as if nothing had ever happened. Like we'd never spoken a word to one another. Except for one last, meaningful glance, before she was absorbed into a group of her friends, it was like I'd imagined the whole thing.

"Where'd you go?" Jane appeared by my shoulder a second later. "I've been looking for you. Were you with Mindy this whole time?"

"Yeah, she needed a breath of fresh air."

"You've got ketchup on your cheek."

"She also needed a hot dog."

Jane laughed. "Leave it to you to be performing maid-of-honor duties at a bachelorette party you don't even want to be at."

"I've had too much to drink," I confessed. "I can't drive myself home yet, or I'd be taking off right now. Though I admit the hot dog helped."

"Then you'd better come with me and burn off the calories."

"Huh?"

"Just follow me."

Jane led me to a small, raised platform in the VIP section that was lit by strobe lights. Colorful smoke plumed around the dance floor. The DJ for the club was located just a few feet away. The only people on the dance floor were ladies from Mindy's bachelorette party. For some reason I'd never be able to explain, when Jane helped me onto the platform, I went along without a fight.

It wasn't until I was out of breath and starting to sweat an hour later that I realized Jane had gotten me dancing the night away. Almost like I was at a true bachelorette party and actually enjoying myself.

"Come on," a voice spoke in my ear. "I found the stash."

"Stash?" I turned to find Mindy by my shoulder.

"I'm the bride," Mindy said bossily. "You have to do what I say."

Still buzzing from champagne and the beat of dance tunes, I followed Mindy away from the stage. She grabbed her jacket again. Then, giggling, she yanked a tablecloth off an empty table near the back of the room and returned to the same staircase we'd climbed before.

"Are you sure you don't want to stay down here with your guests?" I asked. "You are the woman of the hour."

"Half the people have left," Mindy said. "The other half are too drunk to notice I'm gone. They're all having fun dancing. Not to mention, this is my night, and I want to come up here."

It was hard to argue with Mindy's logic. I'd been so wrapped up in the dance party with Jane that I hadn't realized the crowd in the VIP section thinning out.

"Mindy, just so you know, I'm a cop," I said as we reached the roof again. "I won't bust you at your own bachelorette party for having a stash of illegal... well, whatever you might have. But I can't indulge along with you. I hope you understand."

"Man, you really aren't fun." Despite the statement, Mindy winked at me. "Don't worry, I think you'll be tempted."

"I really—"

Mindy slipped her coat onto her shoulders and exposed a plastic bag that had been dangling over her arm. Then she threw the tablecloth onto the ground and plunked herself down on it. She opened the plastic bag, and instead of removing some sort of illegal substance, she pulled out a miniature wedding cake. Also in the bag was another bottle of champagne.

"Join me?" Mindy retrieved two forks, then handed one to me. "It's from *A'more*. The best cake shop in town. I wasn't going to have any because, well, calories, but—"

"But it's your wedding," I said. "You should eat your own cake."

"Screw it. If I need to get my dress altered, so be it."

Mindy took the first bite, then gestured for me to help myself. A sort of comfortable silence settled over us. It had started to snow, ever so lightly, but it wasn't sticking. It would've been romantic with the right partner. For now, it just felt pleasant.

For the next while, we shared the bottle of champagne and picked at the cake with our respective forks. Neither of us felt the need to talk. I'd grabbed my jacket on the way out, too, and found the fresh air to be a welcome relief after the heat of the dance floor.

"I had fun tonight," I said. "I didn't take a Jell-O shot, but I'd say this was a real bachelorette party."

Mindy smiled. "Thanks."

"Feeling any better?"

"I don't know. I'm too drunk to think anything through at this point," Mindy said. "I'll probably regret talking to you at all tomorrow."

"I'm not sure how to feel about that."

"Honored," Mindy said with a teasing wink. "I don't drink too much champagne and then open up to just any-one."

"Well, then you should feel honored too. It's been a long, long time since I've had enough to drink that I can't drive home. I can't tell you the last time I voluntarily stepped onto a dance floor."

"Mission accomplished. You know, Rosetti, I almost wish we were friends."

"We don't have to be enemies."

"I don't know. I'll always think that as long as you're around, I'll come in second place in Gem's eyes."

"That's not true. You can ask him yourself, and I'm sure he'll be honest with you."

"I have asked him. He says I'm being ridiculous."

"Because you are."

"Then let's just forget about this conversation and enjoy our cake before the magic wears off." Mindy took a drink from the bottle and passed it to me. "I'll get you a ride home."

"Yeah, but my car is still here."

"I'm marrying Alastair Gem. He'll figure it out."

"Okay. I should text my sister and let her know not to wait for me."

I pulled out my phone and texted Jane the update. She responded to let me know Wes was picking her up, and that I should let her know when I made it back to my place.

Then Mindy and I sat side by side for a long, long time. The next thing I knew, someone was shaking me awake.

"Detective?"

"Where am I?" I asked, shooting into a sitting position and instinctively reaching for my gun. "What happened?"

The smile that greeted me was not the one I'd been expecting. Alastair Gem was kneeling in front of me, but the second I reached for my imaginary gun, his look of concern faded into one of amusement.

"Oh good, you're not dead." He eased back. "And you already want to shoot me."

"I don't have my gun," I said, feeling dazed and disoriented. "What happened?"

"You fell asleep," Gem said. "So did Mindy."

Gem nodded his head toward Mindy who was still conked out. She was laying on the tablecloth with her jacket wrapped around her. A light snore came from her general direction.

"We fell asleep on the roof?" I winced. "How did you find us?"

Gem looked at the bottle of champagne. It was noticeably close to empty. "That's a lot of alcohol to put away in two women of your respective sizes."

"I'm sorry."

"Sorry?" Gem stood. He extended a hand to help me up. "Why are you apologizing?"

"Because I feel like an idiot," I said. "I fell asleep on the roof at a bachelorette party. What am I, twenty-one? I could've gotten hypothermia. Plus, I should've been looking out for Mindy."

"Do you have feeling in your feet?"

I winced again. "Too much feeling. I am pretty sure my entire heel is bruised."

"I heard you were the dancing queen this evening."

"Crap."

Gem laughed. "It's a bachelorette party, Detective. You're allowed to have fun. I'm so pleased to hear you two enjoyed it. Thanks for being a friend to Mindy."

"I don't know if I'd go that far." I glanced down at her. "She told me repeatedly that she didn't really like me."

"Ah, yes."

"You're aware of that?"

"She's mentioned it to me. It's unfounded. She's a little jealous that you and I had a friendship before she came into my life."

"But there's nothing more than a friendship between us."

"I know, trust me. I've told her that. I think she'll get over it once we're married and settled down."

"Yeah, maybe. I hope so."

Gem looked like he wanted to say more, but instead, he turned away from me. "I have to call your sister."

"Jane? Why?"

Gem was already dialing. "Yeah, Wes, it's me. Is Jane there?"

There was a beat of silence. A moment later, I heard Jane's voice coming through Gem's phone from an arm's length away.

"You were right. They were on the roof," Gem said, unable to wipe the smirk off his face. "I'll make sure your sister gets home in one piece. Her car too. Really, it's no problem. Have a good night, Jane."

I pretended not to have eavesdropped on the phone call. Instead, I leaned over Mindy. She felt warm to the touch, and she was definitely breathing, judging by the decibel of her snores.

"I'll get her home," Gem said. "I have a car out front for you. With your permission—and your keys—I can have a second driver follow behind with your vehicle."

I fished in my jacket pocket for my keys, then tossed them to Gem. "Thank you. I'm so sorry."

"Hey, Detective, wait a minute." Gem's voice was soft, gentle. "Please don't apologize. Thank you. What Mindy needed more than anything was company tonight." He looked down at his sleeping fiancée. "I can see that you provided her with exactly what she needed."

"You'll never take me seriously as a cop again," I said, straightening my dress.

"On the contrary." Gem's eyes twinkled, but on his face was kindness. "It's nice to see that you're human. It was really kind what you did tonight, Kate."

"You don't know what I did."

"No, but I know you didn't want to be here, and yet, you stayed later than anyone."

"Because I fell asleep."

Gem reached down and grabbed Mindy until she slumped into his arms. I picked up the tablecloth and the remnants of our drunken winter picnic. Then the three of us trooped downstairs through a different back hallway and out to where there were two cars waiting—one for Gem, one for me.

Gem got Mindy into the car and passed my keys off to a second man, along with my address. Then he came to my side.

"Have a good night, Detective," Gem said. "I'll see you at the wedding."

Chapter 10

The next morning, I sat behind my desk at the precinct pretending that I felt excellent. In reality, my head pounded, and my stomach churned like a roller coaster that was about to go off the tracks. I turned my computer on, but as soon as the screen blinked to life, I closed my eyes and held my head in my hands. It felt like I was staring directly into the sun.

A few minutes later, I was startled by a voice muttering, "Holy smokes."

I forced my eyes open to see Chloe Marks standing before me. She glanced over to Jimmy's desk where my partner sat, carefully peeling back individual strands of Twizzlers for breakfast.

Chloe turned to look at Jimmy. "Is she hungover?"

"No," I said. "I'm just tired."

Jimmy snorted. "Uh-huh."

"I know what a hangover looks like," Chloe said. "That's no ordinary tired. Not to mention a superhuman like Detective Rosetti doesn't get *tired*."

"I was wondering what was wrong with you," Jimmy said through a mouthful of food. "Some bachelorette party, huh?"

"Oh right." Chloe gave an excited little squeal. "I forgot about that. I can't blame you for being hungover one bit. I don't think it's possible for a person to go to a bachelorette party for Alastair Gem's future wife and not come back looking like you."

"Looking like me?"

"Or worse than you," she added. "They probably served super-fancy drinks, right?"

"I don't remember." I groaned. Then I looked at my partner and Chloe, who were staring at me. "I'm joking. I'm not that bad. Of course they served fancy champagne. And there were hot dogs."

"Ah." Chloe nodded like that was some sort of lewd innuendo. "Right. Hot dogs."

"I'm afraid that Rosetti here probably means real hot dogs," Jimmy said. "Ketchup, mustard, and everything."

"Of course I mean real hot dogs," I said. "What else would I be talking about?"

Chloe's cheeks turned pink. "Forget it. Do you want me to get you my hangover cure?"

"No, I'm fine. I'll be fine. I just haven't had coffee. Once I get some sunglasses, I should be able to look at my computer screen."

Chloe pulled a pair of pink aviators off her head and handed them my way. I took one look at the diamond-encrusted sides and gave a shake of my head.

"Thanks, but no thanks," I said. "I think I'll go blind."

Jimmy snorted behind his desk. I could tell this whole exchange was making it worth his while being in the office on a Sunday morning.

"Where are we on the case?" I asked. "Actually, don't tell me. I need a coffee first."

As I stood, there was a knock on the door to the room. It was a formality since the door was already open. I looked up to find Elizabeth standing there looking uncertain. I frowned, wondering what my mom's college-aged helper from the coffee shop was doing at the precinct.

"Is everything okay?" I stood, my pounding head suddenly the least of my worries. My heart pounded as I worried something had happened to my mother. "Is everything okay, Elizabeth?"

"Yeah, I have a delivery."

"A delivery?" I asked. "What sort of delivery?"

She stepped into the room to reveal a tray of large take-out latte cups. There were at least four of them there. "They're for you."

"All of that coffee is for me?"

"Yeah, I've got a box of doughnuts down by the front door. I couldn't carry them up at the same time without spilling, so I'll grab them."

"I didn't know you guys delivered," I said, frowning. "Is this from my mom?"

Elizabeth blushed. "I guess we deliver for the right price. There's a card. It's for you, Detective."

Before I took the card out of Elizabeth's hand, I already knew who'd sent them. The person who would be okay to pay any sum of money to get exactly what he wanted. I cracked open the envelope and opened a plain white card. On the inside were two words above a name.

Thank you

—Gem

I made a face at Jimmy and Chloe, then I accepted the tray of coffees. "Thanks, Elizabeth. I can grab the dough-nuts."

"Are you sure?"

"Positive," I said. "Thanks again. Sorry to bother you with this."

"Not a problem," she said, then she peered around the room. "So this is where the magic happens, huh?"

"Pretty much," Jimmy said. "You're always welcome here if you're carrying doughnuts."

I quickly ushered Elizabeth out of the building before my colleagues could harass her further. On the way back, I grabbed the box of doughnuts on the counter. The smell of the delicious pastries made me feel like puking. I set them in the conference room and carefully closed the door to contain the smell of fried dough.

"They're in the conference room," I said. "Leave them there if you don't want me to be sick."

Then I grabbed two of the latte mugs and returned to my desk. I nodded for Chloe and Jimmy to grab the other two. They did without hesitation.

"That was nice of Agent Russo," Chloe said, wheedling. "To send you the coffees, I mean."

I glared at her, letting her know her little fishing expedition for information wasn't going to get her anywhere.

"Right," she said. "Well, I'm glad you had a nice time last night."

"If only it'd been worth it," I muttered, then squinted at my computer screen. "Any news from the case? If you sent me an email, it'll be at least twenty minutes before I can stare at my computer screen without my head splitting in two."

"And you tried to pretend you weren't hungover," Jimmy snorted as he returned from the conference room with a plate piled high with doughnuts. "I'll tell you what. You should make this a weekly occurrence if Gem's gonna be buying the office breakfast."

"This is from Alastair Gem?" Chloe looked like she was about to drop her latte right then and there. "But I thought..."

"Don't ask," Jimmy said. "I've been partners with Kate long enough to know that her trigger finger gets twitchy when she's hungover."

Chloe shut up and returned to her desk. There was one blissful moment of silence while I inhaled my first few sips of frothy caffeine. My bliss was interrupted a moment later when Asha strode into the office wearing leather pants and an oversized black sweater. Her braids swung behind her as she stopped before my desk.

"Someone brought coffee and doughnuts?" Asha glanced around at our desks. "Where's the liquid gold?"

Grudgingly, I nodded at the second latte cup on my desk. "You can have one of mine."

Asha took one look at me and let out a laugh. She reached out and patted my shoulder. "You need it more than me, sweetie. Let me know when it's safe to talk to you."

Asha disappeared without another word.

Jimmy looked at Chloe. "That's a smart woman right there," he told her. "Asha knows to let Kate get in her two espresso shots before attempting to discuss business when she's like this."

"I'm right here," I grumbled. "I'm not going to shoot anyone."

Jimmy made a noise in his throat that told me he wasn't totally convinced. It was worth noting that exactly zero people tried to talk to me in the next twenty minutes. The second I tossed my cup in the trash can, however, both Asha and Chloe descended on my desk as if it was suddenly safe to approach.

"I definitely want to hear about last night," Asha began, "but I can wait until Bellini's tonight."

"No Bellini's," I said. "I can't even hear the word Bellini without getting acid reflux."

Asha grinned. "That's what I like to hear. It's been a long time since you had some real fun."

"I'm not sure I'd call it fun," I said, thinking of the conversations I'd had with Mindy. "Complicated, maybe."

"Okay, then I'll buy you a greasy lunch, and you can dish," Asha said. "You know Lassie's salivating to hear how the party went."

"I guess I can wait to read about it on Lassie's blog," Chloe said, sounding left out. "It's fine."

"The case," I said. "We need to focus on the case."

"While you were dancing your tail off last night, Chloe and I were here until two in the morning," Asha said. "We are running into a dead end on this stuff. You need to talk to your boyfriend to see if he can pull a few strings."

"I asked Jack about witness protection. He's working on it, but he didn't sound hopeful."

"My best guess is that something happened fifteen years ago to put this guy in the program," Asha said. "We've scoured the cases that made headlines around that time and put a list together. There are seventeen cases that would make good candidates, and those are only the super high-profile ones. It's by no means all-inclusive."

"It's a starting point," I said. "Good work. Can I get a list?"

"It's in your inbox," Asha said.

"She can't look at her inbox," Chloe said. "It splits her head in two."

Asha grinned. Then she elbowed me out of the way and bent over my keyboard. After a minute or two of furious typing, she backed away. "How's that?"

"What sort of voodoo magic did you work?" I stared at the screen which had vastly decreased in brightness and blueness and glowed in a soft shade of warm yellow. "This is amazing."

"I know I'm amazing," Asha said. "You're welcome. Anyway, take a look at the list of cases that went to court and see if anything pops for you. Otherwise, we're running out of leads. As for the rest of my guesses, I'm thinking that either Charles Marlo didn't trust the witness protection program, or he was extremely paranoid."

"Or both," Chloe said. "The best we can figure is that the guy secured a second fake identity. We think that when he moved up here to the Cities from Atlanta, he set everything up under a different name."

"It was probably originally intended as a precaution," Asha said. "You know, to make the trail a little harder to follow in case anyone was looking for him."

"Got it. Anything else?"

"Melinda came in today to get the autopsy done," Asha said. "She's downstairs now. She's your next best hope to turn up something."

"Nice work. I'll go talk to her."

As Asha and Chloe left my desk, I rose to make my way downstairs to the lab. However, a figure in the doorway stopped me in my tracks.

"Mom?"

My mother took one look at me and frowned. "Your father's missing, and you're out dancing on tables?"

"Huh? How did you know I was dancing on tables? I mean, I wasn't dancing on tables."

My mother marched across the room and stared into my eyes. "I raised two teenage girls. One of them was your sister, lest you forget. I know when someone is still drunk the next morning."

"I'm definitely not still drunk."

"Hungover, then."

I blinked. My mother was so close I could smell her very minty breath. The sweet scent made my stomach do additional flips. I wondered if this was what being pregnant and having morning sickness felt like—every little smell making me nauseous. I forced myself to not lose the contents of my stomach all over my mother.

"I had an outstanding obligation," I said. "Not to mention, I'm an adult. I'm allowed to have some fun at a bachelorette party if I want. I wasn't even late to work today, not that it's any of your business."

"It *is* my business when your father's missing. How's the case going? Any progress?" My mother spun around and looked at the room as a whole. "Anyone? Detective Jones?"

Jimmy cleared his throat. "Mrs. Rosetti?"

My mother took one look at Jimmy's expression and seemed to correctly interpret that he was clueless about the whole matter. She whirled back to face me. "You still haven't told anyone about your father? You haven't made it an official case?"

"It's not that I haven't told anyone," I said. "I'm looking into it. It's a personal thing, Mom."

"Well, I'm making it not personal." My mother turned, a hand on her hip, and faced Jimmy. "I'd like to report my husband missing."

"Ex-husband, technically," I said. "Unless there's something you forgot to tell me."

"It's hard to marry the man when he's disappeared," my mother retorted. "I don't suppose you have any ideas as to where he might be?"

Jimmy cleared his throat. "Angelo Rosetti is missing, ma'am?"

"Yes. I called my daughter on Friday night to let her know. It was around one in the morning. I was worried."

"I didn't report anything because he hadn't even been missing for an hour." I spoke to Jimmy. "He wasn't home by his curfew, so my mom wanted me to send out a search party."

"He wasn't where he was supposed to be," my mother argued. "He wasn't answering his phone. He's not at his place—I went and checked the next morning, and it was obvious he hadn't been there. I'm worried about him. I have been since Friday."

"Were there any signs of foul play?" Jimmy asked. "Any signs of a struggle?"

"No. I know what y'all are thinking. You all think that Angelo ran off on me because he was caught up in something, but I'm here telling you he wouldn't do that. The man is missing."

Jimmy turned on his soothing voice. "We will look into it, Mrs. Rosetti."

"You know I was right, Jimmy," I argued. "We didn't have enough to declare a real missing-persons case after a couple of hours."

"It's your father!" My mother faced me. "You should've made an exception."

"Ma'am, Detective Rosetti did spend most of the day yesterday looking for him," Chloe said. "I went with her to help."

"At least someone was doing something," my mother said with a grateful look at Chloe. "Thanks, darling."

Chloe looked embarrassed. "I meant—"

I waved Chloe off. "I'll file a report today, Mom. But I talked to his friends and didn't get anything suspicious. They say Dad left Gallagher's voluntarily at around ten forty on Friday night."

"Then we know exactly when he was kidnapped," my mother said. "Between ten forty and midnight. Find him, or I shall refuse to serve any of you coffee for as long as you all shall live."

Then my mother stormed out of the room, leaving a wave of silence behind her.

"She's scary," Chloe said. "I mean, I understand her concern, but she's very intimidating. And I do like her coffee."

"Now do you understand why Kate's not afraid of hardened criminals and murderers?" Jimmy raised his eyebrows and shot a glance at Mrs. Rosetti's receding back.

I sighed. "I guess this is me officially filing a report."

"Are you going to tell us the real reason you didn't file one sooner?" Jimmy asked. "Why didn't you mention your mom was worried?"

"I didn't want anyone knowing about it until I found out something definitive," I said. "I didn't mean to tell Chloe. She just stumbled into it and got dragged along for the ride."

"Typical," Chloe said cheerfully. "That's how I find out about most things around here. No one tells me anything."

"I'm sorry, Jimmy," I said. "It's my dad. The situation is complicated. Then with the murder yesterday, I got distracted. I also had to wonder if maybe..." I didn't want to finish the sentence.

"You think there's a possibility our murder situation from yesterday and your father's disappearance are related?" Jimmy asked. "Kate, your dad's not a killer. He was a cop, a good guy who made one bad decision. It could happen to anyone. Except you, maybe."

"It doesn't happen to anyone," I said. "Plenty of cops have made it through their career without making that sort of 'mistake,' if that's what you want to call it."

"Okay, fine. Let's focus on the fact that your father isn't accounted for at the moment. What do you think happened?"

"I don't know," I said. "I honestly don't know. But I intend to find out. Now, if you'll excuse me, I have to talk to Dr. Brooks to see if she's figured out who sprayed our local co-op with bullets."

Chapter 11

"Good morning to you too," Melinda said as I entered the lab. "It looks like you had a great time last night."

"Yeah, yeah."

"I'm happy for you," Melinda said. "I admit I'm surprised to see you stumbling around here since you didn't want to go in the first place."

"Trust me, it was an unexpected night." I moved closer to the autopsy table. Melinda had been working over the body but had straightened when I arrived. "Did you find anything?"

"The victim was hit with five bullets. This one, here, is the one that killed him."

I looked at the place on the man's chest where Melinda pointed.

"I'm running tox screens, but I doubt we'll find much of anything." Melinda gave me a quirky smile. "Most people don't still have alcohol in their system when they're grocery shopping on a weekend morning. Unless, of course, it's you."

"Hey, hey."

"I'm joking. You're definitely below the legal limit."

I rolled my eyes. "No signs of a struggle?"

"None," Melinda said. "This guy was just walking along, doing his morning shopping and minding his business, when he was hit by a bunch of bullets. I'm sorry, but I don't think I'm going to be much help in getting you leads this time."

"I've heard that one already this morning," I said. "We're running into issues on Asha's end too. Have you run this guy's fingerprints?"

"There's no match in the system," Melinda said. "I spoke to Asha about it. I agree with her theory that he might've been in witness protection."

"In that case, it wouldn't necessarily mean this guy wasn't in the system but that he's been scrubbed from it."

"It's very possible. I'm not getting any results, but that doesn't mean there were never any to begin with. It's just not how you're going to ID this guy properly unless you get access to witness protection."

"I already asked Russo," I said. "I'm getting the chief to follow up as well. We'll see if anything comes of it."

"I'm sorry, honey." Melinda gave me a guarded look. "I heard about your father."

I wrinkled my nose. "You talked to my mother?"

"She supplies me with coffee. I had no choice. Is there anything I can do?"

"I hope not. If I need to ask for your help in figuring out what happened to my dad, it's too late."

"What do you think happened, Kate?"

"I don't know," I said. "But I'm starting to get nervous that there's some sort of mob thing going on here and that my dad might be involved."

I hated to admit it aloud, but it had been weighing on my mind. I could trust Melinda more than just about anyone else in the world. She knew how to keep a secret and how to be supportive without being pushy. We'd been friends for years, and working the sort of job we did, we'd seen a lot in our time together.

"Your father loves you girls. And your mother," she added. "Do you really think he'd jeopardize that?"

"Not on purpose," I said. "But if something turned up and my family was threatened, then maybe."

"He's not a killer, Kate. And he does love your family."

"People say that like it excuses bad behavior," I said. "I love my family too, but I'm not in prison because of it."

Melinda decided to leave that alone. "If it makes you feel better, the crime scene crew found next to zero evidence of tire tracks or marks of any sort on the road. I'm not sure the car ever stopped, which suggests there might have been two people in the car. A driver and someone else. It's not a certainty, but it is a possibility."

"You think my father could've been the driver?"

"I think that's still a huge leap," Melinda said. "Why would your dad want this Charles Marlo guy killed? What's his motive?"

"I don't know. I haven't gotten anywhere on motive yet except that this Charles guy was obviously on the run from someone. I just don't know who. I do have to admit that the timing is suspicious. The very morning after my dad never returns home, this guy turns up dead on the sidewalk?" I shrugged. "It could be a coincidence."

"You don't believe in coincidences."

"My dad has ties to the mob; Charles Marlo might've been in witness protection... It doesn't take a genius to make the leap to revenge of some sort."

"Kate, one of your strong suits is being objective," Melinda said. "Look at this case that way. There's not a single thread linking your father to this murder. If it were anyone else, you wouldn't have all of this background knowledge on your father, and you wouldn't be making this leap. You wouldn't even *know* about Angelo Rosetti being missing."

"But I *do* have the background knowledge."

"Don't let it completely cloud your judgment. Follow all the leads that turn up. See if you can make some headway with the US Marshall's Office to get our victim's real identity. That's going to get you further than stressing about some long-shot chance of your father being involved."

"You're right."

"In the meantime, file a missing-person report on your dad, and have a team assigned to the case to take some of the pressure off you."

"He's my own father. I have to look into it."

"Sure, then do it your way, on your own time. It doesn't hurt to have help in a more official capacity."

As I left Melinda in the lab, I realized she was right. So was my mother. It was time to get the professionals involved, especially since I was no longer able to give my dad's disappearance my full attention. Melinda was right, too, in reminding me that I needed to focus on following the leads that radiated out from Charles Marlo's dead body. Making leaps that weren't connected would get me in trouble. The first order of business was to find out who this guy really was. If that path led me to my father, then so be it.

I filed a formal report for my now-missing father and called Chief Sturgeon to give him a heads-up that it would be coming through. It was a personal case, and I figured he'd want to know from me directly instead of through the grapevine.

"It's a little early for a missing person's report," the chief said, "but we'll go ahead with it. I'm sorry, Rosetti. I know things with your father are complicated."

"Yeah, thanks," I said quickly. "Let me know if you hear anything, okay? I'd like to assist on the case."

"I recommend—"

"I'll be looking into it on my own time," I said. "I'll be doing it whether you like it or not, so it's probably best we just kept each other in the loop."

The chief sighed. He knew his hands were tied. He picked the lesser of two evils and agreed. "Fine, I'll call you."

I thanked him, then hung up. My next phone call was to Russo.

"How was the party?" he asked.

"Long. Interesting. Weird."

"Not what I expected to hear," Jack said. "Did you have some fun?"

"It's the first time I've been hungover in a long, long time."

"Should I be concerned with how that happened?"

"*I'm* concerned with how it happened," I admitted, hiding a grin. "Mostly it was Mindy's bad influence."

"I thought she didn't like you."

"She didn't. I still don't think she does," I told Russo. "It's complicated. Honestly, I'm wondering if she's not having second thoughts about marrying Gem."

"Kate."

"What? I'm just repeating what I heard last night."

"What you heard or what you interpreted?"

"I mean, that part's a little bit fuzzy," I said. "I don't remember verbatim what was all said. Mostly just the gist of it. Regardless, she seems like she's getting a little unhinged from the stress of wedding planning."

"Well, it is the week before Christmas. Even completely sane people tend to go a little crazy around the holidays," Russo said. "Not to mention pre-wedding jitters."

"I'm sure that's all it is."

"Last time you got involved in this wedding mess, it didn't end well."

"I'd argue that it actually ended okay," I said. "Gem got to push the wedding back, which was what he wanted."

"What about Mindy?"

"Well, she already didn't like me. Plus, I seriously think she's getting cold feet."

"Again, I'm going to remind you not to—"

"Yeah, yeah. I know. I'm not going to do anything more about it. You forget, I didn't even want to go to the party," I said. "The real reason I called—besides to say hello—was to ask if you'd made any progress on the witness protection stuff I asked you about for our case."

"It was a Saturday night and a Sunday morning."

"This is important."

"I'll follow up," Jack promised, "but if we do hear anything, I wouldn't expect it to be until tomorrow. Have you talked to Chief Sturgeon to see if he has channels to go through?"

"Yes." I sighed. "I'm just impatient. I'm just running out of leads to chase down on this guy."

"Have a little patience," Jack said. "It seems like this was a targeted killing which means whoever pulled the trigger probably isn't planning another random murder. You'll get there. By the way, did you ever get a dress to wear to the wedding?"

"That was an abrupt change of subject."

"Take your mother shopping," Jack said. "It sounds like you both might need a few hours away from this mess to clear your head."

"She's not going to want to go shopping," I said. "My dad's still missing. I just filed an official report before I called you."

"Then it's the perfect time to get out. Let the team get caught up on your dad's case; pick up a dress in an hour, and then resume looking for your father. You can't do everything, Kate. And you can't go to the wedding naked."

"What about we skip the wedding?"

"I wouldn't complain, but I'm pretty sure Gem would hunt you down and drag you there if you didn't show."

I made a grumbly noise.

"Glad to hear you agree," Jack said. "I've got to let you go. I'm working a case too, but I'll keep you posted if I hear anything back."

"Thanks, Jack."

"Hey, I miss you," he said. "I'm looking forward to spending the holiday with you."

"Me too," I said. "I'll see you in a few days."

***

I let Jones and Chloe know that I was stepping away from my desk for an hour or two to be with my mom. They smartly didn't ask questions and told me to take my time. A few minutes later, I walked into the Seventh Street Café and found my mother behind the counter. There were bags under her eyes, and the smile that normally greeted her customers had vanished. I immediately felt guilty, and I couldn't even totally be sure why.

"Hey, Mom," I said. "I wanted to check on you."

"I'm not the one who needs to be checked on." She glanced at me, looking a few years older than her age and completely exhausted. "That would be your father who needs our help."

"I need to get a dress for the wedding this weekend," I said. "Will you join me? This won't take long."

"I'm working. I've asked Elizabeth to cover for me enough this weekend."

"Go on." Elizabeth waved at my mother from the other end of the counter. "I've got this under control."

"You're supposed to be done with your shift in half an hour."

"So pay me an hour of overtime. I could use it, so you'll be doing me a favor." Elizabeth winked. "Go find something nice to wear with your daughter. How often does she ask you to go shopping anyway?"

My mother gave a grateful smile to Elizabeth, then turned to face me. "You know I can't resist a shopping trip with my daughter. Lord knows you've never asked me to go with you before. You made me pick up your prom dress sight unseen so you didn't have to try it on in public."

"Yes, well, I'm asking now. Come on."

I beckoned for my mother to follow me to the car. We hopped in, and I turned the car to the nearest mall—some ten minutes away. I wasn't even sure which stores still existed, but it wasn't like I was picky when it came to clothes. If it had armholes and a place for my head to go, I was pretty well satisfied so long as it covered all my private places.

"I know you only asked me to come with you because you feel bad about your father." My mother glanced over the center console at me. "You don't have to pretend you want to go shopping."

"I *don't* want to go shopping," I agreed. "But I do need a dress. I also wanted to spend some time with you, so I figured we could do both at once. Real mother and daughter bonding time."

My mom gave me a small smile. She wasn't as chipper as she'd normally be under these circumstances. If it were any other day, she'd be plotting to sneak me off for a haircut, a manicure, and a sushi dinner before our girls' day was complete.

"I'm sorry, Ma," I said. "I had no idea how serious you and Dad were getting."

"Even so, it's your father. Whether or not we were back together, I'd have thought you'd want to find him."

"I did want to find him. I still do," I said. "I made an official report just before I left the office today."

"Days later."

"The reason I didn't do it sooner was because I wanted to look into it myself." I kept my eyes fixed on the road ahead. "He is my father, and this case is personal. The second I made an official report, I knew I'd have to hand over the reins to someone else. I can't technically be on the case because I'm too close to it."

My mother nodded. It seemed hard for her to speak.

"I did my best, and I'm going to continue to work on it. I told the chief as much," I said. "The truth is, I failed to find him before I had to turn the case in. I wasn't successful."

"You weren't successful *yet*. You are the smartest, most incredible detective I know. And I serve coffee to a lot of cops."

I flashed her a smile. "Yeah, but you're my mom. You're required to say that."

"It's the truth."

"You should also be aware that people will be coming to talk to you now. Other cops, not me. You know how these things go. Once an investigation is opened, and the police start asking questions, nothing is private anymore. They'll dig into your history, ask you uncomfortable questions, and pry through your things. They'll want to know all about your relationship with Dad. They'll ask about us. It's invasive. Necessary, but not fun."

"I'm from a family of cops. I understand." My mother shrugged. "I don't care about any of that. They can look through all my things. I'll tell them whatever they want to know. It's worth it to have him brought back to me."

"I know, Mom. I'm sorry. I really am sorry."

"You don't have to apologize. Yes, I'm missing a husband, but you're missing a father. I never give enough credit to your feelings on the matter."

"Not true," I said. "Everything you did for us our whole life has been for me and Jane, to make sure we had as normal of a life as possible after Dad left."

"It's just such a shame to have come all this way, and then this. For the first time in years, we were starting to be a family again."

"We'll get him back."

"It's Christmas." A few tears slipped down my mother's cheeks. "I was hoping we'd be able to have our first Christmas dinner together as a family in decades."

"We will, Mom," I promised, hoping against hope that it was a promise I wouldn't break. "We'll make that happen."

"It's so stupid."

"Stupid?"

"I thought he might propose on Christmas. Maybe New Years," she said. "Propose *again*, I should say."

"Really?" I glanced her way. "How did you feel about re-marrying Dad?"

"Excited," she said, wiping the tears from her cheeks and breaking out in a smile. "Giddy. That's why I said it was stupid. The other day I literally scoured my bedroom for evidence he'd bought a ring. I was like a teenage girl looking forward to her boyfriend asking her to prom."

"Mom, he has his own place. Why would he keep a ring at your place?"

"I know," she said stubbornly. "I told you I was excited."

"That's great, Mom. I'm really happy to hear it."

"I didn't find anything. Obviously. Your father was always good at hiding things."

I winced at her connotation, but she didn't seem to piece together the underlying meaning to her own words. If my father hadn't been so good at hiding things, maybe he'd never have gotten sent to prison. Alternatively, if he'd actually been the best at it, he'd never have gotten caught.

"I do love him," she whispered. "I don't think I could bear losing him a second time, not when things have been so good, so promising this time around."

A wave of sympathy rolled over me at the emotion in my mother's voice. She'd always been so strong for us when we were younger. I didn't have a single memory of her crying openly, not even when the police were asking us impossible questions. When they were accusing her of being involved with my dad's crimes. Not even when the case went to court, and my father was found guilty. Somehow, she'd managed to hold it together for all of us.

It wasn't until Jane and I were adults and on our own, or mostly on our own, that she'd started to let her walls crumble. She'd started to let her heart show a little more, to voice her real emotions. Some days, I still wasn't used to it.

As I was about to comfort my mother, however, I hesitated. Something about what she'd said had triggered something in my mind.

"You said you scoured the house for a ring?"

"Yes, Kate," my mother said. "Don't rub it in. I was embarrassed enough about it before I said anything to you. I don't need to be teased about it."

"It's not that. I was just wondering what made you think to look for a ring in the first place."

"I told you. I thought he was going to propose, so naturally I thought he'd do it with a ring."

"Specifically, what made you think that?" I asked. "Did you see a receipt somewhere for a jeweler? Did Dad mysteriously disappear to go shopping for a day? Did he let something slip?"

"No, it was nothing like that. Nothing concrete. Just a few little things. You know how it is, Kate. Women's intuition, if you will."

"Had you talked about the possibility of getting remarried?"

"Not in great detail. Your father's a hopeless romantic at heart. He would've wanted it to be a surprise—the ring, the proposal, everything. A few months ago he'd asked if I'd be open to the idea, and I'd said I'd think about it, but that's all."

"That's it?"

"There were a few other signs, if you must know. I once went to reach in his jacket pocket for his keys, and he just about had a back spasm trying to keep me away from it. Then the other morning, his phone rang, and I handed it to him, and he seemed almost annoyed when I glanced at the caller ID. Which is preposterous because we don't have secrets. I know we don't. We have both agreed that we can use each other's phones freely. This time around, we're all about trust."

There it is, I thought. My mother hadn't yet pieced together what I was getting at, but the fact of the matter was that my father had been hiding something. My naïve, hopeful mother had assumed it was for the positive—a marriage proposal. Her cynical, commitment-phobe daughter had assumed he was hiding something. In this case, I hated to be right, but I suspected I knew my father better than she gave me credit for.

"Oh, I see," she said softly. "You think this has something to do with his disappearance."

"The signs are there. If he'd been hiding his phone, keeping his belongings tucked out of reach..."

"He wasn't having an affair."

"I don't think he was," I said. "That doesn't mean he wasn't involved in something else that could've gotten him in trouble."

"No. Just, no. You're twisting this all around. You always do this. You turn a good thing into something awful."

I knew my mother was lashing out, and it didn't make me feel any better. Possibly because I was worried she had a point. After all, lately, it felt like everything I became involved with turned complicated. The issues with my father. The whole wedding debacle with Gem and Mindy. Even my relationship with Russo.

"I didn't mean that," my mother said, "I know it's your job. I'm talking about your job. That's all. Not *you* specifically."

"I'm not offended," I said quickly, too quickly maybe. "It's true."

"No, it's not, honey. I'm sorry. I just don't want to believe it."

"I'm going to play the bad cop now because someone else is going to do it sooner or later, and I want to make sure you're prepared. Can you think of anything else that Dad was doing that made you think he was hiding a surprise from you? Something that could maybe have been misinterpreted?"

She pursed her lips. "He canceled on me one night. I really didn't think anything of it. Your father called a week or so ago to say he'd eaten a bad sandwich and thought he had food poisoning. He was going to stay home instead of coming over."

"That's good memory, Mom. It's helpful."

"At the time, I didn't think anything of it. I mean, we talked for two hours that night and again first thing the next morning. He did sound pretty miserable. I figured he wouldn't be spending the night on the phone with me if he was off to meet someone else. No, actually, I didn't even think about him going off to meet someone else because his having an affair just isn't even realistic. I'm with him almost every night. He loves me. I know he loves me."

"Of course he does. Nobody thinks this is about an affair. That's actually something I'm certain about, and I'm never certain of anything."

My mother gave me a thin smile. "You're just saying that."

"No," I said, making eye contact with her at the red light before the mall parking lot, "I truly mean it."

I was surprised to find I did mean it. In the back of my mind, I had to wonder if that had something to do with my father's supposed code of honor among criminals. A man couldn't have an affair, but he could kill someone to save his family, and the latter was seen as noble? It still didn't make sense to me, but I could sort of see the logic. Maybe someday I would understand.

"Anything else?"

"The phone call," my mother reiterated, "it was weird. I thought it was maybe the jeweler calling about a fitting. I realize how stupid that sounds now. Maybe you could trace that number."

"Now you're thinking like a cop." I smiled again. "We don't have Dad's phone, but I'll have Asha see if she can get into his records anyway."

"As for the keys-in-the-pocket thing, I don't know what that was about. I really thought it was about a ring. He was so sweet right after and apologetic, and I just thought he was sort of apologizing for overreacting."

"He could've had a name, a receipt, a phone number, something," I mused aloud. "Do you still have the jacket at your house?"

"It's winter," my mother said. "He was wearing it the night he went to the bar."

"Do you mind if I make a quick call?"

With my mother next to me, I dialed Asha and explained to her about my mother's theory and the phone number my father had been uncomfortable to answer in front of my mother. Asha promised to look into it.

We climbed out of the car and faced the mall, which was a whole other beast I wasn't prepared for. I took a deep breath and steeled myself as we faced the entrance which was surrounded by Santas clanging bells and little elves handing out candy canes to kids. I should have known better than to put off finding a dress until the week before Christmas.

"I hate shopping."

"You're a good cop."

"What?" I turned to face my mother. "What are you talking about?"

"You're a good cop and an even better daughter." My mom leaned up onto her tiptoes and kissed me on the cheek. "I'm sorry about what I said earlier."

"Forget about it. I already did."

Then my mom pulled me into a hug, and I hugged her back, and it felt nice. I forgot how long it'd been since I'd taken the time to stop and actually embrace my own mother. We saw each other so frequently, little bits in the coffee shop, in passing as I made my way to work, once in a while when I stopped by her house. It was easy to take it all for granted.

"I love you, Mom," I said. "We'll find Dad in time for Christmas. I promise."

Chapter 12

It was a true testament to how much I was trying to please my mother that I walked out of that mall with not one but two dresses. In her words, "It wouldn't hurt to have two decent things to wear around the holiday season, what with my boyfriend coming to town for the first time in months."

On a positive note, besides getting my outfits squared away for the wedding and Christmas, my mother's spirits seemed to have been buoyed the smallest amount by our outing. She hadn't forgotten about my missing father, but she'd been temporarily distracted, which counted for something. I'd even seen her smile when I'd put on the second dress, and that was the real reason I'd pulled out my credit card and swiped it.

Two hours later, my phone rang as my mother and I exited the cheerfully decorated lobby of the mall. I gestured to my mom that I was going to step away to answer it, and I tossed her the keys to my car so she could start it up and stay warm.

I ducked out of sight of the loudly clanging Santas and their bells and was surprised to find Chief Sturgeon's name on the caller ID. "Hello, Chief?"

"Where are you, Rosetti? A bell choir?"

"The mall," I said apologetically. "I'm with my mom. Trying to keep her busy."

"Good thinking. Though you know we're going to need to talk to her, sooner rather than later."

"I'm dropping her off at the café now. She knows you'll be stopping by at some point."

"We found your father's phone."

I blinked. "Really? I already checked with Asha to see if we could triangulate a location for it, but it was turned off, and—"

"It's not always about modern technology," Sturgeon said. "I had some guys scouring the streets near Gallagher's for any signs of a struggle."

"You found signs of a struggle?" I felt my heart racing in my throat. This could finally be the evidence I needed to truly accept the fact that my father was missing—and not by his choice. "Where?"

"Not necessarily. Sorry, Rosetti. We just found the phone. Crumpled and broken, almost completely destroyed. It was a block from Gallagher's next to a gutter, but it's impossible to say if it was dragged that far by traffic, wind, being kicked, whatever, or if that's where it was left."

"No sign of a struggle?"

"None. Of course, it's possible an assailant overtook him as he left Gallagher's, relieved your father of his phone, and put him in a car he had waiting out front."

"Okay."

"It's also possible your father dropped the phone himself, stepped on it, kicked it into the street, and vanished of his own accord."

"Right."

"I'm afraid it's not a good lead, but it's something."

I told the chief about my mother remembering a phone number my father hadn't wanted to answer in front of her and suggested he check with Asha for any updates. Then I hung up as he promised to keep me informed of any additional developments.

"Rosetti, it would be good if we could get into your father's house too. And it would be good if we can keep your mother close by."

"Are you saying that you want me to tell my mother not to leave town?" I waited a beat as it sank in. "You don't actually think she had anything to do with my father's disappearance, do you?"

"Rosetti, you know how we do things. We explore every option under the sun. I'm not saying your mother's in on anything. Just that we need to ask her some questions."

"That's fine, but she didn't have anything to do with it. I'll tell you that right now."

"This is why you're not on the case." Chief Sturgeon's voice was stern but surprisingly kind. "Did you even consider the fact that your father could've been having an affair; your mother found out, and she wasn't happy about it?"

"That's just not a possibility."

"Exactly. Any other case, you would've already made that leap. It's always the spouse, remember?"

I swallowed hard. Sturgeon had a point even if I didn't want to admit it. I knew with my whole heart that my mother wasn't involved in my father's disappearance, but if I put myself in Sturgeon's shoes, I could understand why he had to ask the questions. Especially considering my father's murky past.

"Call me if you learn anything new," I said. "And you can get the keys to my dad's place from my mom when you talk to her. Do what you need to do to find him."

Sturgeon hung up. I made my way back to the car, feeling like I was moving in some parallel universe to the cheer around me. Santas smiled; elves giggled; lights twinkled. People walked from the mall laughing with loved ones and carrying huge stacks of presents, all preparing for the joyful week ahead.

This week was time that should be spent with family, eating sweets and watching festive movies. Instead, I was dealing with a chief who thought my mom might've killed my father and a murderer who had felt it necessary to shoot their victim upwards of five times. It was days like these I wondered what drew me to my profession.

When I got in the car and greeted my mom, the look on her face told me she knew something had changed. I wasn't sure if it was my expression or something else, but I could tell that she sensed it. There was a change in the air, and our temporary shopping distraction had already lost its impact.

"That was the chief," I said. "He's sending a few people over to talk to you."

"The chief."

"The best people are on the case, Mom. Just be prepared for them to ask you some difficult questions."

My mother folded her hands in her lap and stared straight ahead. "It's nothing they haven't asked me before. I can handle it. In case you're wondering, Kate, I'm innocent. I didn't have anything to do with your father disappearing on us."

"I know. The thought didn't even cross my mind."

I dropped my mother off at the café, then parked and headed next door to the precinct. Asha had sent me a text to call her back, but I figured I might as well swing by in person.

"What's up?" I found Asha and Chloe together, chatting in low tones about something. At my voice, their heads both snapped up. "Did you find something?"

"You didn't have to come in," Asha said. "You could've called."

"I'm here," I said. "Tell me you've got a lead. I need something to do."

Asha glanced at Chloe. "A call came in about half an hour ago."

"From?"

"A woman. She's a local to the area, married with one kid."

I gave a shake of my head. "Okay. Does this have something to do with my dad?"

"No, honey. Sorry. But this woman wanted to report her husband missing."

"How does that relate to my case?"

Asha clicked a few keys on her computer, then nodded for me to look at the front of the room. "I had this woman email me a photo of her husband. This is what she sent."

I looked up at the screen and felt my pulse begin to race, but in a different sort of way this time. The thrill of the chase. A dog with a bone. Finally, I had something I could work with.

"That's our guy," I murmured. "That's Charles Marlo."

"Except, according to this woman, this man's name is Gavin Harris."

"He was married with a kid?" I shook my head. "I wonder if that's why he started up a fake identity. He wanted a new life, a family, and he preemptively wanted to protect them from whatever ugly business was in his past."

"I think that's a pretty good guess," Asha said.

"Either that, or he wanted to keep his history a secret from his wife," Chloe suggested. "This guy, Gavin Harris, has a whole alternate history separate from Charles Marlo. Different schools, occupations, the works. Though there are some similarities between them."

"We think he was trying to tell as much of the truth as he could," Asha said. "It's easier to keep stories straight when there are elements of truth to them."

"Have you checked out the history of Gavin Harris, then?"

"Of course," Asha said. "From what we can see, it's all fabricated as well. Some records clumsily so. It's easy to see the differences between this history and the one prepared by witness protection."

"Meaning he did this one himself."

"That's what I believe," Asha said. "It makes sense it's a patchier job—I mean, he's just one guy. He has a lower budget, less access to government assistance, the whole lot of it. Don't get me wrong, his falsified records are very convincing and quite thorough for anyone looking into his background, but it was no match for me and Chloe."

It was still disconcerting to see Asha partnering together with someone. She'd been such a lone wolf in the years I'd known her, especially when it came to her work. Apparently, Chloe was different. They seemed to feed off one another.

"Thanks, guys. This is great," I said. "Do you have an address?"

Asha hit print and nodded toward the piece of paper spitting out from the machine behind her. "You need someone to come with you?"

"I'll grab Jimmy," I said. "Is he still here?"

Asha nodded. "You don't mind if I keep Chloe working on this? I want to try and piece together what's truth from fiction in this guy's past. It could help us narrow down which court case he might've been a part of—if one exists."

"Please do."

I made my way into the office and found Jimmy at his desk. He really hadn't moved much in the hours I'd been gone. Only his stack of Twizzlers had depleted accordingly.

"Come on," I said. "We've got a lead. I'll fill you in on the way."

Chapter 13

"Well, I can see Charles Marlos's apartment from Gavin Harris's house." Jimmy sat in the passenger's seat of my car. He glanced at the house in front of us, then beyond. "I mean, literally."

"The guy didn't venture far," I agreed. "I can't tell if that helped or hindered him."

Jimmy and I had arrived at a cheerful little house not far from the apartment we'd first visited in search of Charles Marlo. It was also a stone's throw from the little co-op market outside of which he'd been killed.

"I guess in a way it's smart," Jimmy said. "He built up a life in this area, so people would report seeing him if anyone asked. Seems like he had his routine, his grocery shopping schedule, and whatever else that placed him in this area. He could also keep an eye on his old apartment and grab packages."

"He was doing all this to protect his family," I said. "It's sort of sweet."

"Look at you, getting all soft. Before, you'd have been saying he was doing all this to hide lies from his wife."

I gave Jimmy a look. "Don't start psychoanalyzing me."

He winked. "Shall we go in?"

I climbed out of the car and made my way to the front steps. Jimmy was close behind me. It only took one knock before the door swung open.

"Hi, Mrs. Harris?" I asked. "I'm Detective Rosetti, and this is my partner, Jimmy Jones. We're here from the TC Task Force."

She frowned. "Wait a minute, I've read about you guys. Your offices are just down the street."

"That's us."

"No, no. I mean, you guys deal with homicides." She shook her head. "My husband is just missing, not dead. I told them that when I called it in."

"Can we come in for a minute?" I asked. "We just want to ask you a few questions about your husband."

"I-I guess," she said. "Sure, come on in. Sorry about the mess. I have a toddler."

The house was spotless. I wasn't sure if it was the sort of house that was always spotless, or if Mrs. Harris had spent her afternoon stress-cleaning. In the short time it took her to lead us to the living room, she picked up one blanket from the back of a chair, refolded it, and smoothed the already tidy blanket. She didn't even seem to realize she was doing it.

Once we were in the living room, she gestured for us to sit and offered us tea and coffee. Jimmy and I both declined. Then she disappeared from the room for a moment and returned a second later holding a baby monitor. She held it up, gave a smile.

"I was baking when you two arrived. Stupid, I know." The smile slid off her face. "I don't know what to do. I feel so helpless sitting here doing nothing when Gavin is missing. Lord knows the banana bread isn't going to help him, but I needed to keep my hands busy."

"This man is your husband, correct?" I held up a photo to show her, except this photo was actually taken from Charles Marlo's ID. I wanted to see if she'd recognize the man based on Marlo's identity and not her husband's identity.

"I've never seen this photo before," she said, "but yes, that's Gavin. Where did you get this picture?"

"We're looking into your husband's history," I said vaguely. "It turned up in our search results."

She nodded as if satisfied with the explanation. She gave us a feeble attempt at a smile. "Why don't you send me the report of his history when you're done, then?" She laughed, a hollow sound. "He doesn't like to talk about his past much."

I resisted a glance in Jimmy's direction. Mrs. Harris seemed to have her wits about her despite being obviously distracted and upset about her husband's disappearance.

"Please, ma'am, can you tell me what makes you suspect that your husband is missing?" I asked. "When was the last time you saw him?"

I knew that soon enough we'd need to break the news to Mrs. Harris about her husband's death, but I had no clue how she'd react—if she'd become hysterical or unresponsive or what. It would benefit both her and Gavin, and the investigation as a whole, if I could gather some information from her before ruining her life. It felt awful to delay the inevitable, but if we wanted justice for Gavin Harris, we needed to know everything we could about his mystery life.

"Why do I suspect he's missing?" She stared at me. "Because he's not here, and he should be here."

"When's the last time you saw him?"

"Saturday morning," she said. "He went out for a walk. I never saw him again."

"Did you try calling him?"

"He always leaves his phone here when he goes walking," she said. "He doesn't take much of anything except maybe some cash for emergencies. He says he doesn't want to be distracted, that it's his time to think. I always told him he could just put his phone on silent, but it was just one of his quirks. I actually thought it was sort of cute. Wholesome, you know?"

Or secretive, I thought with a glance at Jimmy. It sounded like our guy didn't want any ID on him that would've tied him to his family if it wasn't necessary. "Was he going somewhere specific on his walk?"

"Just exercise," she said. "He takes a walk most days. Once in a while he'll swing by the grocery store on the way back. I didn't even... I didn't even think to check with the grocery store. I've been so busy with Addy—our toddler—and Gavin's disappearance that I didn't even think... He hadn't said he was going to pick anything up that morning."

"You expected him home immediately after his walk?"

"Yeah, I mean, he didn't even take his phone or keys. Where would he have gone? I called yesterday, but they said a few hours wasn't enough to report a guy missing. I called back today and insisted. Now, here you are."

"Has he ever done anything like this before?" I asked. "Disappeared, I mean?"

There was a slight hesitation before she said the word, "No."

"Mrs. Harris, the truth is only going to help us right now. No matter how difficult it is."

"There was one time that he sort of... left in the middle of the night."

"Left?"

"I mean, he left the house unexpectedly," she said. "I woke up at three in the morning, and he was gone. I panicked and called him. He'd left his phone and his wallet again. I paced the house, frantic, and he came strolling in an hour or so later like nothing had happened."

"Did he say where he'd gone?"

"Yeah," she said. "For a walk. I mean, it looked like that was what he'd done. He was dressed in sweatpants, had headphones in, everything. The car was in the garage when I'd looked, so I knew he hadn't driven off anywhere."

"I see."

"He told me he had a project at work that was stressing him out. I mean, he's a mechanic, so I was a little surprised, but sometimes he does get larger projects—old cars to fix up, things like that. He said he couldn't sleep and just needed some fresh air."

"You believed him?"

"I had a healthy amount of skepticism as any wife might have, but yes, I did believe him. He wasn't having an affair. I know that's what you're thinking."

"That wasn't what I was thinking, but why would you suggest it?"

"A husband disappearing in the middle of the night? I know that's the first conclusion every detective jumps to. I watch TV. It's always the spouse."

I was actually wondering if Gavin's middle-of-the-night disappearance had something to do with his other life, but I wasn't ready to share that theory quite yet. He could've popped over to his other apartment to see if he had any packages or met with someone from his past. Not many people went for a neighborhood stroll in the middle of the night—insomnia or not.

"That's why I... I waited," she said, playing with her hands. "To call back, I mean. Gavin is a wonderful husband and an even better father, but he has his quirks. He doesn't like to talk about his past. He's very anti-technology. No social media, no internet on his phone, that sort of thing. He'd do things like go for long walks where I couldn't contact him, and then there was the middle-of-the-night walk. None of that made me doubt how much he loved us though."

"You thought maybe your husband would come strolling in that door any minute like nothing had happened because he'd done it before."

"I *hoped* that was what would happen. That it was all a misunderstanding." She gave a tearful nod. "It's stupid, but what's the alternative?"

"How long have you known your husband?"

"Four years. We dated one year, got married shortly after, then had Addy not long after that."

On an impulse, I nodded to a photo on a shelf behind her. "Is that a wedding photo? Did you have a small wedding?"

"Yes, his idea. I mentioned he wasn't big on social media and the like. Well, he has no living family and very few friends around except for a couple people he works with. I wanted a bigger ceremony, so we compromised."

"How so?"

"We had a small thing here in our backyard for only my immediate family," she said. "Then he spent a lavish amount of money to take me on a destination wedding, an elopement-type honeymoon. It actually turned out to be a nice choice."

"How so?"

"I didn't have to lift a finger to plan the wedding at all," she said, leaning forward and whispering as if she were telling me trade secrets. "I didn't have to find a person to officiate, I didn't have to book a single plane ticket—nothing. The only thing I booked was my hair and nail appointment, and that's because... well, men. You understand."

I nodded as if I understood. Then I thought maybe Gem and Mindy would've benefitted from the same sort of plan. It might've saved a lot of heartache—and dieting—in the planning stages of their looming nuptials. Then again, I believed Gavin had a different sort of reason for a small ceremony, one that had everything to do with privacy and fake identities and nothing to do with planning and practicalities.

"You said he doesn't talk much about his past. Any idea why?"

"Oh, don't get any negative ideas from that," she said quickly. "I don't mean he's hiding something. He had a tough childhood. His parents died young. He never went to college and was embarrassed about his lack of education. In his words, he 'didn't do anything with his life' and was always trying to change that. When I'd pry about his younger years, he'd just tell me there was nothing pleasant to talk about from back then, and that the best part of his life was now, here with me and Addy."

"That's romantic in a way."

"I just gave up asking. I didn't want to make him uncomfortable."

"Mrs. Harris, I'm going to get into a few more questions about your husband's disappearance," I said. "Do you have any guesses as to what might have happened, before I do?"

"Honestly, not a clue. It's like he just walked off into the sunset and vanished. That seems like the most likely scenario in my mind."

"Did your husband have any enemies? Difficult friends? Issues at work?"

She shook her head. "He's quiet and easygoing. That's why people like him; he just fades into the background and doesn't cause problems. In a good way."

"I know what you mean," I said. What I didn't say was that her husband had likely tried very hard to create this persona. A persona where he was never more noticeable than the background of any room he was in. "There's nothing wrong with being easygoing."

"I like it. We complement each other very well. I'm a little more outgoing, but at heart, I'm an introvert. We like to stay home quite a bit. Then once we had Addy, our entire social life has basically consisted of being together as a family. We both love it, though."

"What about work?" I asked. "You mentioned it could stress him out?"

"Gavin takes pride in his work. Not many people do that, you know," she said. "It's a rare trait these days. I already mentioned he's self-conscious about not having a college degree, and I think that leaks into his work. He always does meticulous work, whether it's an oil change or a complete restoration of a classic car."

"Sounds like the sort of employee that's hard to find."

"Absolutely. He's underpaid, but he isn't treated poorly at the shop," she said. "I've always encouraged him to ask for a bonus or a little increase in pay, but he isn't bothered by it. He isn't greedy. He tells me that he has everything he needs right here. So long as he can support us and bring home a little extra, he's happy."

"Nobody at work has problems with him?"

"Not that I know of. He's never complained. If he did mention anything, it was about an interesting project he was working on or something. It seems like his boss sort of leaves him alone. Gavin works better that way, putting in his headphones and plugging away in silence. I've seen it myself. If you want my opinion, that's the only smart way to treat Gavin as an employee—trust him to do his own thing, and it'll be done right."

"Could I get the name of the auto shop?"

"Tom's Auto Repair," she said. "It's right down the street. Tom's the owner. He's owned it for years. He's retired now and doesn't step foot on-site much, but he's the one who hired Gavin. Now, there's a manager named Chris, but I think Tom must have told Chris to leave Gavin pretty much alone, which works well all around."

"Thank you for your time, Mrs. Harris. There is something that I'd like to discuss with you now, but I'm afraid it's not pleasant."

"My husband is gone. No offense, but nothing about this visit is pleasant. I'm worried sick about him."

"The man I showed you earlier in the photo, the picture you didn't recognize..." I pulled it out again and showed it to her. I waited until she got a good look. "This man goes by the name Charles Marlo."

"That's not possible." She raised a finger and pressed it against the photo. "I recognize the little freckle on my husband's temple. Are you telling me he has a twin or something?"

"I'm afraid I'm telling you that your husband had a second identity."

She took a sharp breath. "That's preposterous. My husband doesn't even know how to work the internet. How could he have even managed to get a fake ID? It makes no sense."

"We're still investigating why he might have had two separate lives, two separate IDs, two separate addresses," I said, "but the reason we know about this person at all is because he was killed yesterday."

"Th-this person?" She winced. "You mean my husband?"

"We didn't know it was your husband until today when you reported him missing," I said. "We'd only ID'd the victim as the man named Charles Marlo. We were trying to find out more information about this man, next of kin, anything, really. We were having a difficult time."

"You're telling me that my husband is dead?"

"I'm so sorry, Mrs. Harris. I'm sure you have a lot of questions."

"How did he die?"

"He was on a walk, and he did stop by the grocery store," I said. "Unfortunately, he was killed outside of it in a drive-by shooting."

"My husband was killed? Murdered? Oh my God," she said. "No. That can't be possible. Absolutely not. Was it random? Random street violence? It must have been. Nobody would have done that to my husband. Poor Addy, her father. No, this can't be happening."

As if the toddler could sense her mother's distress, a cry sounded from over the baby monitor. It resonated through the whole house, rendering the monitor useless.

"I've got to get her," she said, standing, distractedly wiping at her face. "My poor baby."

"Is there someone we can call?" I asked. "Someone to be with you?"

"M-my mom. I'll call her. She only lives twenty minutes away."

Jimmy and I sat in silence for a few moments, listening to the sounds of Mrs. Harris lifting her toddler from the crib and shushing her. The choked sound of sobs followed. A moment later, she was on the phone asking her mother to come by. When she returned, Mrs. Harris had somewhat composed herself, though her face was as white as a sheet.

"Why?" she murmured. "Why did this happen to him?"

"We're looking into that," I said. "We're going to find out what happened. I promise you we'll find out who did this to your husband."

She nodded, a blank look on her face. She patted her daughter's back. A shock of dark hair stood up on Addy's head. The little girl stuck a thumb in her mouth and snuggled against her mother's chest.

"Would you like us to wait here with you?" I asked. "Just until your mom gets here?"

"No, no, it's fine," she said briskly. "I need to feed Addy. There are arrangements, I'll have to—oh, please tell me I can have his body back to bury him. I'll have to—"

"Yes, of course," I said. "It will be released to you as soon as possible."

Mrs. Harris nodded, then walked toward the door, assuming we were following behind her. She pulled it open and stood there, still obviously in shock.

"I'm really sorry," I said. "It sounds like your husband really cared about you."

"He did," she whispered. "Gavin was a good man. He didn't deserve this."

Jimmy waited to speak until we'd made it back to my car. On the drive back to the precinct, he glanced over at me. "Feeling sentimental?"

"What do you mean?"

"You're not usually into the sympathy thing with the victim's family."

"Yes, I am," I argued back. "I hate notifying the family. It's awful. They've just lost a loved one."

"That's what I mean," Jimmy said. "You hate it. You try to keep as businesslike as possible. I'm not saying I blame you. We've all gotta deal with this stuff in our own way or we'd be a lot more dead inside than we already are. But it just seemed different for you this time."

"Maybe. I don't know," I said. "It just felt like the right thing to say. It did seem like he cared about his family, despite whatever this Gavin guy might have done in his past. It seems hard to reconcile a nice, hardworking family man to the sort of guy who gets shot up on the sidewalk."

Jimmy nodded. "You'll find your dad, Kate. The chief's got the best people on it."

"I know, Jimmy," I mumbled. "I know we will."

"Angelo cares about you guys too," Jimmy said. "It's okay to forgive the guy."

"Remember what I said about psychoanalyzing?"

Jimmy raised a hand. "Just saying, Rosetti. It's Christmas."

***

After our interview with Gavin Harris's wife, Jimmy and I returned to the precinct. Asha had taken off for some Sunday evening plans with her family. Chloe was still at the office, to my surprise, leaning over her computer and staring at lines of letters and numbers that made no sense to me.

"I think I found the number that called your dad," she said. "It belongs to a shop."

"A shop?" I asked, heading closer to her. "Not a jewelry shop by chance, is it?"

"A mechanic type of shop."

I frowned. "Why would my dad care if my mom saw the name or the number of something like that?"

"Maybe he just didn't want her to answer," Chloe said. "I don't know, maybe he knew someone there. Or maybe your mom misinterpreted the situation."

"Can you get me the name and number?" I asked. "I'm curious if I might know why the shop was calling him anyway."

"Maybe it was nothing," she said. "Maybe he was just getting his oil changed and was annoyed. You know how those places always try to screw you over—they call you to let you know the oil's done, but then they're all like, 'Oh, by the way, we also need to fix your brakes and filters and repaint your entire car, and it will cost you one million dollars.'"

Jimmy snorted behind me. "Just say no when they ask if you want that extra stuff done."

"I get scared," Chloe said. "What if my brakes really do need replacing, and I blow it off, then I skate right through a red light and hit another car?"

Jimmy just shook his head. "Have your boyfriend answer those calls."

"That's sexist," I said. "I can say no to those people just fine. They don't even ask me half the time."

"That's because you rarely service your car," Jimmy said. "And also because people are afraid of you."

"That's true," Chloe said. "I was scared of you until I learned that you're actually a softie inside."

"Softie?"

Chloe's cheeks turned red. "That was a joke. Sorry. I'm still scared of you. A little. A healthy amount."

"Me too," Jimmy agreed. "But in a good way."

"Send me that information, will you?" I asked. "I'm going home for the night. Shopping is exhausting, and I'm not going to be able to fit any more interviews in on a Sunday night. I'll take a look into it tomorrow."

"I just sent the files to you," Chloe said. "Just so you know, I also have to send it to Detective Young since he's leading the investigation into your dad's disappearance."

"I get it. Thanks, Chloe."

"How'd it go today?"

I quickly filled Chloe in on our interview with Mrs. Harris. I assured her that Gavin Harris and Charles Marlo were almost certainly the same man. Before we'd left the Harris house, I'd also asked Mrs. Harris to pack up a few items of her husband's that I had dropped off in the lab downstairs. Hopefully, Melinda would be able to match the DNA from

Gavin Harris's hairbrush to the DNA of the man known as Charles Marlo to confirm the two men were without a doubt the same person.

"It's weird," Chloe said. "I mean, it's obvious this guy was hiding something, but *what*? It's driving me nuts not knowing."

"Well, now that we know the identity he was living under, maybe we'll be able to figure it out," I said. "Not to mention, we're all following up with witness protection to see if we can get some information on Marlo's original identity."

"It just seems like a guy who has a wife and a daughter and works a normal job shouldn't be involved in a mess like this, you know?" Chloe said, more to herself than anyone else.

"I guess he got his second chance and didn't want to waste it. He straightened out his life and was trying to live simply," I said. "But I guess sometimes it's not enough. Sometimes the past catches up with us all no matter how far we run."

"Don't I know it," Chloe muttered. "Okay, well, I'll take more of a peek into Gavin Harris's current life and family."

"Go home," I said. "You and Asha can do that first thing in the morning."

"But—"

"It's fine," I said. "Go get some rest. You've been here all weekend."

"I'll just type up what you told me for the report. Then I'll take off."

I studied her closer. "You're avoiding something."

"Huh?"

"What is it, family problems?" Jimmy asked. "Boyfriend issues?"

"There are no issues," Chloe said, swiveling to face her computer. Then on second thought, she swiveled back. "I'm getting nervous about seeing Maxwell."

"Why?" I asked. "Rough patch?"

"The opposite," Chloe said. "It's amazing every time we're together. It's just, I don't know, I can't help but feel like this is sort of a big step."

"A weekend trip?"

"I'm spending a full week with him. We're going to a cabin in the mountains. I'm going to meet his family. We're spending a major holiday together. It's just a lot of stuff."

"Meeting the family," I said. "You could've just said that. I'd be hiding out at work too."

"You haven't met Jack's family yet?"

I shook my head. "The opportunity's never really presented itself. Plus, we see each other for such short periods of time, we usually try not to arrange a lot of stuff to do when we're together."

"Interesting."

"It's right for us," I insisted. "We're doing just fine."

"No, no, I know."

"So do you feel like your relationship is moving too fast?" I asked, switching the focus back to Chloe. "You guys have only been dating for what, a little over three months?"

"That's not the problem at all. It could go faster, if you ask me," Chloe said, her eyes shining. "I'm really excited for it. I definitely love him, and he loves me. Agent Brody is just perfect, plus he's a major hunk. I guess that's why I'm nervous. He's *so* perfect, I don't want to mess things up. I suck at skiing, and I just really want his family to like me."

"They'll like you," I said. "I wouldn't worry about your skiing prowess."

She gave a soft smile. "Thanks, boss. Anyway, I don't need to bore you with this stuff. I'll just get this report finished and turn in for the night. I should start packing anyway."

"I'll stick around a few minutes and then take off," Jimmy chimed in. "See you tomorrow, Kate."

I said good night to my colleagues, then made my way home for the evening. At the last minute, I changed directions and swung over to my mother's place. She would have closed up the café and gone home by now if my calculations were correct. I couldn't say exactly what made me stop, but it had to have been something about the way I'd left her after shopping. She'd seemed like she might need some company.

I was surprised to find another car already in the driveway. My sister must have had the same inkling I'd had. I parked my car behind Jane's and headed to the front door. I knocked out of formality, then let myself inside. I immediately smelled pepperoni pizza, the thick kind with the cheese stuffed in the crust, and I knew I'd made the right decision.

The smell of pizza and the ambiance of my parents' house brought back memories of high school with a vengeance. Stuffed-crust pizza had always been Jane's comfort food of choice. Bad test result? Stuffed-crust pizza. Boyfriend problems? Stuffed-crust pizza. Missing father? Stuffed-crust pizza.

I found my mother and sister in the living room. A chick-flick movie was on the television screen, and snack debris littered the coffee table.

My mother looked up at me and smiled, but there was surprise in her eyes. "Kate! What are you doing here? Any word on your father?"

"Nothing yet, Mom," I said, easing into the room. "I thought you might need some company tonight, but it seems like Jane beat me to it."

My mother's eyes crinkled as her smile grew wider. "Come on. There's more pizza and root beer."

"Anything stronger?"

"Oh yeah, that's in the kitchen," Jane said, raising a martini glass. "Help yourself."

I went into the kitchen and grabbed a cold beer from the fridge and helped myself to a still-hot slice of pizza. I returned to the living room and found a space on the couch on the opposite side of my mother. My mom had hit pause on the remote when I'd entered the room, and she hit play the second I pulled a blanket over my lap.

Jane looked across my mother at me and gave me a smile. My mother reached over and squeezed my hand. For once, I was glad I'd left work on time. This was where I needed to be tonight.

Chapter 14

"Good morning, good morning, what an amazing morning," my mother chirped. "Wake up girls, I've got breakfast ready."

I threw the covers off, taking a moment to place myself in the guest bedroom of my mother's house. My sister had fallen asleep on the couch downstairs, and I wasn't sure where my mom had camped out for the night—or if she'd even slept at all.

"Did they find Dad?" I asked groggily. "What's so amazing?"

"Both girls waking up under my roof again?" my mom practically trilled as she opened the blinds in my bedroom. "This hasn't happened since Jane was in high school. Even then, she was sneaking out more nights than not, so I never really knew who was sleeping under this roof."

"Yeah, sorry about that," Jane said, appearing in the doorway to the guest bedroom and rubbing her eyes. "I was pretty dumb."

"I like the term rebellious. Or maybe adventurous," my mother corrected. "Then again, that's easier to say when those years are in the rearview mirror. You gave me more heart attacks than I cared for in those days."

I waggled my eyebrows at Jane.

"Oh, you should talk," my mother snapped at me.

"Me?"

"You still give me heart attacks," my mother said. "Out there facing criminals every day."

"You like my job when it benefits you," I said. "Remember when you wanted me to do a background check on the guy you were trying to internet date?"

My mother looked sheepish, but it quickly passed when a ding sounded in the background. "That'll be the cinnamon rolls. Hot and fresh. Coffee's ready."

I sat up in bed. Jane had slipped into some sort of night-shirt that I vaguely remembered from high school years. It didn't totally fit her anymore.

"I get the shower first," I said. "I've got to be at work."

"Not if I beat you in there and lock the door," Jane said. "You can't call dibs on the shower. You know that."

"Dude. I'm a homicide detective," I told her. "You really don't think I know how to pick a lock?"

"Who doesn't know how to pick the lock?" Jane retorted. "It takes a bobby pin for crying out loud."

"Oh, I love this." My mother clapped her hands together. "All of this bickering. My two sweet baby girls." My mother moved from one of us to the other, giving both me and Jane little pecks on the cheeks. "Just like the old days. What a treat. Almost makes me forget your father is still missing, for a few minutes."

The room grew quieter as the truth as to why we were all there reemerged.

"You can shower first," Jane said. "I'm hungry anyway."

Twenty minutes later, I'd showered and changed into one of Jane's old pairs of sweatpants and a sweatshirt. It mostly fit; it was clean, and it'd last me until I could get home to switch into new clothes. I met my mother and Jane down at the breakfast table where the cinnamon rolls were still hot. My mother was just pouring me a cup of coffee.

The three of us sat in the kitchen, quietly savoring the rich breakfast meal together. When we were almost finished eating, my mother burst into tears. I paused, mid-refill of my coffee.

"Mom?" I asked cautiously with a glance at Jane. "Everything okay?"

"It's snowing," she said with a sniff. She nodded outside to emphasize her point.

"Right," I said slowly. "It's December."

"It's a nice sort of snow," she continued. "The real Christmas type of snow. Look at us. We've got Christmas music, lights, cinnamon rolls..." My mom nodded toward the living room where she'd set up a tree. Lights twinkled along the kitchen counter. Her Santa collection had been set out at various intervals around the house. "Meanwhile, your father is somewhere, probably miserable, and I just can't bear to think about it."

"We're making some progress, Mom," I said. "I'm going to look into it more today. I told you the chief has a great team on it. We're closing in on him; I can feel it."

My mother nodded. She rose and brought some plates to the sink. She started to do the dishes. Jane offered to help, but my mother waved her off.

"No, no, it's good for me," she said. "What will I do all day when you girls leave anyway?"

"Um, run your café?" I suggested. "You have plenty to do, Mom. You don't have to sit around here and wait. That will only make things worse."

"Would a little sympathy kill you, Kate?" Jane hissed. "Mom, I made us appointments to get our nails done. I asked Elizabeth and a couple of the other girls to cover for today. We can pick up those sub sandwiches you like on the way back."

"And a bottle of wine," my mom added. "One of the big kinds."

"Sure," Jane said. "That sounds perfect."

I rose and made my way over to kiss my mother on the cheek. "I love you. Thanks for the delicious breakfast. I've got to head out and get to work. I'll keep you posted if I hear anything."

My mother set an extra cinnamon roll or two for the road in a Tupperware container and shoved it at me before I took off. "For Jimmy," she said. "You know how his wife doesn't let him eat these."

"For a reason," I muttered, but when Jane flashed me a look, I shut up and accepted the Tupperware with a smile. "Thank you. He's going to love these."

"I know," my mother said absentmindedly. "Be safe out there, honey."

I hopped in the car and made a quick stop home to change into a new outfit that wasn't leftover from the 90s. Then I hopped right back in the car and headed to the precinct to pick up Jimmy. I texted him to let him know I was on the way, and he was waiting outside when I got there.

"Tom's Auto Repair?" Jimmy asked as he opened the passenger's side door. "Is that a cinnamon roll I smell?"

"Which question would you prefer I answer first?"

"No need to answer the latter as I can see the answer right here." Jimmy grabbed the Tupperware and cracked open the top. "Can I assume you're not going to eat these?"

I wrinkled my nose at him. "You already breathed on them."

"Good," Jimmy said. "Now for the former."

"Yes," I said, pulling out of the parking lot. "I thought we'd hit up the auto repair shop, and see what they have to say about our mystery man."

"If he was just a good employee trying to stay under the radar, I doubt we'll find much."

"Touché, but it's about all we've got. By the way, Asha sent me some info on a number that my dad had received a call from. The file's on my phone. Can you pull it up for me? I didn't get a chance to look at it last night. I went to my mom's, and we watched movies, drank beer, and ate pizza. I didn't think about work for a few hours."

"Sounds like you made the right choice with that decision."

"Pull up the file on my phone for me, will you?" I asked, handing my device over to Jimmy. "I didn't think about this yesterday, but what are the chances it was Tom's Auto Repair calling my father?"

I had a bad feeling slithering down my spine that this coincidence was suddenly going to become very un-coincidental. I would've noticed it last night if I'd gone home like I'd planned, but I'd been so distracted by keeping my mother company, I hadn't made the connection.

"I'm sorry, Kate," Jimmy said. "The number on your father's phone was Tom's Auto Repair shop."

"I guess we've got questions on a few cases to ask, then," I said grimly, ignoring the sinking feeling in my gut that the auto repair shop before me might hold some answers—both to the truth behind the killing and the secrets to my dad's disappearance.

"Keep a cool head, Kate," Jimmy said as we emerged from the car. "Don't jump to any conclusions."

"It's not much of a jump when every lead we have right now is pointing us to this exact location."

"You're upset." Jimmy stopped walking. "It's not a good idea to go in there when you're worked up."

"We need answers, and I'm not going to sit around and wait for them."

Jimmy expelled a breath. "I'm just saying, if someone really is guilty here, or if someone knows where your dad is, we don't want to seem too eager. It could lead to bad things down the road."

"But—"

"We need to operate under the impression that your father is still alive, Kate," Jimmy said, waiting until I made eye contact with him.

He was saying my first name a lot, which was unusual. It took me a minute, but I finally registered what he was saying and managed to read between the lines. "You think that if I go in there angry and convinced someone is guilty, the kidnapper might be tempted to start tying up loose ends and get rid of my father?"

"I'm just saying. It's not a risk I'm willing to take."

I took another second to calm myself down, then I nodded. "You're right. I'm okay, Jimmy. I promise."

Jimmy studied me, then he nodded too. "I know you are. Let's go."

We made our way into the auto repair shop. The smell of old coffee and gasoline and paint was strong. There were more employees than I'd expected lingering about in the lobby around the coffee machine. It looked like we'd broken up some sort of get-together.

"Good morning," Jimmy said, introducing himself first and then me. "Any chance we can speak to the manager around here?"

"Good time to come in here," one of the guys said. "I'm the manager, but you'll probably want to talk to Tom if you're looking for the head honcho."

"Tom of Tom's Auto Repair?" Jimmy asked. "I thought he was retired."

"He is, but he keeps an eye on things," the man said. "He comes in for our weekly staff meetings. We just finished up this morning. That's why everyone's hanging around."

"Someone say my name?" A man somewhere in his mid-fifties came into the room. "Who's looking for me?"

"You're Tom?" I confirmed. When he nodded, I took a turn handling the introductions. "Can we talk somewhere private for a minute?"

"Come on back to my office," Tom said. "I've got an acupuncture appointment in an hour, so let's make this quick."

I glanced at Jimmy, who shrugged his shoulders. Apparently, acupuncture was a new excuse to get out of questioning early.

Tom led us into a back office. He sort of offered us coffee by waving a hand at the empty pot. Jimmy and I didn't even bother to formally decline. We took seats in the plain office chairs across the desk from him. Tom took a seat as well, then he waited for us to speak first.

"I understand you're not around the office much since you've retired," I said, "so I'm not sure if you can help us, but—"

"'Course I can," Tom said gruffly. "This is my place. I built it from the ground up. Just because I'm not spending my days tinkering under the actual cars themselves doesn't mean I don't know everything that goes on around here."

I caught Jimmy's smile out of the corner of my eye. My gut had been right. With one question, I'd established that Tom was not only defensive and proud of his place, but I'd caught him saying he knew every detail of what went on around here. Which meant that once we got into asking the harder questions later, he couldn't plead ignorance.

"Great," I said. "Seems like you've got a good place around here. My father actually comes here himself."

"Really? He got a name?" Tom asked. "I know every long-term customer. We're like a family around here."

"Angelo Rosetti?"

Tom's face was blank. "Haven't heard that one before. Are you sure this is the right place?"

"He's actually a new customer," I said. "He just brought his car in for the first time a week or two ago. He mentioned the name of your shop to me with a glowing recommendation."

Tom's eyes lit up. "That'd be why I don't know him, then. Like I said, I don't tinker as much as I used to, so I don't get to know the new customers as much as I'd like."

"Would you happen to know who worked on his car?"

"Not offhand, but we keep excellent records around here. Let me check. I'll be right back."

Tom disappeared, and when he returned, he was carrying a large three-ring binder that was bursting at the seams with what appeared to be sheets of ledger paper. I noted there wasn't even a computer in his personal office. There was one at the front desk, but I was also pretty sure it belonged in a museum.

"We do things old school around here," Tom said. "I don't trust technology. The internet is bad for your brain."

"Okay," I said.

"I make all my guys take notes in here whenever they work on a car," Tom said. "Sometimes I glance over it at the end of the week. They know if I find missing details or crappy notes, they'll be hearing from me."

"Sounds like you keep good tabs on your employees."

Tom was already running his finger down the worn pages of the booklet. "You said the name was Rosetti? No one in here by that name."

"Oh, weird," I said. "Maybe I misunderstood. I know he said he called to find out about your services. Maybe he was planning to bring the car in?"

Tom shook his head. "I don't see any name looking like that on the list. We only schedule a few days out because we keep so busy with walk-ins. The list isn't that long."

"Could you tell me who was working the front desk on this date?" I named the date in the memo from my phone. The date the number had called my father's phone.

Tom looked in the log again, then glanced up when he found what he needed. "I had three guys working that day. Any of them might've answered the phone. It's mostly George who's on the phone, but everyone pitches in. I can't say with certainty that he answered everything that day."

"Can I get the names of everyone working that day?"

"George Flores, John Neely, Patrick Hamilton."

"Wait a minute, Patrick Hamilton works here?" I asked. "You're sure?"

He looked at me like I'd grown two heads. "'Course I'm sure. I hire everyone myself. I take pride in my employees and only hire the best."

"Is Patrick here today?"

"Remind me how you know Patrick?"

"Hey, buddy, she's the cop," Jimmy said. "Detective Rosetti's the one asking questions today, Tom."

Tom barely looked at Jimmy.

"He's a friend of my dad's," I said. That part wasn't a lie. "That must be how my dad found out about this place. My dad trusts Patrick, so I bet that's why he recommended this place."

"Good man, Patrick," Tom said proudly. "I knew I was right to take a chance on him."

"What sort of a chance?"

"Patrick came out of prison and couldn't get a job any-where. It was a risk hiring him, but it paid off. He's a genius on the older vehicles. He's got a whole roster of people who come here just to work with him specifically."

"Have you ever had any problems reported about him as an employee?"

Tom frowned. "Is this investigation about Patrick? Did he do something?"

"Have you ever had any issues with Patrick?"

"I just told you, he's a good worker."

"But you must have kept an eye on him. He's fresh out of prison, and you were the only person willing to take a chance on him."

"He's a reformed guy," Tom said. "I know it. He's got a family at home. Just because someone came out of prison doesn't mean they're a bad person."

"Answer the question," Jimmy prompted. "Did you keep tabs on the guy?"

"There's no evidence to show Patrick was falling into old habits."

"But you were watching," I said. "You practically just said so yourself."

"I've got a big heart. I'm not an idiot," Tom said. "I keep my eyes on everyone. Patrick included. So far he's been nothing but an exemplary mechanic."

"Let's talk about Gavin Harris," I said. "I understand he works here too?"

"He does."

"What sort of employee is he?"

"Up until today, I'd say he was a great employee."

"Why has that changed?"

"He didn't show up for the meeting this morning or his shift afterward. I was just going to call him after we were done, as a matter of fact."

"Well, there's a pretty good reason for that," Jimmy said. "On account of he's dead."

"What?" Tom looked to me as if he wasn't about to take Jimmy at his word. "Dead? Gavin Harris?"

"I'm sorry," I said. "He died on Saturday. I take it he wasn't scheduled to work on Sunday?"

"No, he never does." Tom shook his head. "We have shortened hours on Sundays—Gavin used to work weekends, but he started taking them off when he had his kid. He worked Friday, then wasn't scheduled again until today."

"When's the last time you saw him?"

"That would've been a week ago," Tom said. "He was at the staff meeting. I wasn't in a lot last week. I had some friends in town."

"How long has Gavin been working here?"

"Almost three years now. My understanding was he was new to town when I hired him. I'm just glad he moved in close to this place. He's probably my best employee. Don't go saying that aloud, though. The others think he's weird."

"Why do they think he's weird?"

"He's quiet and keeps to himself. Perfect employee in my mind, but the other guys don't get it. I told you, it's almost like a family around here. The guys usually go out for drinks Sunday after their shift since they end early. Sometimes they do barbecues after we close Saturday. Friday night is bowling league and chicken wings."

"Busy social schedule," I noted.

"Not everyone goes to everything, but we've got enough guys interested in hanging out that it happens most weeks. Sometimes the wives come with. Not often, but every now and again."

"Did Gavin participate in these events?"

"Never. Not once," Tom said. "I like to take guys out for a little meal to welcome new employees, and Gavin wouldn't even do that. I ended up just bringing a bunch of bagels into the shop one morning and calling that his welcome party."

"So they think he's weird because he's a private person?"

"It's that, but it's a little more than that," Tom said. "I admit, the guy has barely uttered a word during the entire three years he's worked here. To me, that's not a bad thing. He was zero drama. Never had a complaint against him from a customer. Impeccable work ethic. I gave him the expensive cars and longer-term projects. He'd just tuck himself in a back corner, show up on time, do his job, eat his lunch at a picnic table outside if the weather permitted—alone—and go back to work."

"Did his behavior change at all recently?" I asked. "Did he skip shifts? Show up late? Anything like that?"

Tom shook his head. "Nope. Not that I can think of."

"We'd like to talk to a few of your other employees while we're here," I said. "Could you give us the names of anyone who worked closely with him?"

"You can talk to the manager, Chris. He handles day-to-day operations. Other than that, I don't know anyone particularly close to Gavin. You can ask all the questions that you want if it'll help. How did he die?"

I ignored the question. "Do you do a background check when you hire new employees?"

"Sure do. I told you, though, I hired Patrick even though he was fresh out of prison. I got a nose for personality types, see, and I could tell he was a reformed guy. It's not like he was even armed, robbing that bank. Nobody got hurt."

"Did you find anything when you looked into Gavin?"

"No. Should I have? I dunno; it's not my fault if I missed something. We just run the check and go off what we get. I remember every person I ever hired, and I never had a doubt about Gavin."

"Thanks for your time. We'll be in touch if we have any more questions," I said, sliding over my card. "Give us a call if you think of anything else that might be helpful. In the meantime, is it okay to use your office to talk to a few more of your employees?"

"If you're wanting to talk to this many people, his death wasn't an accident. Am I right?" Tom scanned back and forth between me and Jimmy. "What happened to Gavin? Did someone kill him?"

"He was murdered," I confirmed. "We're just trying to trace his day-to-day life at this point. That's all."

"You think someone here did it?"

"That's not what I said," I repeated. "We're just trying to understand his daily movements."

"Well, I'll tell you that I can't think of a reason anyone here would've killed him," Tom said. "Why would they have? He kept to himself, didn't cause waves, and did his job. Not worth the hassle."

"Okay then," I said. "Thanks for your time."

The next person to enter the office was the first person who'd spoken to us as we'd entered the auto repair shop. The guy had orange, curly hair and was shorter than both me and Jimmy. He introduced himself as Chris Dunlap and explained he'd worked here for ten years and had been manager for the last four.

"What's your schedule like?" I asked. "How closely do you work with the employees here?"

"I'm here all the time," Chris said. "This place is like home to me. I'm not married, no kids. It's part of the reason Tom trusted me to run this place. He knows I give it my everything."

"So are we talking nine to five?" Jimmy asked.

"I'm here most days of the week during main business hours," he said. "I pop in on the weekends. I'm always here early on staff meeting days to get things ready. Then there are some of the events we have on the weekends that I help with too."

"You mean bowling and barbecues and all that stuff?" I asked. "Tom mentioned you guys did a lot of things together."

"Yeah, that sort of thing too," he said. "Why?"

"Can you tell me about Patrick Hamilton?" I asked. "Have you ever had any trouble with him as an employee?"

"Did Patrick do something?" Chris's eyebrows furrowed. "I told Tom he never should've hired a guy just out of an orange jumpsuit, but he didn't listen to me. Seems he thought Patrick had changed."

"It seems like you're pretty skeptical of him," I said. "Is there any particular reason why?"

"I'm just saying, I'm of the mindset that people don't really change. Not when it comes to the big stuff." He shrugged. "It's not like he ever did anything here, at least that I know of. Why? Is he in trouble?"

"No, he's not in trouble," I said. "I'm just asking about people who work here. That's all."

"Oh. Well, okay."

"What about Gavin Harris?"

"Now, that guy didn't do anything. I mean *anything*," Chris said. "He came to work and did his stuff and left. That was it."

"So by anything, you mean he didn't join you for festivities outside of work?"

"Not once. He was sorta weird about it. We tried to include him, but he didn't want to be included."

"Do you think he might've just been busy with family and things?"

"Walter has three kids and a wife and still manages to meet with us once a month," Chris said. "You ask me, Gavin just had no interest in hanging out with any of us."

"That's not exactly a crime," I said. "Did anyone ever have actual complaints about him? Aside from the fact that he was quiet and withdrawn?"

"No, I guess not," Chris said. "He was an easy guy to manage. Just give him the job and let him run with it. I guess I can't complain really."

"Did Gavin ever have any beef with anyone here?"

"Not until today," Chris said. "I've got a beef with him today."

"Why's that?"

"He didn't show up for his shift. Totally blew off the staff meeting. That makes me look real bad in front of Tom. Like I'm not doing my job keeping the employees in line."

"Well, it's probably because he's dead," Jimmy said. "Gavin Harris died on Saturday."

Chris's eyes grew wide. "What? Dead?"

I nodded. "He was killed. That's why we're here asking questions."

"Oh crap," Chris said. "That's not good."

"No," Jimmy agreed. "Not good. Still got a beef with the guy?"

Chris shook his head, not realizing the question was rhetorical. "No, man. That sucks."

"Sure does," I said. "Now, can you think of anyone who might've had an actual beef with Gavin? Either an employee or maybe a disgruntled client?"

Chris gave a short laugh. "Aside from his wife, I don't think we've had a single complaint lodged against the guy."

"His wife?" I asked. "What do you mean by that?"

"I just mean, well, I figured you already knew." Chris looked worried as he glanced between us. "I don't want to snitch."

"We're homicide detectives," I said. "You're not snitching. If we find out you weren't truthful at any point during our conversation, we can arrest you for obstruction of justice."

Chris held up his hands. "I didn't mean it like that. I just meant I don't get into others' domestic disputes. Whatever Gavin did to tick off his wife, I didn't want any part of it."

"How do you know his wife was upset with him if he didn't talk about personal things at the office?"

"Because she stormed in here not two weeks ago," Chris said. "I was at the front desk. She came in asking to see him. More like demanding," he corrected. "I told her she could go on back, then I sort of melted into the office because I didn't want to get caught in the crosshairs. She was in a rage, man."

That was new and interesting information. Quite different from the impression I'd gotten from our previous meeting with Mrs. Harris. She'd left out the little detail about a big argument with her husband when we'd been speaking with her. Because she'd forgotten about it in her grief? Or because it pointed to her guilt?

"I understand," Jimmy said. "I've been married a long time. Did you hear what the fight was about? The gist of it?"

"I didn't, but some of the guys were talking about it that weekend at the bowling alley. Something about him having a second cell phone. Not good, man, not good. There's no legitimate reason for a secret second cell phone."

"Is there anything else you can think of that might be relevant to the investigation?"

"Not really," he said. "Of anyone, I knew Gavin the least of all the guys. Then again, maybe the guy was full of secrets. Sorta might explain why he was so quiet. Maybe he just didn't want to risk saying the wrong thing."

"Is Patrick here today?" I asked. "He should be here for the meeting, right?"

"He had a dentist appointment," Chris said. "Cleared it with me about three weeks ago. He won't be in until tomorrow."

"Great," I said, then I looked down at the other names Tom had given us who might've worked during the window of time my father had received a call from the shop. I requested to speak with both of the employees listed.

Chris sent both men in, one after the other, and Jimmy and I questioned them about Gavin and the phone call. Both men claimed they hadn't used the phone to make any outgoing calls, and my gut told me they were telling the truth. That left me to suspect that Patrick had been the one to call my dad, which really made sense. They knew each other.

After the initial interviews were finished, Jimmy and I had a brief chat with the rest of the employees still around. Nobody had much to say about Gavin aside from the fact that he was a hard worker and a quiet guy. We left the place an hour later.

"Back to Mrs. Harris?" I asked Jimmy. "Then Patrick?"

Jimmy didn't answer until we were in the car. "You want to fill me in on this Patrick guy? Do you think he's connected to your father's disappearance or Gavin's murder?"

"I'm not sure," I said. "Either, both. Whichever it is, we'll find out."

Chapter 15

On the way back to Gavin Harris's home, I filled Jimmy in on the details we knew of my father's disappearance. Admittedly, it wasn't much, but it was a start. By the time I finished, we tabled the discussion to focus on our visit with Gavin's wife.

I knocked on the door. It was opened a minute later by Mrs. Harris with her daughter on her hip. Mrs. Harris looked tired. Almost comatose.

"Detectives," she said. "Have you found out information on the man who killed Gavin?"

I noted her use of the word "man" in conjunction with the killer. It begged the question if she was using it as a general placeholder for the unknown, or if she was purposefully trying to lead us away from the possibility of a woman as the killer.

"Do you mind if we come in for a few minutes?" I asked.

"Of course not," she said. "I apologize for our appearances. We haven't had much energy to get dressed in real clothes, much less leave the house. Mascara is useless since I cry at least once an hour."

"We won't take up much of your time."

Mrs. Harris led us into the kitchen this time, a compact, bright space with robin's-egg-blue walls and a coastal vibe with white trimmings and a cozy breakfast nook. She set Addy in a highchair and absentmindedly gave her a few crackers that seemed to occupy the toddler's attention.

"Thanks for having us back," I said. "I know this is a difficult time for you."

"I didn't know you were coming," she said, looking up at me. "Did you find information about Gavin's killer?"

"We're working on it," I said. "Unfortunately, I can't get too into the details of our progress as it's an active investigation."

"Sorry, then why are you here?"

"I need to ask you a few more questions."

"Oh, okay. Sure."

"Do you know if Gavin might have had a second phone?" I asked. "Maybe a work phone or something?"

"I don't think he had a work phone." Mrs. Harris stood and grabbed a box of Cheerios from the cupboard even though her daughter was still busy with the crackers on her tray. She poured a few into her hand. "At least not one that I knew of."

"What about a second personal phone?"

"Why are you asking this?" She deflected again. "Did you find out something? Was Gavin having an affair?"

"I don't know; you tell us," I said. "Did you suspect something?"

"I-I don't know what you're talking about."

"Mrs. Harris, why didn't you tell us you confronted your husband at work?"

Her face paled a few degrees. "That was a personal, marital matter. It's not relevant to the investigation."

"You had a huge argument with your husband in front of his colleagues a week or two before he was killed," I said. "You don't think that's relevant?"

"You can't possibly think I killed Gavin." Mrs. Harris's eyes were wild as she glanced between us. "There's no way. I loved Gavin. That's why I confronted him."

"We've got eyewitnesses—"

"Yes, I argued with him," she said. "I'm not denying that. It doesn't mean I didn't love him. In fact, that's why I argued with him. I thought maybe he was having an affair."

"Why'd you confront him at work?" I asked. "Why not wait until he got home?"

A sheepish expression crossed her face. "I was angry. I didn't want to wait until he got home."

"Did something trigger your confrontation? I find it hard to believe you would have suddenly stormed into his workplace accusing him of having an affair for no reason."

"I didn't storm," she said. "Okay, maybe there was a little storming. But we have a young daughter. We're a family. If you found a second phone for your husband, wouldn't you be upset too?"

"Can I see this other phone?"

"I don't have it. I found it and threw it in the garbage can. They took the garbage out the next day."

"Is there any chance that your husband retrieved it and kept it for himself?"

"Zero chance," she said. "I checked the next morning myself to be sure."

"Did you look through the contents of phone?"

"Not much."

"Now's not the time to be modest or embarrassed," I said. "This phone could lead us to your husband's killer."

"So he *did* have a mistress? And you think she killed him?"

"I'm just saying we'd like to understand what was on that second phone."

"There was nothing," she said, pouting her lower lip defensively. "I'm not stupid enough to think he didn't use it, though. This phone was newer and fancy. It had internet access and all the bells and whistles that Gavin swore he'd never use. He couldn't take his cell phone on a walk around the neighborhood because he didn't like carrying Wi-Fi, but he could have a whole secret phone he could use whenever he wanted?"

"What do you mean there was nothing?"

"I mean I looked at the phone. Who wouldn't have? He must have deleted his messages as they came in. He wasn't totally stupid. If he was having an affair, he hid it from me for a long time. Who is she? Do you have a name?"

"We're not convinced he was having an affair. We do think there's a reason he had a second identity, and we're trying to figure out why he would have needed one."

"I just can't believe that our entire life together was a lie."

"I'm not saying that his life here with you and your daughter was a lie. Just that he had a complicated past. You're sure he never told you about it, never let anything slip?"

"No, I swear this is the first I've ever heard about it."

"Mrs. Harris, I need to ask you where you were on the day of your husband's murder."

"I was home with my daughter."

"Can anyone corroborate your story?"

She glanced between me and Jimmy again. "You really think I killed him? You think I'm capable of killing the father of my child?"

"Mrs. Harris, you had just learned your husband was hiding a second phone from you. If you'd learned he was hiding more than that..."

"I thought he was having an affair! If he was, I would've been upset, but I wouldn't have *left* him, let alone killed him. I would've wanted to work through it together."

"You were angry enough to storm into his place of work and confront him there."

"You don't know the full story." She shook her head. "The reason I was so angry that day was because I'd taken a pregnancy test that morning. I'm pregnant, Detective."

I gave a slow nod. "I see. I'm sorry, Mrs. Harris. Congratulations on your pregnancy, though I'm sorry the circumstances aren't different."

"You think?" She teared up. "I have been sick to my stomach; my hormones were going wild, and then I found potential evidence my husband was having an affair? That's why I stormed into the shop like that. I'm not proud of it, but that's where it ended."

"Did you tell your husband about the baby?"

"Yes. That night when he came home from work, I was waiting for him. I'd ordered our favorite takeout and told him over dinner. I apologized for acting the way I had earlier, and he apologized for keeping a secret from me."

"What secret?" I asked. "Did he explain the phone?"

"He said it was complicated, but that it wasn't an affair. That he'd never have an affair."

"You accepted that as a reason?" I asked, skeptical of her easy forgiveness. "That doesn't exactly explain anything."

"He wasn't lying. I told you my husband had his quirks. I could usually tell when he was directly lying to my face. I knew he was telling the truth."

"That's it? You just trusted him?"

"He said he'd explain more when he could, but that I needed to trust him for a few weeks. He said there was some sticky business going on at work, and he needed the phone for emergencies. He told me it was safer the less I knew and that he'd explain once it was over. Honestly, I just thought he was looking for new jobs on the sly and didn't want to worry me."

I didn't mention the fact that he probably wouldn't need a second phone to apply for new positions. Mrs. Harris had enough on her plate to deal with. And it might be getting worse before it got better, depending on what the investigation turned up on the man she knew and loved.

"Do you think this could have had something to do with that? His workplace stuff?" she asked. "I mean, he worked as a mechanic. How much trouble could he get into there?"

"I'm sure there are ways."

"Yes, I suppose that's true. And honestly, it shows you how desperate I was to believe him that I just took his word for it. I *wanted* to believe him. We have a daughter together, and soon we'd have two kids. I knew he loved me. I never doubted that. I thought maybe he'd made a mistake. I guess maybe he did, just not in the way I thought."

"We're not sure your husband did anything wrong at all," I said. "We're doing our best to find out the truth."

"Why would my husband have a second name? Why would he not have told me about his real past?"

"That's exactly what we're trying to figure out."

Chapter 16

"She didn't do it," Jimmy said as we drove back to the precinct. "I know I shouldn't say that without an airtight alibi, but c'mon. Can you see that woman driving down the street and shooting her husband five times? With a toddler in the back seat or grandma at home babysitting?"

"You're right. I don't think she did it either. What I think was happening, though, was that Gavin's past was starting to catch up to him. It seemed like his life was starting to implode, and he knew it. He was probably panicking."

"His wife was noticing things were falling apart, so something was definitely going on in Gavin's secret life. I wonder what spooked him."

"What do you say we pay a visit to Patrick, and see what he meant by having a dentist appointment this morning?"

"You don't believe him?" Jimmy looked over at me. "Chris said the guy cleared it weeks in advance."

"It could be Chris covering for him," I said with a shrug. "Or it could be a real dentist appointment. We won't know until we ask."

"You're pretty convinced this Patrick guy is caught up in this mess, huh?"

"Sometimes the simplest answer is the right one. In this case, we've got a couple of different threads all leading to one person: Patrick."

"What'd he have to say the last time you talked to him?"

I filled Jimmy in on the details of my conversation with Patrick Hamilton. "The thing is, though, Patrick was one of the last people to see my father before he disappeared. Then we find a suspicious phone call to my father that leads us back to the shop where Patrick works? *Then* the morning after my father disappears, a guy's shot up on the sidewalk. Turns out the dead guy and this Patrick guy work at the same shop. No, I don't think any of it's a coincidence."

"Do you have any theories on how they're all connect-ed?"

"No," I said grudgingly. "The only thing I can think of is that they all have a history."

"You mean prison?"

"Well, the two guys who spent time in prison aren't dead—at least that we know of," I said. "But the guy with the secret past, who was probably in witness protection, ends up killed? Yeah, I can see a connection."

"What do you think about your father?"

"What do you mean?"

Jimmy took a breath. "Don't take this the wrong way, Kate."

"Spit it out, Jones. You've never walked on eggshells around me before."

"Which side do you think your father's on?"

"Do I think he's in trouble, or do I think he's on the run?"

"Yep."

"I don't want to guess. This has turned into a profession-al case, and I'm walking a fine line on it," I said. "I don't want to start bringing my personal life into things. I don't want to risk getting kicked off the Harris case too. I've already been booted officially from my father's."

"I don't think your father killed anyone. Just my two cents. Professional and personal."

"You can't separate your professional and personal opinions either. You know me. You know my dad."

"I stand by it."

"Just because he didn't pull the trigger doesn't mean he's innocent. He knew that from the last go-round."

"Do you think they might've met in prison?"

"Who? My dad and Patrick?" I asked. "I know they met in prison. My mom told me as much."

"I mean the other guy. Gavin. What if he's not actually in witness protection? What if he was in prison, and we just haven't found that name yet?"

"I suppose it's possible," I said. "We won't know more until we learn this guy's real identity. With Melinda's findings from the autopsy, though, I'm still leaning toward witness protection. How else could the guy get his fingerprints removed from the system?"

By the time our discussion of Patrick had wound down, we were in front of his house. I led the way to the front door and knocked. Patrick's wife answered shortly after.

"Hi there," I said, quickly reintroducing myself, then introducing Jimmy. "I've got a couple more questions for Patrick, if that's all right."

"Actually, it's not a good time," she said. "Patrick had a dentist appointment this morning, and he's still pretty numb. He can hardly drink through a straw."

"I'd still like to speak with him. It's official business. I'm sure you understand."

She looked hesitant but eventually nodded. "Sure, come on in. I'll have to grab him from bed. He's upstairs watching a movie unless he fell asleep. You can wait in the living room."

Patrick's wife left us in the living room as she went upstairs to get her husband. Jimmy and I waited in silence until we heard one set of footsteps come down the stairs, then another. Hushed whispers were exchanged in the next room. Then a stomping could be heard as another set of footsteps went back upstairs. I assumed Patrick had asked his wife for some privacy, and she'd grudgingly agreed.

A moment later, Patrick appeared in the living room. He wore flannel pants and a black T-shirt. "Hey, Rosetti," he said, though his words were somewhat slurred. His eyes were a little blurry as if he'd been woken from a deep sleep. "Sowry about the mouth."

"We won't take up too much of your time. We're just here to talk about Gavin Harris."

I dropped the name on him quickly, before he could adjust. Before I could even introduce my partner. I watched Patrick as his eyes shifted between me and Jimmy. He tried to swallow, but it didn't appear to be successful. He raised a hand to his lower lip and dabbed at it as if checking to see if he was drooling. I'd have felt bad for the guy if I didn't suspect him in my father's disappearance and a man's murder.

"I see," he said, his words still sounding crumpled and unnatural. "What about Gavin?"

"What do you know about him?" I asked. "I understand you work with him."

He nodded. "You're not here with the other woman this time. Different guy, different case?"

"I'm afraid so. This one's a homicide."

"I wondered if you'd be back." Patrick sighed, then lowered himself into an armchair as if he were extremely tired. "I didn't do it. I swear."

It was interesting that Patrick knew about Gavin's death. That in itself told me something. After all, nobody else at the auto repair shop had seemed aware that their colleague had died over the weekend. While there had been press reporting on the death, the name had never been released—partially because we hadn't known the real name of the victim until much later.

"Yet you're not surprised we're here."

"I get it. I'm an easy target," Patrick said. "I always knew that idiot Chris watched me at the shop more than anyone else. Like I was going to steal fifty bucks from the cash register."

"That idiot Chris?" I asked. "You don't sound fond of him."

"He didn't want Tom to hire me. Ex-convict and all."

"Right. Do you have problems with anyone else at your job?"

"What, do you mean Gavin? No, I didn't have a problem with him. He was a quiet guy, did his job, didn't interfere with anything. Sort of like me."

"Do you hang out with the other guys from the auto repair shop?"

"I see you've been talking to them already."

"Part of the job," I said dryly. "Would you say they've accepted you into their circle?"

"Look, I've had to work a little harder than most to become one of them," he said, wincing as he tried to pronounce his words clearly. "Everyone was a little skeptical of me. I put in enough face time there to show them I was just one of the gang. I'm the newest hire, see. They already had their clique, then here I come, a new guy with a record. So yeah. I had to suck up a little bit."

"To Gavin?"

"Gavin didn't care what anyone thought of him. He never said more than two words to me."

"You knew he was dead before we got here today."

"It was on the news."

"Not his name," I said. "That wasn't on the news."

Patrick sat back in his chair and folded his arms across his chest. "I heard it through the grapevine."

"Any chance you want to let me know who this grapevine might be?"

"I hear things," he repeated. "Your dad's the same way. It's not like you can live the sort of life we've lived and not keep an ear to the ground. It's second nature. It's practically a safety measure."

"I don't know, I think cutting ties with old mob connections would be a good thing," I said. "Less temptation."

"I already told you, I'm not tempted to do anything," he said. "I've got a life here, a family. I'm in the doghouse already with my wife just because the two of you are at my door again. I didn't even do anything wrong."

"How'd you find out Gavin was dead?"

"I recognized his picture."

I didn't believe Patrick for a minute, but the way his eyes were set on me, I was pretty sure he wasn't going to budge on this one. We were back to that secret criminal honor code where Patrick wasn't going to snitch on old friends whether the cops were involved or not. My dad would've done the same thing. I was sure of it.

"Isaac?" I asked, trying one more attempt. "Would he know anything about it?"

"Don't bother him." Patrick waved a hand dismissively. "It wasn't him. Gavin was after his time."

"What do you mean by 'after his time'?"

"Nothing."

"Patrick, I understand you were a friend—or something—to my father, but I won't hesitate to arrest you. I didn't come here trying to make life difficult for you, but I'm pretty sure I can find a charge to bring you in on if I try really, really hard," I said. "I doubt your wife would be happy about that."

Patrick glanced over his shoulder toward the room behind him as if his wife might be eavesdropping. "Fine. I'll tell you what I know, but leave me out of the rest of this."

"I'll do the best I can," I said, "but you'll understand if I'm not exactly sympathetic, seeing as my own father is still missing, and now a man you worked with is dead. Let's not forget you were one of the last people to see my father before he vanished."

Patrick rubbed his forehead. "I knew I shouldn't have said anything."

"Said anything to who?"

"I mentioned something to your father," Patrick said. "It was a couple of weeks ago now, but the minute the words came out of my mouth, I regretted them."

"Why?"

"This little light went on in your dad's eyes. Like a dog catching a scent or something. I don't know. I should've kept my trap shut."

"About what?"

"I told him I'd been seeing a guy hanging around the shop." Patrick looked petrified as he worked up the courage to say the name. "I recognized him. A lot of us guys would recognize him."

"Guys at the shop?"

"No, guys like me and your father."

"You mean criminals, mobsters, and bank robbers."

"Sure, fine, whatever." Patrick shrugged. "The name Nick Ralphio mean anything to you?"

I shook my head. "Unless he's killed someone or been accused of it, I wouldn't have met him on the job. As for my personal life, I don't tend to fraternize with my dad's friends."

"You're related to half of them," Patrick shot back. "You think the Bellinis are innocent?"

I swallowed back my retort. "Tell me about this Nick Ralphio."

"The reason you wouldn't have heard of him is because he's so high above everyone you deal with that you couldn't touch him with a ten-foot pole. He has people to kill people for him."

"I see. Mob connections?"

"Yeah," Patrick said. "He's friendly enough with the Bellini group, so there hasn't been much trouble on your side of town. He stays more to the Minneapolis side of things, which was why it was weird to see him in the auto repair shop."

"Getting his car fixed?"

"I guess you could say that," Patrick said. "First time I've ever seen a Bugatti in Tom's Auto Repair."

Jimmy raised his eyebrows and gave a low whistle. "He took his Bugatti to Tom's Auto Repair for an oil change?"

"You can see why I was skeptical," Patrick said. One glance in my direction told him I didn't quite get it. "You don't bring a car that cost you six figures to the little mom-and-pop shop on the corner."

"Ah."

"I wasn't working the front desk when he came in," Patrick continued. "I was rotating the tires for some grandma on her Chevy. The second I recognized Ralphio, I ducked into the office and kept out of sight. I still heard every word of the conversation, and he asked specifically to work with Gavin."

"And you don't think it was because of his stellar reputation as a mechanic?"

Both Jimmy and Patrick glanced at me.

"Right," I said. "Fair enough."

"So why do you think he wanted to work with Gavin?"

"I don't think he wanted to *work* with him, if you know what I mean," Patrick said. "There was something going on there. Ralphio's presence at Tom's place was more like a threat."

"What else did he say?"

"It wasn't like he bared his soul to the dude at the front desk," Patrick said. "Ralphio just gave a load of crap about how he'd heard about this place from a friend. He said this friend mentioned Gavin Harris specialized in unique types of cars. He wondered if Gavin had any availability that day."

"Did he?"

Jimmy gave a snort. Patrick gave him an appreciative little smile.

"What's so funny?" I asked.

"Someone drives a Bugatti into your shop," Jimmy said in low tones, "you make time for them."

"Exactly," Patrick agreed. "Tom cleared the project himself. He was just about wetting his pants with excitement and instructed Gavin to drop everything and give this client his full attention."

"Did that catch Gavin's attention?"

"That's the thing. The second the guy walked into the shop, Gavin disappeared."

"Disappeared?"

"Went to lunch," Patrick said. "No matter it was about ten in the morning. Tom was pretty annoyed about it, but everyone's entitled to their breaks. Still, he said he was going to make Gavin stick around when Nick Ralphio came to pick up his car. Sometimes the guys with the super expensive cars want to meet the mechanic, talk to them, ask nitty-gritty detail-type questions. That sort of thing."

"Did that happen?"

Patrick shook his head. "Ralphio never even left the shop, which is weird in and of itself. He sat in the lobby and read a paper and drank our crappy coffee the whole time."

"Gavin obviously returned to work after his break?"

"Had to or Tom would've fired him."

"Do you know what needed fixing on the car?"

"Nothing big. Routine maintenance. The job took Gavin maybe an hour start to finish."

"And after?"

"Nothing, really. Gavin went into the lobby to meet with Ralphio. Nick just shook Gavin's hand and smiled, politely thanked him for fixing up the car. That's it. Haven't seen the guy since."

"How did Gavin seem after that meeting?" I asked. "Did he seem shaken up? Distressed? Annoyed?"

"I didn't notice anything off, but the guy doesn't say much."

"You never saw Ralphio again?" I asked. "What do you think he was doing there?"

"I told you I don't know. But I've got this sixth sense for things, and my senses were tingling that day. Something didn't add up, and it wasn't just the Bugatti being in Tom's shop. It was something else. Ralphio was either sending a message, or he wanted something."

"I thought you said he didn't do his own dirty work," I countered. "Wouldn't that mean he'd have sent someone else to check out Gavin if that's what he was after?"

"Exactly," Patrick agreed. "That's why it's so weird. I can't figure out why Nick Ralphio was there in the flesh. It doesn't make any sense to me, but I'm telling you it wasn't a good thing. I knew that wasn't going to end well."

"Like him getting sprayed with bullets while doing his weekly grocery shopping for his family?"

Patrick swallowed. "Yeah, an ending like that."

"Why wouldn't Gavin have run?" I posed the question to anyone, really, including myself. "If he felt threatened, why wouldn't he vanish that day after Nick Ralphio left the shop? Ralphio obviously left Gavin alive, so why'd he just continue going about his business?"

"Maybe he needed the money?" Patrick took another moment to think. "The guy had a wife and a kid. I feel like he was a good dude. Maybe he didn't want to leave them stranded. Maybe he didn't think it was as serious as it really was."

"Getting killed *is* leaving his family stranded," Jimmy said. "Permanently."

Patrick shrugged in agreement.

"He had also just found out he was having another baby," I said. "I bet that's why. He loved his wife, and he wasn't going to leave his family if he could help it."

"I understand," Patrick murmured. "I'd have stayed. I'd have done the same thing."

"You'd have taken your chances? You wouldn't have run?"

Patrick nodded. Another glance back at the kitchen. "I've been on the other side—I've run plenty before. There's nothing there for me. I don't care to live all that long if I can't do it my way. Not anymore."

There was a moment of somber silence.

"Kate—" Patrick stopped himself at my sharp glance upward. "I mean, Detective Rosetti," he quickly corrected, "your father is the same way. Me and him, we understood each other. We got our priorities straightened out. Whatever happened to your dad, wherever he is, it wasn't his choice to be away from you. I guarantee it."

I cleared my throat, not willing to get into a sentimental situation with one of our best suspects for Harris's murder. After all, the best criminals were the best liars. Charming, handsome, suave. While Patrick couldn't exactly be described as suave with Novocain in his jaw, he'd already proven he was good at lying before he went to prison. What if he was lying about everything else?

"Speaking of my father, you said you thought something spooked him. What did you say that you thought might scare him off?"

"I mentioned Nick Ralphio's name in passing," Patrick said. "I swear I didn't mean to. We were just shooting the breeze about random stuff: work, family, friends. I happened to mention that we'd gotten a Bugatti in the shop. Isaac's a big car buff, and he got a kick out of it. When he asked who it belonged to, I didn't hesitate to say. It was only after the name came out of my mouth that I recognized my mistake."

"Why would Nick Ralphio be relevant to my father?"

"I can't figure it out. I mean, I guess your father used to run in similar circles, but I really don't know. Their sort of gang wasn't my area of expertise."

"No, your area of expertise was robbing banks," I said, trying to drive the point home that we were here on a murder investigation and not sitting down for tea and friendly chitchat. It felt to me like Patrick was starting to get confused.

He sighed. "Right. You're not going to let that go."

"It's sort of my job." I stood. "Where were you on Saturday morning?"

"C'mon, you don't really think I killed Gavin, do you? I feel bad enough for potentially roping your father into this. Even at my worst, I never killed anyone."

"There's a first time for everything."

"You really don't ever let things go, do you?" Patrick sounded annoyed as he stood too. "Your poor father. No wonder his relationship with you is strained."

"What's that supposed to mean?"

"It means that your dad's not a bad guy. He made one mistake," Patrick said, heated, flinching with the pain in his jaw. "It was a long time ago. Are you going to hold that against him until he's in the grave?"

I looked into Patrick's face and saw a flash of pain. As if he knew what my father felt, as if he wondered if his wife might hold the same grudge I did. Then the pain disappeared, and he looked mostly sad and frustrated.

"That's all I know," he said. "Please don't bother me and my family again."

"If we have more questions—"

"You can go through my lawyer," Patrick said. "You're not getting back in here without some kind of warrant. So you're either going to have to charge me or leave me alone."

"C'mon, Kate," Jimmy muttered. "Time to go."

We let ourselves out of the house. I closed the door quietly behind me. When we reached the car, I gave a shake of my head.

"He sort of overreacted there, don't you think?" I asked, pulling the door open and sliding inside. "I was just doing my job."

"That's the thing, Rosetti." Jimmy reached across the console and put a hand on my shoulder. "You're always doing your job."

"Not you too," I grumbled. "This is literally what I'm paid to do. I've dedicated my entire life to catching criminals. I'm not married; I've got no kids, and my work is what fulfills me in life. Why does everyone seem surprised by that now, all of a sudden?"

"No one is surprised," Jimmy said. "I think that's the point. No one is surprised."

I tried to swallow my annoyance. I rarely felt annoyed by my partner, and even now, I knew my frustration was misdirected. I trusted Jimmy to always tell me the truth, no matter how difficult. If I was annoyed at the way his feedback was sounding, it was simply because I didn't want to hear it.

We drove in silence back to the precinct. Eventually, the silence became overwhelming, and I hit dial for Asha. She answered on the second ring.

"Nothing yet, honey," she said. "You got something for me?"

I quickly explained our two visits of the morning.

"You want me to look into Ralphio?" Asha asked. "I'm doing a quick Google search now, and it looks like there's a lot to find about him. Which somehow makes me think I'm not going to find anything."

"Huh?"

"He's a big, handsome, rich mobster. Seems like half the time people are fawning over him and half the time people are wanting to arrest him. Sort of like your buddy Alastair Gem," Asha said. "Minus the mobster part."

"Uh-huh."

"But these types are too smart to leave any sort of real trail," Asha said. "It's all fluff pieces and covered-up garbage they want us to find."

"Well, you're the best."

"If there's something to find, I'll find it. I'll get started. Chloe's going to help, is that okay? She's got a flight out tomorrow morning, so I figure I'll have her help me wrap this up, and then I'll send her home to pack for her week of lovin.'"

"You're on speakerphone," Jimmy groaned. "I don't want to know that. Chloe's young enough to be my daughter."

Asha laughed. "Anything else?"

"Actually, there is something else," I said. "I told you that Gavin Harris's wife mentioned he had a second phone."

"Yeah. Right before you mentioned she chucked it in the garbage and made sure it was hauled to the dump."

"Any chance you can look into that?"

"What exactly would you like me to look into?"

"I don't know. I know I'm grasping at straws here, but maybe you can turn up some sort of account. He had to pay his bills, right?"

"Honey, I'm betting it was a burner phone," she said. "Even if it wasn't a complete burner phone, unless you can get the name on the account, I'm going to have a hard time linking anything to Gavin Harris. Harris wasn't his real name. Neither was Charles Marlo. I've turned up everything on their accounts. I think it's safe to assume this guy had a few more disposable aliases. Not necessarily big, built-up backstories—just little fake names for things like secret burner phones."

"I figured you'd say that."

"Yet you asked anyway," Asha said quietly. "You're getting close, aren't you?"

"I don't know," I said. "Just when it feels like we're getting close, everything comes collapsing down. We caught Harris's wife in a lie, so I thought maybe her, but now I doubt it. Then there was Patrick Hamilton."

"And?"

"I don't know," I said. "I just can't shake the feeling he didn't do it either. But he's clammed up and asked for a lawyer, so we're not getting any further with him for now."

"You had a feeling?"

"I prefer the word hunch," I said. "It feels more police-like."

"Honey, it's not against the law to have a feeling or two. Even if you're the most accomplished, cold-hearted homicide detective in town."

"Thanks for your advice. I'll keep that in mind."

"Hey, what are your plans for tonight?"

I glanced over at Jimmy, confused, then replied to Asha, "I don't know. I don't think I'm in the mood for a drink. Sorry. Maybe we can rain check?"

"I've got a date, sweetie," Asha said. "But if I were you, I'd get yourself in the mood for a drink. Real slinky dress, the more low-cut, the better."

"I don't think that's going to help me feel any better."

"Maybe not," Asha said, "but it might help you catch a killer."

"How do you figure?"

"Strap on your heels, baby. Nick Ralphio's got a table booked at a new bar opening downtown tonight. He paid a couple grand for bottle service. Even a guy like Ralphio's not going to skip out on those plans."

"I guess I could flash my badge to get in there," I said. "It might be worth checking him out."

"Better idea," Asha said. "Use your charms to sweet talk your buddy Gem into getting a table next to Ralphio."

"Gem?"

"It's his club," Asha said. "I bet he can get you inside without you alerting everyone to your presence as a police officer. Especially if you wear that really slinky number I mentioned. Jane will know the one I mean."

"No, I don't want to use Gem," I said. "I'll just flash—"

"Call him," Asha and Jimmy said together.

"It's not just *any* case," Asha said. "If your father is wrapped up in this, you could be racing against the clock to save his life. Now's not the time to nitpick your friendship with Gem."

I swallowed, glanced at Jimmy, and he gave a nod of confirmation. "Fine," I said. "I'll call him. But let the record show that I heartily object."

"Right, babe," Asha said. "Slinky dress."

Chapter 17

"That'll do," Jane said. "Yes, yes. That'll do."

I groaned. I took a glance in the mirror, then groaned louder in protest.

"You're going to have to start paying me," Jane said. "How much do you think stylists make? Maybe I should consider a career change. I really think I have a knack for it. Nobody will guess you're a cop if you're dressed like that."

"Because they'll be too busy staring at my cleavage."

"That's the point," Jane said. "Just don't argue with me. You're going to one of Alastair Gem's new club openings. What's more, you'll be sitting in the VIP section, probably next to Gem himself. Sorry, but nobody would believe that Gem brought a date wearing a tank top and slacks to the club."

"My boots have a little bit of a heel," I said. "Also, I'm not Gem's date. I'm his fake date."

"And it will look very fake if you don't sell it a little bit. At least with your clothes."

"Why won't Mindy be there tonight?"

I took one more glance at myself in the mirror before Jane elbowed me out of the way to reapply her lip gloss. She frowned, then dabbed bright red gel across her lips.

"It's not really her thing," Jane said. "She supports Gem and everything, but it's not her business. It's Gem's business, literally, so he likes to make an appearance at these things if he can. Honestly, though, I don't think he was planning on going tonight until you called him."

"What?" I spun around and faced Jane. "That's not what he told me."

Jane shrugged. She was wearing a tight, sparkly number. It had long sleeves, and the hemline went to her feet, but somehow it seemed even more revealing than my dress. She glittered like a disco ball, and the V-neck in front practically showed off her belly button. No curve was left un-flaunted.

In contrast, I'd gone with a shorter option, mostly because it was the only option in black that Jane had offered to me. If I had to wear a short dress with fringe on the bottom that tickled against my thighs, it wasn't going to be in bubblegum pink. The spaghetti straps on the thing were so tiny Jane hadn't even let me wear a normal bra. There had been a strapless bra and tape involved, and that's all I was at liberty to say. I wasn't even going to discuss the underwear situation happening underneath.

Fortunately, Jane let me get away with some chunky wedge heels under the argument that I might need to move quickly. She'd given a huge sigh when I'd brought up the possibility that I might need the stability over stilettos, but eventually, she'd caved. On the condition that I let her curl my hair.

"Of course, Gem wouldn't tell you that," Jane said. "He wouldn't want to make you feel bad. What'd you do, call him and ask for a police favor type thing?"

"Essentially. I said I'd heard he had a new club opening, and I mentioned the name of the guy I'm trying to keep an eye on. Gem said he knows Ralphio and that it wouldn't be a problem to accompany me to the club so I could get my work done."

I frowned, realizing that with the way he'd framed the words, he hadn't technically said he'd be going already. I realized Jane was right.

"He shouldn't have done that," I huffed. "Especially since you and Wes were already planning on going. I could've just gone with you. All I needed was a guarantee that I could get inside and close to Ralphio."

"Thanks for that, by the way," Jane said. "You got us the best table in the house. Wes called me this afternoon to let me know about our upgrade."

"How did you not have the best table in the room already? You're dating the manager of the club. He can put you wherever you want."

"Yeah, but when people pay thousands of dollars for bottle service at one of these tables, you don't take up one yourself," Jane said. "That's pretty stupid in terms of a business sense."

"Was the table already taken up?"

"I think it was some prince from the Middle East," Jane said. "They bumped him a few tables back."

"So my little favor is costing Gem thousands of dollars?"

Jane put down her gloss, smacked her lips, and looked at me. "Don't sweat it. He wouldn't have agreed if he didn't want to help you out."

"This was not my intention. I knew I should've just used my badge to get in there."

"Hey, I think it's sweet. Gem's willing to pay thousands of bucks to hang out with you for a night."

"It's not like that. This is official police business."

"Yeah? Then where's your gun?" She waggled her eyebrows.

"Jane."

"I know, I know. Lighten up a little." Jane reached for her half-empty glass of champagne. "You really should have a drink."

"I'm on the clock."

"You've made that clear," Jane said. "I'm just teasing you about all this Gem stuff. You know how he feels about it. He says he likes to help you because you make the world a better place. A couple grand here and there to better the world? Probably the best money he's ever spent. I'm pretty sure his accountant writes these losses off as donations to the police force anyway."

"But—"

"Dude, Kate. He flew you on a private plane to a prison because you asked," she said. "You don't think that cost him some cash? Just relax. He can afford it. Plus, you said it yourself. This is about Dad. Don't forget that."

"I suppose you're right."

Jane's playful look slid away, leaving her expression radiating nerves. "The only reason I'm going out at all tonight is to have a distraction. Mom's got a book club tonight, and I didn't want to sit at home, twiddling my thumbs and worrying about Dad. Gem knows the situation. He knows if you're asking him for a favor, it's important. This might be the most important favor yet if getting close to Nick Ralphio could save Dad's life."

There was a moment of quiet in which I realized Jane had a point. It helped to get a glimpse beneath her exterior—beneath the frivolity and playfulness of this evening was fear and nerves. I wasn't the only one struggling to find a balance and an outlet for the way I was feeling. Eventually, I nodded.

"You're right," I said. "I know."

Jane reached out to squeeze my arm. "I appreciate this. So does Dad and Mom. Heck, I'll happily pay Gem back a couple of grand if it gets Dad safe. I might max out my credit card doing it, but it would be worth it."

I smiled. "You're right. Easy to forget why I'm doing these things when I'm wearing three-inch wedges."

"Four inches," Jane said, wrinkling her nose. "I lied to you. They really make your legs look great, though."

"Jane!"

"They're here," she said, glancing down at her phone. "They're out front. Are you ready?"

I grabbed a small purse, which Jane had assured me was clunky and sort of ugly. It had been nonnegotiable, however, so I could carry my phone and my keys. I'd called Russo on my way home earlier in the evening to explain my plan to him and update him on the case, but he hadn't answered. Instead, I'd left him a quick message to call me back. A few hours later, and he still hadn't called me back. I wondered if he was still on a case.

I quickly texted Russo that we were heading out as part of a case and that I might not be home until late, so not to worry if he called. Then I slipped my phone back into my purse and headed downstairs to the waiting limo.

Outside, Gem was standing beside the car. He was dressed in a suit without the jacket. His hair was curly, mussed, and the second Jane and I appeared on the front steps, his trusty smile brightened his features.

Jane hurried on ahead while I locked up. She was in the car by the time I turned around and found Gem waiting for me at the bottom of the stairs.

"Detective," Gem said softly. "Thank you for joining us this evening."

"You're a liar." I stalked up to him. "You weren't going to the club tonight until I asked you for the favor."

"Did I say something to make you think otherwise?"

"No," I said, still sour about it.

"That's why you're mad about it, then, because it's not my fault." Gem gave a gentle laugh. "It's no problem, Detective. I wasn't doing much tonight anyway."

"Sorry to take you away from Mindy during the week leading up to your wedding. You guys are probably very busy."

"She's been away at a spa day all day and is sleeping at her best friend's tonight," he said. "Apparently her skin was awful after all of the hot dogs and alcohol she consumed at her bachelorette party and she's panicking."

"It was one hot dog," I said. "And you say it like it was my fault."

"If the shoe fits."

"These shoes do not fit," I retorted. "I can't believe we're doing this. I'm sorry I made you come out with us."

"Don't apologize. I like to put in face time at my businesses when I can. This is a good excuse."

"Yeah, but you didn't have to kick the King of Egypt off his table to make room for us."

"He was a prince, and he happily accepted my personal apology, as well as a comped executive suite at the Diamond Hotel."

"Great. I'm costing you even more money than I thought."

"I'll have my accountant write it off, if that makes you feel better." He winked. When I didn't so much as crack a smile, he stilled. "Detective, are you okay? I was just joking. Of course I don't mind helping you out. The money means nothing. I donate millions of dollars a year. This, actually spending money to take real action in my community, is a welcome breath of relief from simply signing checks to other organizations."

"It's just that the stakes are higher this time."

"I understand. They always are when family is involved."

"Do you know Nick Ralphio?" I asked. "I mean, personally?"

"Know is a complicated word."

"You've obviously heard of him. You know *of* him."

"I know *of* a lot of people."

"What's your take on him?"

Gem considered. "He's a powerful man."

"Powerful? How about you be more specific? Is he a good or a bad guy? Nice or evil? Loyal, or will he stab you in the back?"

Gem laughed softly again. "I don't view good and bad like you do, Detective. Can Nick Ralphio do very bad things? Yes. Is he loyal, possibly to a fault? I believe the answer is also yes."

"Why'd you invite him to your club tonight if you think he sometimes does bad things?"

"As a show of goodwill."

"Making nice with the enemy?" I asked. "Or in bed with the mob?"

"Or simply two businessmen showing one another some sort of respect."

"Again with this stupid respect and loyalty code among criminals."

"Are you calling me a criminal, Detective?"

"No, I didn't mean it like that. It's just this case that's getting to me. I'm sorry."

"It's personal."

"It's not that. It's this little song and dance people do out of respect for each other, even though some of these people are bad people, that I just can't understand."

"It *is* personal," Gem insisted. "Mostly because that's the code your dad lives by. I don't think you're confused, Detective. I just think you don't like it because it doesn't fall neatly in the lines of your ordered world."

Gem's words stung. I was used to Jimmy being brutally honest with me, and I could handle that. He was a work colleague and a friend, and our lives often depended on one another—literally. We had to be honest and have complete trust in one another.

But Gem's nature was often joking and lighthearted. Money was like a plaything to him. Items, possessions, things—they were all just that. Toys. His curly hair and sparkling eyes, along with the quirky British lilt to his voice smoothed over the hard edges behind the businessman. It was easy to forget how intelligent and ruthless the man standing before me could be. I'd rarely seen that side of him, but I knew it was there. One didn't build themselves an empire without those qualities.

"Maybe," I said, trying not to let myself sound offended. A part of me suspected that he was right. And extremely perceptive, though it still didn't make the truth easier to swallow. "I'm sorry I linked you to Nick Ralphio."

"You didn't link anything," he said nonchalantly. "I did that myself by inviting him to the club. I can handle any links you might draw from that action. You are a detective, and connecting the dots is your job."

"Yeah, but you're here as a favor to me, so I should lay off you."

"What if I *was* a criminal? Would that change things?"

"What things?" I looked up at Gem. "What are you talking about?"

"You and I, we're friends. If you found out I'd broken the law, would you break off all contact with me?"

"That's not a fair question. You haven't killed anyone. The people I'm talking about have committed murder."

"Your father hasn't."

"I don't know that for a fact," I muttered. "I'm also convinced he'd be capable of doing it if the circumstances were right."

"Who wouldn't be?" Gem asked, his eyes shining against the moonlight as he studied me carefully. "When we love something so much we can't bear to lose it, and that something is gravely threatened, I believe humans are capable of things we can't even imagine."

I swallowed hard at the piercing stare in Gem's eyes. "I hope you're not trying to justify murder to a homicide detective."

Gem smiled, breaking the serious moment, but he didn't laugh, didn't shrug it off. "I'm just saying that the world is all shades of blacks and whites and grays. I understand there's a spectrum, and frankly, I don't think it's all wrong."

"Do you think my father deserved to go to prison?"

"Sure," Gem said. "He blatantly broke a law and was caught."

"Okay," I said hesitantly. "So we agree."

"But I think your father only broke the law to provide for his family. I respect him for that. I don't hold a grudge. He did his time and was released. End of story in my book."

"You think I'm wrong to be mad at my dad?" My voice raised slightly. "You sound just like Jane and my mother. How can you people not understand by trying to 'take care of our family' my father left us alone for years? For the majority of my life?"

"I'm not justifying his actions, nor am I saying it was worth the risk. I think your father would agree. But in terms of mistakes made, I consider his a relatively small blunder. He wasn't trying to hurt anyone. He wasn't being malicious. Selfish and wrong, sure. Evil? I don't think so."

I took a deep breath. "You didn't have to watch my mom go through what she did to raise us alone."

"No."

I was surprised by Gem's simple response.

"I'll never pretend I can walk a mile in someone else's shoes because the truth is, I can't," Gem said. "I'm sorry you didn't have that time with your father."

I shifted uncomfortably under his earnest words. "I guess I should stop complaining to the guy who's been on his own for ages. At least I had a really great mom who was around."

Gem leaned in and brushed his lips against my forehead in a display of sympathy. "I'm thankful for that."

There was a long moment of silence as we stood a foot apart from one another. It was cold outside, and I pulled my coat closer to my body. Somehow, I hadn't noticed the temperature until there were no more words to fill the space between us.

"Shall we?" Gem asked, moving to open the door. "We have a table waiting."

As I climbed into the car behind Gem, I was filled with a swirl of unexpected emotions. That was exactly what bothered me about Gem. He threw me off. He tilted my view of the world on its axis, unsettled me, made me think about things in ways I hadn't before. I didn't like it.

But I was the one asking him for the favor, the one costing him money by requesting a seat at an exclusive table. So as we settled into the limo and rode downtown, I focused on keeping my head on the case and not on the dizzying effect that Gem seemed to have on my life.

Chapter 18

Gem's new club was dressed to the nines in festive decorations. This time around Gem had gone all out on exterior pizzazz. The name of the club was Sapphire, and neon, sparkling blue lights lit up the sky for miles around announcing the presence of the new facility. The line to get inside extended around the block.

A glance at the people waiting in line made it seem like short dresses and skirts were required for the women. When I'd visited Rubies—another of Gem's clubs—I'd complained that all the women waiting outside would be freezing in their high heels and bare legs all winter. This time around, I noted that Gem had installed an electric fire right into the wall of Sapphire's to provide heat to his waiting guests.

"Genius move, don't you think? Having warmers for the guests." Gem gently rested his hand on my back as he steered me through the crowded front walk and toward the entrance to the place. "Whoever thought of it should probably get a cut of royalties."

"Probably should."

Gem smiled and withdrew his hand from my back as we reached the front door. We whizzed right by the bouncer and were ushered straight to the host, a beautiful woman who seemed to be about six feet tall and couldn't have weighed more than a hundred pounds. She smiled at us, tossed her lush red hair behind her back and then, without a word, led us down a private hallway that curled around the edge of the building. We popped out onto a raised, roped-off platform that I assumed was some sort of VIP area.

"Your table, Mr. Gem." The woman's voice was honey smooth. "We'll have drinks brought out immediately. Is there anything else we can prepare for you?"

"Has the prince arrived yet?" Gem asked. "I'd like a word with him when he gets here."

"Not yet," she said. "I'll let you know the second his car pulls up out front."

Gem nodded, and the woman melted into the crowd of people, disappearing as quickly as she'd arrived. Then Gem gestured for us to take seats at a booth that circled a round table. Beneath the table were hints of blue lights. I glanced around the room, and it seemed half of the ice cubes were glowing blue. It made for an interesting, almost otherworldly ambiance.

"You really went all out on the sapphire theme, didn't you?" I asked, studying a blue Christmas tree off to one side of the dance floor.

"What you have to understand is that people come here for an illusion, Detective." Gem sat back in his seat and surveyed the people entering his newest venue. "They don't come here for more of the same. They're escaping their everyday lives."

"I didn't mean—"

Gem leaned one elbow on the table and looked over at me. "They come here expecting an experience. They want things to feel dark, dangerous, sexy. But in reality, they don't want too much of any of those things—especially the dangerous. They want to have a few drinks and let the music take them away."

"Yeah, but the reality is that most of these people will end up sweaty and making out with a drunk stranger whose name they don't remember in the morning."

"Maybe, but that's not what they're concerned about at the moment." Gem winked. "Who am I to burst their bubble? That's what their alarm clocks are for."

"You really do understand people and their desires, don't you?"

Jane elbowed me to signal that she and Wes were headed to the dance floor. A waitress stopped by and set a bucket of ice cubes on the table along with a chilled bottle of high-end champagne. She wore what looked like a bra and boy shorts—both encrusted with sapphires. Gem barely glanced at her. He nodded his thanks briefly, and she disappeared as silently as she'd arrived.

"What do you mean by that?" Gem asked.

I was so distracted by the sparkling outfit of the retreating server that I could hardly remember the original question. When I turned to face Gem, however, his piercing eyes drew me back to our previous conversation like the snap of fingers.

"You understand people," I said. "Not only people who are like you, but people who are different from you too. It's a talent."

"I think you understand people too, Detective. Just in a different way."

"I beg to differ. I can't for the life of me understand what everyone is talking about when it comes to my father. Him taking some sort of moral high road just because he hasn't killed anyone yet makes no sense to me."

"You think he's capable of killing?"

"Yes. I agree with your point earlier. I think most people are capable of killing. I think my dad is higher on the list than most."

"Because of his gray moral code?"

"Because of how he justifies things. The truth is he took money that didn't belong to him. Even worse, it was while he was on the job. A job that requires honesty and loyalty above all else. He was supposed to be a role model, but he made a choice that was no better than the criminals he was supposed to be busting. It's a deeper betrayal."

Gem blew out a breath.

"You think I'm being too harsh?"

"I already told you what I think," Gem said. "I think you *do* understand. It's just hard to see past it because it's personal. You'll never get that time back with your father from when he was in prison. You'll never be able to unsee the heartbreak in your mother's eyes when she had to scrimp and struggle to make ends meet for you and Jane."

"Correct," I said, then hesitated. "This, this moment here, is an example of what I meant earlier. It feels like you really understand me, even though by your own admission you said you couldn't possibly understand."

"I think empathy is gained from bad decisions."

I couldn't help the funny expression I felt creeping onto my face. "How do you figure that?"

"When you make bad decisions or wrong choices, when you stumble and fall, it humbles you." Gem reached for the empty glass sitting in front of him and played with the stem of the champagne flute. "You think you'd never be the sort of person to make a certain decision. Then once you find yourself there, in the throes of the consequence of that decision, it shakes you to the core."

"I guess."

"It makes you question everything you've ever thought about yourself. You wonder if change is truly possible, or if you're just a horrible person."

"Gem, I don't think—"

"You wonder if you deserve any of it, your happiness or success. The family who loves you, the friends who care about you."

I reached over and gently set a hand on Gem's arm. I gave a squeeze, then drew my hand back.

"You have to hope against all hope that change is possible. Some people have a whole crisis about who they are. Some people move away, leave their current life behind. Some people find religion. Others find friends. Of course, some people will fall back into their patterns over and over again."

I nodded, knowing the last part to be all too true through my work.

"And for those of us who don't fall back into our patterns over and over again, we mostly spend each day simply trying not to make the same mistakes again."

"If that's true, then you don't think change is possible," I argued. "You're just saying that people have to work on their willpower and fight against their natural instincts."

"Maybe at first. Change isn't instantaneous, nor is it all encompassing. First it's one day at a time, then a week at a time, then maybe a month. Eventually, hopefully, years will pass. But the thought never disappears. It might get easier to ignore; we might go days without thinking about it, without feeling the guilt that goes along with it. Then it all comes right back."

"I've made mistakes before, Gem. I'm getting the impression that you think I don't understand what it's like to screw up."

"You don't."

"That's stupid, Gem. And not true. I'm human. I make mistakes all the time."

"Sure, little mistakes. How about the kind of mistakes that you spend your whole life wondering how to fix?"

I took a deep breath and felt uncomfortable trying to come up with a response.

"Detective." Gem's voice was soft but stern. "You're as close to morally perfect as any person I've ever met."

"That's ridiculous."

"It's true, and I've met a lot of people."

"I've still made plenty of mistakes."

"Not like the kind I'm talking about," Gem said sharply. "No, you simply haven't. I think you know that too."

My breath came out shaky. "You say that like it's a great thing. Some huge accomplishment."

"Isn't it?"

"Gem, I've played my whole life safe. I could blame my dad, but it's not all his fault."

"I agree. His choices influenced you, but they influenced Jane too. The two of you are impossibly different, considering you had very similar upbringings, not to mention your similar genetics."

"Don't you think I've ever wondered what it'd be like to be different than I am?" I raised my shoulder, surprised to find myself opening up to this billionaire. I'd never voiced these thoughts aloud to anyone before him. "I've never taken a vacation by myself. I've never moved away from family or friends. I've lived in the same twenty-mile radius my whole life. I have never had a one-night stand with a stranger. The most I've ever done is have a few too many drinks, and, well, you saw what happened that night."

Gem gave a small smile. "How did it feel letting loose at the bachelorette party?"

I shrugged. "I don't know. I remember the hot dogs tasted really good."

"Most people have to go through the trials and tribulations of heartache and loss and guilt and mistakes and rebuilding to get to the place where you are."

"Yes, but that's what you're saying," I said. "You have empathy because of it. You don't think I can truly understand what it's like to be in someone else's shoes because I haven't made those same mistakes."

Gem considered. "That's mostly true."

"So how is it a good thing that I'm like this?"

"I'm just explaining why I am the way *I* am," Gem said. "It wasn't actually a commentary on you. If you want to take it that way, frankly, Detective, I think that's a reflection of what's on your mind. Not what's on mine."

I felt a little stung by his words. Once again because they were probably true, and I didn't want to admit it.

"We started this conversation talking about this club," Gem said. "The reason I think mistakes give a person empathy is because I've been on the other side of things. Young, cocky, bold. I made a lot of money very fast. A lot of money plus the näiveté of youth is a dangerous combination. I made a lot of mistakes."

"Like?"

"Oh, I'm not nearly drunk enough to go down that road." Gem gave me a dark little smile. "Maybe a different day."

"What changed?"

"I used to look at my clients like sources of money. How could I get them to come to my club and order top-shelf liquor and stay all night long, spending more and more money so that I became richer and richer?"

"That's not a sin. That's mostly just good business sense. You need to make a profit to run a profitable business. Obviously."

"Yes, but the growth of my companies started to stall. I was throwing tons of money at advertising and promotions. Ladies' night. Two-for-one Thursdays. College-night Wednesdays."

"Again, another smart business tactic."

"Things didn't start changing until after I dug myself into a hole, then another hole, then finally a few more holes until I hit a rocky sort of bottom." Gem shifted and pulled his eye contact away from me. "It was not a pleasant time."

"But it made you grow. Or change."

"Both, hopefully," Gem said. "I started seeing these customers as people—not customers. I started seeing them as human beings with desires and hopes. The thing was, I understood these people. I still understand them. No matter how much money I accumulate; at this point, it's just that. Numbers on a scale. It goes into my bank account and out of it. I have accountants to manage it."

"A lot of people would kill to have that problem."

"There are phases of money," Gem said. "There's the first phase where you have none of it. Then you start working, you get a little money. You can afford some bare-bones necessities. Then maybe you get a new job, a bonus, a little more cash. You don't have to watch your grocery budget so closely."

"Okay."

"Then some lucky people will be fortunate enough to start making more. More than enough to be comfortable. Vacations start happening, then lifestyle creep. You hire a maid at home; you get used to new luxuries. This new wealth starts to feel normal. You expect it."

I nodded along.

"A few years of this, and a person might realize they can spend money on whatever they want. They go a little wild, let the power that money can bring go to their heads. This is the most dangerous phase to get stuck in."

"What comes next?"

"The sobering realization that money isn't everything," Gem said. "The realization that some days, you wish you were back in that first phase with no money but a lot of hope. Where you scrimped and saved and appreciated every little purchase you made. Where buying a coffee felt like Christmas morning because it was such an indulgence."

I gave a fond smile. "I know what that's like."

"As do I," Gem said softly. "And I know the alternative. Happiness is a lot harder to come by when you have more money than most people in the world. What can someone give you that you can't buy yourself?"

"Is that a rhetorical question?" I asked. "Because I don't know. My car doesn't even work right most days."

Gem laughed. "That's where it becomes about other things. Companionship. Helping people."

"You mean, helping people like me. You like to be in on the whole catching-the-bad-guy thing."

"When you put it like that, it sounds a little pathetic."

"Trust me, we appreciate it. I appreciate it."

"I appreciate it too," Gem said. "Believe me. Some days, I think it would be easier to have never made millions."

"I dunno. I think money can buy a little happiness."

"It can buy comfort. And, sure, maybe a little bit of fun," Gem said, a nostalgic smile on his face. "I remember the day I bought my first brand new sports car. That was pretty fun."

I couldn't help but grin at the joy dancing behind his formerly serious eyes. "See?"

"But I'd rather be in the first category with no money but a family who loves me than the latter category with nobody by my side."

"Yeah," I murmured. "I get that too. Which is pretty obvious, seeing as I chose a profession that'll never get me rich."

"You don't need to be rich when you have everything you could ever want in your life." Gem's eyes ran over me.

"I'm not saying your life doesn't have problems, Detective, but you have a mother who loves you. A father who does, too, whether you'll admit it or not. A sister who adores you. A man who loves you. A career you're passionate about. You make a difference in this world."

"You make a difference too, Gem. Look at all these people here enjoying themselves. You're giving them that experience."

"Ah, yes, full circle," Gem said. "That was my whole point. When I started thinking about what my customers—these people—actually want, the dollar signs started to disappear. I set out to create an experience for people."

"You mean, you added custom fire warmers into the side of your club that probably cost thousands of dollars just to make people more comfortable."

He gave a funny smile. "It's interesting how my bottom line began to explode once I stopped thinking about the dollar signs. I had enough money by that time that it just didn't matter as much to me. It was an experiment."

"One that obviously paid off."

"It's common sense in retrospect," Gem said. "I had to put myself into the head of my eighteen-year-old self who would've stolen ten dollars to get the entry fee to get inside. I could've bought food with those ten dollars or I could've saved it for school. I could've bought a nice book or paid some of my utility bills with it. But why would I have even considered spending it to come to a place like this when I had much more pressing needs?"

I didn't say anything, sensing Gem wasn't finished.

"It was because I wanted to escape my life—the life where I was forced to worry about what to do with those ten dollars. I wanted to believe, for one night only, that a bigger, better world was out there." Gem surveyed the dance floor thoughtfully. "I wanted to disappear into a fantasy land where nobody knew who I was. I wanted to escape from the fact that my mother had died and I had no one left who wanted me. I wanted to escape from the fact that my rent was due the next morning, and nothing I could do would change the fact that I had no money to pay it."

I glanced down at the table. Gem wasn't looking at me. It was like he'd forgotten I existed.

"Her, over there," Gem said, nodding toward a group of girls around one another. "It looks like she's just getting sloppy drunk and trying to make out with strangers."

I winced at a young woman whose skirt was inappropriately hiked up as she leaned over a man who looked entirely unappreciative of her slurred advances. I watched as two of the woman's friends hurried over to pull her off the guy. One of them swiftly tidied up the skirt situation for her friend.

"She's probably trying to get over a bad breakup," Gem said. "Or maybe she failed one of her classes, lost a scholarship, and doesn't know what she'll do next. She's trying not to think about it."

"It's nice she has friends with her," I said. "That will help a lot with whatever she's going through."

"Touché."

"Do another one," I said after a moment. "Another scenario. This is interesting."

Gem nodded toward another corner. "That guy over there lives in his mom's basement, but only because he's going to community college and knows his mother has worked two jobs all her life to afford him this opportunity. He doesn't want to waste more of her hard-earned money by living on campus even though he feels like he's missing out big time because of it. He probably works a job too, but instead of spending the cash on rent at his own place, he contributes to the household finances so his mom can quit the overnight shift she's worked for ten years."

I raised my eyebrows as I studied the nervous-looking man Gem had selected for his assessment. The guy was probably in his early twenties, toying with a glass of water at the very end of the bar.

"He's nervous to meet women because he feels young and inexperienced, but in a few years, he'll fill out some and make a great husband." Gem made a tsking sound. "Unfortunately, most of the women won't be interested in him tonight, which is a shame because he's probably got a lot to offer someone."

"Your scenarios assume most people are good people."

"I think most people are," Gem said. "Don't you?"

"I think my perception is skewed because of my job," I said. "Okay, one more. What about that guy right there?"

I pointed out someone in the middle of the dance floor with a shirt deeply unbuttoned. His hair was slicked back. I felt like I could probably smell his cologne from across the room.

"Wait, no, let me try," I said quickly. "He's a young guy who's going to school to be a ruthless lawyer but really, underneath, he's a teddy bear."

Gem burst into laughter.

"What?" I asked. "You didn't like it?"

"I liked your analysis. I think you're wrong."

"Wrong?" I said defensively. "Well, we don't know that."

"No, I suppose not. It's just a game after all."

"Fine, what do you think his story is, then, if mine's so stupid?"

Gem shrugged. "I think he's just a douche who grew up with too much money."

It was my turn to grin. "Really? No sob story behind that fake tan?"

"Not everyone has a sob story. I can see my reflection in that guy's hair. No, he's just an idiot who's failing all his college classes but doesn't care because his parents are paying for it. He'll try to scoop up the prettiest girl he can get tonight and never call her again. Maybe he'll learn someday, and maybe he won't."

"Wow. Okay."

He shrugged again. "I told you my job is to read people. Not to pretend everyone is a good person."

"Fair enough." I wrinkled my nose and studied the guy again. "You know, I think you're right."

"Your analysis has changed?"

"Yep," I said, watching as the guy reached out and pinched some random woman's butt. The woman swatted him away with a look of disgust. "I don't think he'll ever learn." I gave a sideways glance at Gem. "You know, you could've had a second career as a detective. Most of my job involves reading people. Trying to determine if they're lying or telling the truth. Figuring out the motives behind why people do what they do."

"The next time you need someone to swoop in and make up backstories about your murder victims or your best suspects, you know who to call."

I hid a smile. "We can't afford your consultant fee."

"For you, Detective, it's free of charge."

I cleared my throat and sat back in my seat. I was relieved that our conversation had wound its way around to lighter territory, but now that we'd sort of wrapped up our discussion, my mind was whirling. I felt like I'd gotten a lesson in both business and anthropology from one of the richest men in the country in the space of ten minutes. Bonus points because we were in a club full of sapphires and blinking blue lights with bass-filled Christmas songs pulsing around us.

"There he is." I nodded at a table two rows away. "That's him, right? Nick Ralphio?"

"That's him, all right," Gem said. "Him and his posse."

"Do you know who's next to him?"

Nick Ralphio was one of those dangerously handsome men. The sort of men who didn't have to try, and he'd still draw women to him. Dark hair, neatly pressed white shirt, and black slacks. Expensive shoes. Probably subtle-smelling cologne that insisted it was expensive even to someone like me, whose most expensive perfume purchase was a bottle of body mist from Bath and Body Works in high school.

He seemed like the sort of person whose eyes you'd look into and know that he'd seen things. That he could be ruthless, that his words could be magically alluring or sharply cutting. I shivered.

"Yes, that's an appropriate reaction," Gem said.

I wasn't aware he'd seen me shiver. Then I realized that he must have felt it since we were sharing a bench. "I've never seen him before. My father knew of him."

"That doesn't mean much," Gem said. "I know of him too."

"I know, I know. You have to befriend other powerful players in the city."

"The circle is small at a certain level."

"I'd have no idea," I said, "but I'll take your word for it. What can you tell me about him?"

"Not much that you wouldn't already know. He's been linked—loosely—to a lot. Murder, extortion, mob ties, drug trade, you name it. Nothing's ever been proven."

I took a deep breath. "Okay, well, I'll keep an eye on him for a bit. I want to get a feel for him before I decide what to do next."

"Good idea." Gem looked up as Jane and Wes came back to the table. "Don't rush into anything. He's dangerous. Especially if he realizes you're a cop who's onto him."

"He won't realize that," Jane said with a laugh. "Come on, Gem. I picked out her dress. Haven't you seen the way she looks? Nobody's looking for a gun on her tonight."

Gem gave a polite nod. "I have noticed, actually. You look very beautiful, Detective."

"Now, you're just laying it on thick." I rolled my eyes.

At that moment the host reappeared at our table. "Sir? The prince has arrived."

"Great. Excuse me for a moment," Gem said. "I'll be right back. Detective, please wait for my return before doing anything. Like I said, he's a dangerous man."

Chapter 19

"You guys didn't crack open the champagne yet?" Jane wiggled up next to me. "Mind if I do the honors?"

I gestured for her to go ahead.

"You're not going to give me that lame excuse about being on duty or something, are you?" Jane winked as she grabbed the bottle out of the bucket of ice. "What a Debbie Downer."

"I'd argue the Debbie Downer is the person who shot up my victim on the sidewalk, but who am I to judge?"

"Now, now," Wes said teasingly. "We appreciate your service, Detective."

I was happy to see Jane enjoying herself. It made Gem's point about the importance of entertainment as an escape hit home in a way that was a little more personal. The illusion of an escape was just what Jane needed for tonight.

There was nothing she could do about her missing father. There was nothing she could do about the guy found dead on the sidewalk. The alternative to her enjoying her time here would be sitting at home and feeling miserable. The outcome wouldn't change, so she might as well escape from her misery for a few short hours before the morning light hit and reality came flooding back. It always did.

"I'm going to use the restroom," I said. "I'll be back in a minute."

"You're not doing anything dumb, are you?" Jane asked. "You heard Gem."

"I promise. I want to feel out this guy before I approach him. I'm not going to rush anything."

"Gem might be able to help," Wes said. "They used to be friends."

"Used to be friends?" I halted in my tracks. "Gem and Nick Ralphio?"

"Not best buddies, but they got along."

"How?" I blurted. I couldn't help it. "I mean, I've heard Nick's into some dangerous businesses."

"Gem has a way of being able to separate a person from the things they've done." Wes shrugged. "Honestly, I've met Ralphio. If I didn't know any better, I'd like him too."

"That's the most dangerous kind of guy," I said grimly. "He'll be your friend until you tick him off. Then he'll kill you."

Wes wagged a finger in my direction. "Correction. He'll hire someone to kill you."

"Is that supposed to make me feel better?"

"It's the truth."

"Maybe you need a new job." Jane poured herself and Wes a glass of champagne. "Then you can hang out with whomever you want and you can forget all about these criminal guys."

"Then who'd catch 'em?" Wes asked. "Everyone knows Kate's the best. Without her, this city would fall apart."

"Uh-huh," I said with a groan. "Not an exaggeration at all."

"When's Jack getting in town?" Jane asked. "The wedding's in a few days. I thought he might be here a little earlier. You know, Christmas spirit and all."

"Let me lock up the murderer I'm chasing first. Then I'll find our father. And then maybe I'll be in the mood for a sugar cookie. I'm going to hit the restrooms before Gem comes back. Are you going to be here?"

"We'll wait for you," Jane said. "Make sure you don't get yourself into any trouble."

"I think I can handle using the restroom by myself."

I left the table with Wes and Jane behind. I really did need to use the restroom. My intention this evening wasn't to get in any trouble despite what Jane thought. My intention was only to get a feel for the guy, under the guise of being some random girl he'd met at a club.

I'd work my way around to the whole detective thing later, on a different day, when I had my gun, a badge, and backup. I was considering this to be a little fishing expedition to understand what I was working with. Off-duty perks of being friends with the richest man in the city.

I found the restrooms just behind the back of the bar. As the night was still young in terms of club time, the bathrooms were mostly empty and still somewhat clean. As I washed up, I glanced into the mirror and caught sight of the person Jane had made me into for the night. I had to admit I didn't look like a cop.

My phone rang then, and I glanced down and saw Russo was calling. I answered as a woman with pink hair slipped into the bathroom and made her way to the last stall.

"Hey," I said. "How's it going? I haven't heard from you in a while."

"I'm sorry," he said. "I don't have time to talk now. I just wanted to touch base and let you know I'm on a case. We're getting close to breaking it. I might be off the grid for the next twenty-four to forty-eight hours. Just didn't want you to worry."

"I appreciate it."

"It sounds like you're inside a boombox," Jack said. "Everything okay?"

"Long story. I'm on a case too."

"I've got to go," Jack said. "I just wanted to say I'll see you in a few days. I'll call you once things lighten up here."

"Okay, I'll talk to you—"

The phone line went dead before I could murmur a proper goodbye. It was rare for Jack to sound so focused, so business-oriented on a phone call. He was much better than me at separating his work life from his personal life. Even in the throes of a busy time, he could usually carve out a few minutes to talk to me without hanging up mid-sentence.

Those were the perks of dating someone in the same industry as me. I completely understood where Jack was mentally, and I wasn't upset in the slightest about our brief and abrupt phone call. I could hear the concern and worry in Jack's voice.

In the past week or so, he had been unusually vague about the case he was working on, which told me it was a very high-profile case with lots of security clearances. In a way, it was almost better our busy times were lining up. He'd catch his bad guy, I'd catch my bad guy, then we could worry about sipping hot chocolate and opening presents together.

I was slipping my phone back into my clutch as the toilet flushed in the last stall. I headed out from the bathroom and let the door swing shut behind me. Zipping up my purse, I took a few steps down the hallway before I felt a hand on my shoulder. I tensed, but the other person had caught me off guard and had me pinned against the wall before I could take a breath.

My clutch fell to the floor as my head banged lightly against the padded walls. I wasn't hurt, but there was no question the movement was a threat. When I glanced into the person's eyes who'd startled me, I knew why.

"You're pretty, you know." Nick Ralphio's voice was low and sultry. "Smoking hot, actually. But you're not his type."

The woman with the pink hair pushed her way out of the bathroom, took one look at the two of us, and grinned. She was gone before I could think of a way to signal to her that I needed help.

To any bystander, we looked like two people in the throes of a passionate conversation. Nick had both of his hands on my wrists, pinning them against the wall. His body was just about pressed to mine. His lips were an inch away from my skin, fluttering between my ear and my cheek. An ironic thought flashed through my mind as I realized he smelled just like I'd thought he would. Expensive, understated, strong. It was an appealing scent. But considering the circumstances, it made my stomach turn.

"What are you talking about?"

"I know Gem." Nick's breath was minty and fresh. "I can see right through you. Are you sleeping with him, or has he simply had a 'come to Jesus' moment?"

"What are you talking about?"

"Alastair Gem comes to the opening of his own club with you on his arm." Ralphio shook his head. "I knew something was up the second I spotted him with you. You're a cop. The Gem I know doesn't fraternize with cops. Unless you're screwing him."

"Feel free to check me for a gun and badge," I said as his hands slid down my waist. "Oh wait, you already have. I'm not a cop."

Ralphio reached for the clutch on the floor with one hand without letting me go with his other hand. He peeped inside. "Good. I didn't think you were that stupid. I'd be offended if they just picked the prettiest intern to send my way. But you're not an intern, are you? No, you're Detective Kate Rosetti. You're starting to get pretty famous in my circles."

"What circles would that be? Criminals? Killers? Enlighten me."

He gave a smile, a soft laugh. Up close, he was very handsome. I could see how people would be drawn to him. His looks, his appearance, the way he carried himself and spoke as if he were being modest and friendly. Beneath it all, however, I could feel his anger as his fingers gripped my wrists.

"I always knew Gem wasn't one of us. Even if he walked the walk, talked the talk, he never truly fit in with us."

"You mean he'd never kill anyone?"

"How well do you know him?" Nick asked. "I was leaning toward the idea that the two of you were sleeping together. After all, Gem's always had a weakness for beautiful women. Then again, who doesn't?"

I swallowed back a retort.

"Then I saw the two of you sitting next to each other, and I knew that wasn't it."

"How could you possibly know that?"

"The sexual tension between the two of you is thick enough to slice with a knife," he said. "That all goes away the second you hop in bed with him. Enjoy it while it lasts. Nobody escapes the clutches of Alastair Gem once he's got his sights set on you."

"He's getting married in a few days. To someone else," I added. "There's nothing between us. We're just friends."

"Friends?" Nick said the word as if the very taste of it in his mouth was foreign to him. He appeared to be considering whether or not I was telling the truth. "I'm surprised."

"What do you mean you're surprised?" I asked. "Friends. It's when you're loyal to a person. Never heard of it before?"

"I have plenty of friends."

"It doesn't count if they're on your payroll."

He laughed again, a genuine gleam in his eyes this time. "I'm starting to see why he likes you, Rosetti. You've got spunk. Gem's always loved the thrill of the chase. Wants what he can't have. Just a word of warning... the real thing is never as good as the anticipation. The second you give in to Gem is the second he stops being interested in you."

"You don't know anything about my relationship with Gem," I said. "For that matter, it doesn't sound like you know anything about Gem at all. You've got it all wrong."

"Sweetheart, *you've* got it all wrong. You want him just as badly as he wants you."

"Not true," I said. "I have a boyfriend."

"Is your boyfriend Alastair Gem?" Nick wrinkled his nose. "No? Well, then that boyfriend doesn't stand a chance. Sorry."

"Tell me what you want with me or let me go," I said. "While our little conversation has been pleasant, I have people waiting for me."

"Gem's talking to the prince. Your sister's making out with her boyfriend. Your boyfriend is—where? Not here. Nobody's waiting for you, sugar."

"Who is Gavin Harris?" I asked. "Why did you kill him?"

I was hoping my abrupt change of subject along with an accusation tossed his way would at least cause him to blink. To pause. To show the first fissure in his coolness. To my dismay, none of that happened. It was easy to understand how Nick Ralphio had climbed the ranks to power and wealth so quickly. Ruthless, composed, intelligent—he was everything that Gem was, except he had a black streak in his moral code that was missing from Gem's.

"Oh, you're here about Gavin. I thought you were here about your father. I'll tell Angelo you say hello."

It took a moment for the words to register. Then the anger hit. A second later, I felt the rage and frustration and discomfort of our entire exchange as it welled up in my chest. I raised my knee as hard as I could into Nick Ralphio's groin area. Before he could bend in half to protect his manhood, I drove my forehead onto his nose and felt a satisfying crack when we connected.

As Ralphio bent in half and slunk to the ground, he exposed a figure standing behind him. Alastair Gem was standing there frozen, his arm extended as if he'd been about to grab Ralphio by the collar when I'd taken him down.

"Sorry," I said. "I didn't see you standing there."

A small smile curled up the bottom of Gem's lip. It quickly turned into disgust as he looked down and stepped over Ralphio's body to me. It then softened as he ran a hand over my forehead. When he pulled away, there was blood on his thumb.

"Are you okay, Detective?"

"That's not mine," I said, glancing at his hand. "I think I broke his nose."

"Just about cracked his skull, I'd say."

"I'm sorry. I didn't mean to cause a disturbance on your first night at the club."

"Stop apologizing, will you?" Gem said briskly.

He retreated from me and reached down to where Ralphio was still groaning on the ground. A small crowd had started to appear around the outskirts of the hallway leading to the restrooms.

Gem seemed to be oblivious to any onlookers as he grabbed Ralphio by the collar. Nick Ralphio wasn't a small, skinny sort of guy, so it was an impressive display on Gem's part that he was able to haul the full-grown mobster to his feet. I wondered if it was adrenaline or if Gem was stronger than he looked beneath those tailored suits.

He thrust Ralphio against the wall. The mobster could barely stand by himself. His bloodied face was scrunched in pain. It was almost pathetic. But after what he'd said about Gem and his threat against my father, I wasn't exactly feeling charitable.

"Get the hell out of my club," Gem murmured to Ralphio. His voice never broke above a whisper. The crowd around couldn't hear. But it was visible to anyone watching that Gem was a step beyond livid. "If I see you step foot in-side one of my properties again, I will end you."

Then he let go of Ralphio. The mobster slunk back to the ground. Gem turned to me and whisked me away by the arm through the now-crowded passageway and back into the club. He didn't say a word, but I could feel him practically trembling next to me with everything he didn't say.

I wanted to apologize again, but even I was intimidated. For once, my intimidation had nothing to do with the fact that I didn't have my gun on me, and everything to do with the fact that I might've finally pushed Gem a step too far. That I might've finally broken the tenuous bonds of the thing we called friendship.

We made it back to the table where Wes and Jane were mid-toast with glasses of champagne. Jane took one look at me, and her jaw dropped.

"Kate?" she gasped. "What happened to you?"

"I told you. I went to the bathroom."

"You have blood on your face."

"Accident," I said, reaching for a cloth the waitress had hung over the side of the bucket of ice. I dabbed it against my forehead. "Don't worry. It's not mine."

"Um..." Jane looked up at Gem.

"We're going," he said. "Now."

It didn't take another word for Jane or Wes to under-stand the gist of what was happening. Within minutes, we'd been shuffled outside and ushered into a limo. Only Gem remained standing on the sidewalk outside of his club. He spoke in low tones to two bulky bodyguards, gesturing agi-tatedly every few minutes with his hands. The guards nodded, their faces serious. Finally, Gem clapped one of them on the back and spun around, heading toward the limo. He slipped in and sat next to me without a word.

The ride was silent for five minutes before anyone spoke. Finally, Jane mustered up the courage. "That was some party, huh?"

Nobody so much as blinked an eye. Wes squeezed her leg. Gem mildly looked like he registered that someone had spoken. The rest of the ride continued in silence. Gem instructed the driver to head to Wes's apartment first.

"I-I think I'm going to stay at my sister's place tonight," Jane said as Wes shot her a questioning look when we arrived. "I'll call you in the morning, babe?"

"Go on," I said to Jane. "I'm fine. Really. Stay with Wes."

"But—"

"I told you, this wasn't my blood," I said. "It was just an average day on the job. I'll call you in the morning and explain. It's probably better if you stay with Wes tonight anyway."

Jane looked a little confused at the explanation. Wes took one look at Gem, then another look at me, and he seemed to understand something that even I couldn't quite comprehend. Eventually he reached for Jane's hand and tugged her out of the limo. We said our goodbyes, and then they were gone, and Gem and I were left alone.

The ride to my place crawled slowly by. For a minute, I'd thought that maybe the unspoken reason Wes had insisted Jane stay with him was to give Gem and me a moment to talk alone. But that didn't seem to have worked out since Gem didn't say a word. Eventually, the limo parked outside of my house. I sat for a moment, unsure of the proper way to say goodbye after all that had happened.

"Stay," Gem said finally. He must have seen the confused look on my face because he added, "for just a minute."

I hesitated.

"Please."

"Gem, I'm so sorry," I said. "I didn't go looking for trouble, I swear. I just went to use the restroom and Ralphio cornered me when I came out. I was hanging up from a phone call and was distracted when he..." I took a breath and hesitated again. "I know that's not an excuse."

"Kate."

"I knew it was a bad idea to ask you for a favor like this. Everything I touch seems to turn into trouble. I'm sorry if I ruined the opening night at your club."

"Ruined the opening night?" The faintest edges of a smile turned up Gem's lips. "A stunt like that will only help things along."

"Well, then..." I squirmed uncomfortably under his piercing gaze. "Then you're welcome, I guess."

Gem gave a soft laugh. It was still missing the true charm, the lightness that his voice normally carried. I hated seeing that spark dulled in him. Over time, that little quirk of his—his optimism and humor in the face of tough times—had grown on me.

"Kate, I don't think we can do this anymore."

The use of my first name shook me. Gem had taken to calling me Detective, and it was jarring to hear him use my given name. "I agree," I said. "I don't think it's wise for me to ask you to help on official business. Even if it wasn't completely official. I wasn't planning to confront Ralphio without backup, and somehow, things blew up anyway."

"That's not what I'm talking about."

"Then what?"

"Spending time together," Gem said. "I realize tonight was spent in a professional capacity, and I completely respect that."

"I'm sorry if I made you uncomfortable—"

"You did," Gem said quickly, interrupting me. "And you need to quit apologizing."

"But—"

"When I saw Ralphio with his hands on you like that, I can't tell you what I felt inside." Gem rested a hand against his chest. A pained look crossed his face as he glanced out the window. "To know that you could've been put in danger, at my place of business no less..."

"I asked you to bring me there. None of this was your fault."

"It wasn't your fault either. You went to use the restroom and were assaulted by a patron. No, worse. By a guest I'd invited there personally."

"You couldn't have known. He pegged me for a cop right away. He knew who I was. He mentioned my dad."

Gem's eyes switched on to mine, piercing and curious. "He did?"

I nodded. "It's sort of what triggered me to, you know, knee him in the crotch."

"A good reason."

"I thought so," I said. "I think he knows what happened to my dad. Whether or not he's actually behind it, I'm not sure."

"I'll find out," Gem said. "I will make sure he knows in no uncertain terms that your father should be returned safely to you. Or else."

"Gem. I'm a cop. Don't tell me these things. You realize if anything happened to Ralphio, I'd have to come forward with what happened tonight."

"It wouldn't be the first time you've questioned me in a murder investigation," Gem said evenly. "Who knows? Maybe it won't be the last."

"Don't say that."

"I have to say that because of the way I feel when I'm around you," Gem said. "That's why, I'm sorry, but this has to end. I'm marrying a woman I love, in several days."

"You didn't do anything wrong," I said. "You just told Ralphio to stay away from your club. Is it because I asked you to come out tonight? I will call Mindy and personally apologize. I'll let her know it was all my fault."

"It's not that. It's how protective I felt when I saw you in danger."

"It's because we're friends," I said. "When Ralphio started saying things about you, it upset me too. Because we are friends, and we are loyal to one another. That's what friends are, what friends do. They defend one another."

Gem again looked puzzled. "What'd he say about me?"

"Nothing," I said, thinking about the conversation with Ralphio and shivering. "I mean, it's not important right now.

It was a load of bull anyway. He was just trying to get a rise out of me. I suppose it worked."

"Kate—"

"You did what any upstanding gentleman would've done if he saw a woman cornered in a hallway," I said. "Jimmy would've done it for me. Russo. My dad. The guy coming out of the bathroom. Don't beat yourself up, Gem, for feeling how you did. You were just worried about a friend. That's all."

Gem nodded, though he didn't seem convinced.

"With that said," I continued, taking a deep breath, "as a friend, I only want what's best for you. I think it might be best at this point if I decline the invitation to your wedding."

"That's not what I meant."

"No, but it is my choice. If my presence makes you uncomfortable, or if Mindy feels uncomfortable with me and you being together at all, then I want to respect that. You're right, you know: you're getting married. A marriage should come first above all else. I might not have personal experience, but I get it. As much as I can."

Gem expelled a breath. He ran a hand over his face. I could tell whatever he was feeling was complicated. I felt guilty and frustrated at myself. After all, it was my selfishness to solve a case that had gotten Gem wrapped up in this situation anyway. If it weren't for me and my inability to let things go, he'd be tucked safely at home tonight—oblivious to Ralphio and Sapphire and everything else.

"I'm going to go," I said quietly. "Thanks for everything, Gem. I'm sorry."

I climbed out of the car. It seemed that Gem couldn't quite look at me.

"I wish you only the best," I murmured. "You're a good person. I appreciate the friendship we've had."

I turned away from the limo and walked up to my front steps. Gem had scooped my clutch off the floor after the altercation with Ralphio, so fortunately I'd walked away from the situation with my keys, wallet, and phone intact.

After unlocking the door, I slipped inside. Before I could close it, however, my phone jangled. I reached for it and answered without looking at the name on the screen. At this hour, I could only assume the call would be important.

A curse word sounded on the other end of the line. A moment later, I recognized the voice.

"Lassie?" I asked. "What's going on?"

"Oh, thank God," she gushed. "I'm so glad to hear your voice."

"Huh?"

"Where are you?"

"Home," I said. "Just walking in the door."

"Oh, thank God." She seemed to be saying the same things on repeat. She followed up with another curse word. "That was a close call."

"Lassie, take a breath. What are you talking about?"

"I thought you might be toast."

"How'd you hear about the Ralphio thing already?" I asked. "I didn't think that would exactly be newsworthy."

"Ralphio?" she asked. "What are you talking about?"

"What are *you* talking about?"

Finally, we reached a standstill. I heard Lassie expel a breath it seemed like she'd been holding since I first answered the phone.

"I thought you were literally toast," she said. "I thought you were blown up."

"Why would I be blown up?"

"You haven't heard yet?"

"I've been in the car."

"Oh, good," Lassie said. "Tell me your sister left Sapphire too."

"Yes, she's home with Wes. What's going on?"

"I got a phone call from a bouncer at Sapphire on my payroll. You know what I mean."

I knew that as a blogger, Lassie had eyes and ears all over the place giving her the juiciest gossip in the Twin Cities on any given night of the week. It was a talent of hers to know what was going on—no matter how big or small.

"He called me saying there was a fight at Gem's new club," Lassie said in a rush. "He thought the guy might be somebody important, but he didn't know his name. I went to do some research and see if I could figure out who this guy was from the picture when, *bam*, I recognized the girl who'd beat him up. That's you, sweet cheeks."

"Oh, yeah, that," I said. "It wasn't a big deal."

"I'm going to skip right over the part where you pretend beating up a murderous mobster isn't a big deal because I don't have time for that right now," Lassie said. "The important part is that Gem's club just exploded."

"What do you mean?"

"I mean *kaboom*." Lassie paused to take a breath. "They think it was a bomb. At least those are the super-duper early rumors. I haven't even had a chance to print anything yet. It's breaking news."

"Wait a minute. Gem's club blew up?" I asked. "Sapphire?"

"Yes," she said. "Fortunately, the bomb was mostly contained to some hallway, but still..." She let out a shaky sigh. "There are at least two confirmed dead, Kate."

My blood ran cold. Everything about the night came rushing back to me in a blur. The multiple warnings that Nick Ralphio was dangerous. The way he'd pegged me for a cop instantaneously, which couldn't have been an accident. The way he'd cornered me in the hallway. The blood gushing from his nose. The words about my father.

Had the entire thing been a setup? I felt a chill run down my back. Had the bomb been meant for me? For Gem? As a warning to stay away from the case? Or had it been somehow planted after we'd left?

A brush of cold air blew in from outside, and I realized my door was still partially open. I pushed it the rest of the way open and saw Gem's limo still parked at my curb.

His door had opened, and he stood there, the phone up to his ear, his face completely unreadable. Solid, stony, dangerous. His gaze met mine.

I felt myself finally breaking down. After going years and years without crying, I felt the tears fall down my cheeks. A moment later, Gem pulled me into a hug. We stood there for a long second in the snow, two friends in the frigid cold, under the moonlight, not entirely sure what had gone wrong in the world tonight.

Chapter 20

Twenty minutes later, Gem was standing in my kitchen. His phone had been ringing off the hook. Somehow, he'd managed to find the electric kettle and had put it on to boil. When the water was hot, Gem poured two cups of tea, and we sat across from one another at the kitchen table.

A glance in the mirrored side of the electric kettle told me I looked like a mess. I had a tiny smear of blood on my temple that had smudged when I'd tried to wipe it off earlier. My mascara was streaked from my tears. I excused myself for a moment and went to the bathroom.

Once there, I scrubbed my face clean. I took a few deep breaths and splashed myself again with cool water. When I returned, Gem was sitting at the table in the same position I'd left him. His phone continually lit up, but he didn't seem keen to answer anyone's calls.

"Two dead," he murmured when I sat down.

"Two confirmed dead," I corrected automatically, having switched into business mode. "I'm sorry, that's not helpful. Habit of the job."

I'd already felt plenty embarrassed for letting Gem see me cry. But something had broken inside of me. In this festive season of cheery lights and sparkling snow, my father was missing. Another woman had lost her husband, a child had lost her father. Then my friend's place of business had been attacked, leaving two innocent people dead, and in some way, I felt responsible.

It was exhausting. The exhaustion had finally gotten to me and allowed the fissures that'd been hissing to break loose to finally crack. Fortunately, Gem hadn't made a big deal about seeing my tears. He'd held me in a hug for a minute until I was able to compose myself. Then we'd gone inside the house and had taken a quiet moment in which we were each obviously trying to digest what had happened.

"It's not your fault," I said. "If anything, it's my fault. I need to get back down there to the scene and help out."

"No, you don't," Gem said. "You've had a difficult enough night already. Let the other police do their jobs. You won't know much until morning."

"Maybe. Don't you think we already know everything we really need to know?"

Gem gave a short nod.

"Do you have any doubt Ralphio was behind it?"

He shook his head.

"Do you think the bomb was planted before I interacted with Nick as an attempt to frighten us? Or do you think it came after?"

"You mean after you took him down."

"Right."

"Kate, you don't have to look sheepish when I say that." Gem looked at me seriously. "You defended yourself against an assault. If you weren't a cop, I'd have filed a report myself. I figured you wouldn't appreciate my filing a report, however, seeing as you are the police."

"Fair point. But don't you think blowing up a club is a bit of an overreaction to what happened tonight?"

"No, unfortunately, I don't think so. Not for him. For anyone else, sure, but Nick Ralphio's got an ego and something to prove. In his line of work, signs of weakness are not tolerated."

"Still."

"You're a woman, Kate. Yes, an accomplished detective, but tonight you weren't looking like a detective. You were looking like a beautiful woman who bested Nick Ralphio by kneeing him in the nuts. If that wasn't embarrassing enough, you then proceeded to bash in his skull."

I shifted uncomfortably again. "He had his hands on me."

"It was entirely justified, but that's not my point. I'm telling you what it looks like to outsiders who don't know the situation. Outsiders who have been watching Ralphio for years, outsiders who want what Nick Ralphio has and are willing to do anything to get it."

"You think the explosion was a retaliation," I said. "Against me. It's my fault."

"No, I didn't say that. A normal person would've left the club feeling embarrassed about their actions. Nick Ralphio had his boys set up a bomb." Gem shook his head. "If anything, it's my fault. If I had to guess, his reaction was as much to me threatening him as to his embarrassment. You heard what I told him."

"You shouldn't have done that, Gem. I wasn't trying to drag you into things. You didn't have to ruin your friendship—or whatever understanding you had with him—for me."

"There's no better reason to ruin a friendship. Not that what I had with Ralphio was a friendship," Gem said. "We had a mutual understanding. The second he laid his hands on you, he broke those rules."

"You mean he left that little criminal club where he abides by some unwritten moral code?"

"If that's how you want to say it, then sure. He's no better than any other thug now. To survive in this world, both as a person and as a business, one needs to adapt. If I learn new information about someone, my opinion changes. My opinion has changed of Nick Ralphio."

I gave a shake of my head. "What does this mean? What happens next?"

"The police are already on the scene." Gem stood. "I should head down to Sapphire. They'll require a statement from me. I'd also like to see the..." He cleared his throat. "See the damage."

"I'll come with you."

"Please stay," Gem insisted. "Get some rest. I have a feeling your case is about to blow wide open, Detective. Get a little sleep so that when it does, you're ready for it."

"I want to be there with you, even if it's only as support. Not to mention, I'm a cop. I can help, Gem."

"I think it's best if you stay away from this part for now. Get some sleep. Focus on finding your father and your killer."

"But—"

"If Ralphio is involved in this mess, you'll need your rest and your strength. This bomb is just the beginning."

A shiver went down my spine. "My father is probably in danger. If Ralphio is willing to kill two innocent people because of a bloody nose, I don't want to think about what he's going to do to my dad."

Gem didn't offer any words of encouragement. There were none. We were both so embedded in this mess that it was useless to offer false hope when the truth was simply that my father was in danger, and if I didn't find him quickly, I might break my promise to my mother. The promise that he'd be home in time for Christmas. I didn't know how I'd ever be able to look my mother in the eye if that happened.

Almost at once, both of our phones rang. I glanced down and saw Russo's name. Gem held up his phone to show me Mindy's name. We both answered at the same time.

"Kate?"

"Yeah," I said, turning away from Gem as he spoke into his device. "How are you?"

"Me? I'm fine. I'm so relieved to hear your voice. I heard that you were involved in an explosion tonight."

"How'd you hear that? Never mind," I said. "I wasn't there. I was out at a club tonight trying to look into this guy. Long story short, we suspect he got upset and set some sort of bomb after we left."

Russo sighed. "Kate..."

"I'm fine. I didn't even approach the guy. Something went wrong. Nick Ralphio knew who I was from the start. I think he might be involved with my father's disappearance."

"You need to be careful," Russo said, his voice tight. "I don't like the sound of this case. Where are you now?"

"At home."

There was a beat. "Who's with you?"

"Gem," I said. "It was his club we were at tonight with Wes and Jane. He'd just dropped me off when we got the news the bomb exploded. He's heading down to the club now."

"I see."

Russo didn't sound happy, but it was hard to say if it was because of the fact Gem was in my kitchen or because of the fact I'd almost gotten blown up tonight. Or maybe a little bit of both.

"I'm sorry I didn't call you sooner," I said. "Everything's been happening so fast, and—"

"You did call earlier," Jack said sharply. "I didn't answer. Kate, I'm sorry. I've been kicking myself all night. Then I got word of the explosion, and the minute I heard that you were there, my heart just about stopped."

"I'm okay, Jack. Take a breath. I'm right here. I was already home when it happened."

"That's not the point. The point was that I chose my job over you. I should've taken your call so we could've actually had time to talk earlier." He paused for a beat. "Then later, when we talked while you were at the club, just thirty minutes before the explosion, I hung up on you."

I could hear heavy breathing on his end of the line.

"I didn't even say goodbye," Jack said. "I didn't mean to be so abrupt, and I knew you wouldn't take it that way. But still, if something had happened to you, I don't even know what my last words would have been. Call you later? Maybe? Before I hung up on you?"

"You're beating yourself up over nothing. I completely understood the situation. I know you're on a case. You're doing important work."

"I chose work over you. I almost lost you, and I couldn't even find the thirty seconds it would've taken to properly say goodbye on our phone call."

"Jack—"

"I've started taking you for granted. I mean, look at us. We've let months go by without seeing one another because we're each so busy."

"It's not your fault. It's more my fault than yours if anything. I'm the one who's reluctant to put more labels on things."

"I don't like this, Kate. It's not working for me."

"What are you talking about?"

"I love you. I care about you," Jack said. "My world was completely rocked tonight."

"You're blowing things way out of proportion." I didn't like the feeling I was getting in my stomach. "This was nobody's fault. You and I put our lives in danger every day we go to work. That's the nature of the job. We both understand that."

"Yes, I agree. We went into this relationship with open eyes, and I have no grudges against you for any of it. I hope you feel the same."

"Of course, Jack. I love you. I love our relationship."

"How is this a relationship?" Jack asked. "We see each other every few months, and as much as I push us to talk about what comes next, let's face it. Neither of us is willing to take the next step. You and me both. It's nobody's fault. It's the job. We knew this was a risk going into our relationship."

"So we wait longer to figure things out," I said. "I'm not unhappy with how things are going."

"I am," Jack said. "I'm not unhappy with you, Kate. The opposite. I'm unhappy being apart from you. I want to kiss you in the morning before we leave for work. I want to meet for lunch on a random Tuesday when we both have light workloads. I want to climb into bed with you at night knowing you haven't just been blown up at some stupid club."

"I don't know what to tell you. This is the way things have been our whole relationship. What changed?"

"Nothing," Jack said. "That's the problem."

"What are you suggesting? Is this you telling me that you don't want to be together anymore?"

"It's me telling you that I want to be together too much," Jack said. "Until we can both make that commitment, I think we need to take a break. Not forever, but I need some time to think. Maybe some time apart will help us both figure out what we want."

"I do know what I want," I said. "I want to be with you."

"I promised you I'd never make you pick between me and your job, Kate," Jack said, his voice pained. "This is me making good on that promise."

"There have to be other options."

Jack waited for me to expand. When I couldn't offer him other options that would satisfactorily solve the problem, he sighed.

"I love you, Kate."

"I love you."

"I'm going to let you get some sleep tonight," Jack said. "Let's talk again in a few days."

"Are you..." I wasn't sure how to phrase the next question.

I wanted to ask if he was still coming to town for Christmas, but I also didn't want to know the answer. He'd also been intending to come for Gem's wedding, and since I'd just declined my invitation, there was no longer a wedding to attend.

"I don't know, Kate," Jack said. "You finish your case and find your father. I'll finish my case. Then we'll talk."

It wasn't lost on me, the symbolism of how Jack ended our conversation. That we both needed to focus on work first. To take care of our careers before we could take care of our relationship. I suddenly felt stupid for ever thinking a relationship could've worked when it always took second place to our professional lives.

I said goodbye and hung up feeling numb from our conversation. I marginally processed the fact that Gem's conversation didn't seem to be going a whole lot better than mine.

"Yes, I'm just leaving Detective Rosetti's house now. I'm heading downtown to Sapphire." He waited a beat. "You knew I would be with her and Wes and Jane tonight. I was just dropping her off when the news of the bomb reached us. We were discussing next steps. She's involved in this. She's a cop."

Gem let out a huge breath, his back turned to me.

"Mindy, let's talk about this in the morning. Two people are dead, and I need to be there," Gem said. "I'll be home in a few hours."

Gem hung up and turned to face me. His face had taken on an annoyed pinch, but one look at my face, and it dissolved. I must have looked like a soggy puppy. My shoulders had slumped, and I felt like I could hardly hold myself standing upright. It took every inch of energy not to burst into tears.

"I'm so sorry," I whispered. "I hope I didn't cause trouble for you or Mindy."

Gem looked at me. "No."

I just shook my head. I took a moment to compose myself, hating that I was human. Hating that my emotions were wreaking havoc on my ability to think and feel things rationally. I hated that I was exhausted and needed sleep. Most of all, I hated how it felt like my life was falling apart around me.

"I'm coming with you," I said firmly. "We're going to nail Ralphio for this. Merry Christmas to me."

***

I felt like a zombie walking through the crime scene at Sapphire. The club had been closed down. Local police were working their way through questioning the patrons, taking down names, checking IDs, trying to figure out if anyone had seen anything fishy.

I found Melinda at the scene of the blast site. The two victims who'd been killed were a woman and a man, both who were waiting in the corridor to use the restroom. The lines had been so long, they'd both been standing outside in the hallway until the stalls emptied out. I didn't think the location could possibly have been a coincidence.

It seemed that Gem felt the same way, judging by the way he raised his eyebrows when the location of the bomb was pointed out to us. The bomb squad was there analyzing the blast zone. One of the techs informed us that it seemed someone had dropped some sort of purse or bag in the hallway. They figured it was either on a timer or used a remote detonator. They wouldn't know more until they could get the material back to the lab to analyze it.

Jimmy was on the scene when we got there. I assumed he'd been in contact with Asha and had linked the explosion to my little outing with Gem.

"Hey," I said to my partner. "Where was my phone call?"

"Don't start, Rosetti," Jimmy said. "You're supposed to be home getting some sleep. I heard enough about what happened."

"You're here. You're my partner."

"I know, Rosetti." He studied my face. He must have seen the same sort of resolve that Gem had seen on it because he quit arguing immediately. "Right. Well, you're here now. Look who else made it."

I turned, surprised to see the chief himself arriving behind me. He rarely came out to active crime scenes anymore.

"Chief?" I said. "What are you doing here?"

"What are you doing here, Rosetti?" he asked. "Is this relevant to your case?"

"It might be."

"I heard Ralphio might be involved," the chief said. "We've been watching this guy for years. He's untouchable. If he's involved, I want this investigation run by the book. We're not letting him slip through our grasp this time."

"There's something else you should know, then, sir."

The chief raised his eyebrows.

"I saw Nick Ralphio earlier tonight," I said. "Here, in the club. He confronted me and said something about my father."

"What did he say?"

"Something about saying hello to Angelo for me." I swallowed. "I was a little distracted. That's the gist of it."

"A threat?"

"I think so, sir. I think he might be involved in my father's disappearance."

The chief cursed. "Why'd he set off this bomb tonight, Rosetti? Was it because of you being here?"

"No," Gem said, stepping into the conversation. "It was me. Kate was here tonight as my personal guest. She was returning from using the restroom when she was cornered and assaulted by Nick Ralphio. I walked into the situation and threw him out. I'm afraid I uttered some harsh words to him, and I believe he retaliated against me."

The chief surveyed Gem. I noticed he didn't ask what Alastair Gem was doing in the middle of a police investigation even if this was his club. I suspected the chief's leniency with Gem's presence might have had something to do with the amount of money Gem had donated over the years to the local force.

Then the chief nodded and moved on. He spoke to Melinda in low tones, dismissing his prior conversations.

"What'd you really do to Ralphio?" Jimmy muttered in my ear. "I don't buy it that some guy assaulted you, and you walked away without doing something about it yourself."

"I, uh, defended myself accordingly."

Jimmy looked over toward Gem.

Gem clasped his hands behind his back and gave a grim smile. "She made sure he'd never have children. Then she broke his nose."

"Ah," Jimmy said, looking entirely unsurprised. "Okay, now things are adding up."

We spent another two hours at the club, but no big discoveries were made. With the extent of the damage, it would take a while in the lab before we'd learn anything about the specifics of the bomb and the person who'd made it. It didn't seem like the rest of the cops were having much luck getting any leads from the patrons. It seemed that most people had been having a good time—meaning they were sufficiently drunk. Drunken memories plus dim lighting and strobe effects did not make it easy to recognize a person passing by in the blink of an eye.

"Come on, Rosetti," Jimmy said eventually. "I insist you get home now. We'll pick this up in the morning but not if you're dead on your feet."

I didn't argue. It was late, and I was tired, and I really did just want to sleep. I found Gem talking with yet another cop and told him good night. Then I let Jimmy drive me home. He waited at the curb while I unlocked the door.

I specifically shielded the little note that'd been taped against my doorknob from view. Using a tissue, I gently removed the envelope before turning to wave to Jimmy.

As my partner pulled away from the curb, I let myself inside and closed the door behind me. I locked it, then double-checked to make sure it was locked tight. I slipped a glove on from my bag and carefully opened the envelope. Inside was a thick piece of rectangular card stock. On it was a simple message.

Hello back.

Chapter 21

"Kate. There you are," my mother said. "I was worried sick about you. Of course I called Jane, and she said that she'd left that place with you. But the explosion on the news had my mind racing all night. I could hardly sleep."

I felt like I'd been hit by a semitruck minus the broken bones. After my shower this morning, I'd looked in the mirror and decided it was better to just pretend I didn't know what I looked like today. The bags under my eyes were dark enough to resemble bruises, and my cheeks looked hollow, like I'd forgotten to eat for the last three days. Then again, I couldn't exactly remember when I'd last sat down to a full meal that didn't involve a latte as my main source of protein.

The last thing I felt like doing was having a heart-to-heart conversation with my mother. I'd had plenty of difficult conversations in the last twenty-four hours, and I was pretty sure my body was physically aching from the stress of it.

I sighed. "Nonfat latte please."

My mother frowned at me. "No extra sugar?"

"I'm on a diet."

My mother studied me closer. "Something's wrong."

"You're right. I should have ordered two. Can I order like an extra-extra-large, or should I just get two? Might as well get about six. I'll probably share one with Jimmy and Melinda."

My mother gave me a curious look. "Are you okay, sweetie?"

"I barely slept. We're on the tail end of a big case."

"Your father's case?"

"I'm not completely sure if it's part of it," I lied, "but we're working on it."

"You know there's less than seventy-two hours before Christmas is here."

"I'm aware, thanks. I guess my shopping will be last minute again."

"That's not what I mean, Kate. Forget it. Just try and take care of yourself, will you?"

When Elizabeth finished the tray of lattes, I opened the door to my mother's shop with my foot and made my way to the precinct. I handed out coffees to Asha and Jimmy. I brought the tray back to my desk and started in on my drink, reserving the final two lattes for Chloe and Melinda.

I took a few minutes to sip my coffee before turning to Jimmy. "Any news?"

"I should be the one asking that," he said. "What happened to you?"

"Love you too, pal."

"Kate, what's wrong?"

Chloe entered the room and came to a standstill. She looked at Jimmy. "Did someone fish her out of the lake this morning? I'm sorry, but you look a little bit like a drowning victim. Except you're not wet or dead. No offense."

"Yeah, none taken," I said with a heavy dose of sarcasm. "I didn't sleep well. Thanks for noticing."

"I can guess why. I read about the explosion," Chloe said. "It's all over Lassie's blog. I've actually been here since five a.m. working with Asha on it. I just popped out for some bagels."

She gestured to the box in her hand. She passed out the bagels like she was handing out Valentine's in a first-grade class. Two landed on my desk. I realized I wasn't hungry for either of them despite the lovely scent of fresh bread.

I pushed the bagels away and focused on the caffeine as I booted up my computer. "What now?"

"The chief sent people over to Nick Ralphio's house," Jimmy said. "They got there early this morning. No sign of him. He never went home last night."

"Perfect. Our main suspect's in the wind."

I thought about the note on my door. Reluctantly, I fished it out of my pocket. "The chief should probably have this."

Jimmy looked down at the note. His usually bright smile flattened out. "You think this is a message from your father?"

"I think it's a threat from Ralphio."

"That's what I meant."

Chloe watched quietly from her desk. Even she seemed to sense now was not the time to insert her usual running commentary.

"I think you should give this to him yourself," Jimmy said. "He's at his desk."

I glanced at the clock. It was just after seven in the morning. I'd barely slept more than two hours the previous night. I reasoned I could sleep when the case was over. It would be my Christmas present to myself.

"The chief's in already?" I asked. "This office?"

"He's taking this case seriously," Jimmy said. "He wants to catch Ralphio. And find your father."

"You mean, now that Nick Ralphio is involved in this mess, the case is officially important," I said darkly. "A name like that, and there's a big chance for some favorable publicity. The mayor will like a big arrest right before the holidays. I can see the headlines already. 'Jingle All The Way to Jail' with a nice big picture of handcuffs and Ralphio's face beneath it."

The room had gone silent as I'd been speaking. I glanced toward the door. Normally, my stomach would already be sinking as I realized the chief was standing in the doorway, listening to every word I'd said. Normally, I'd be worried for my job. I'd be itching from the embarrassment of the situation even if there was a kernel of truth to what I'd said.

I was already rising from my seat, latte in hand, when the chief asked to see me in his office. It was a true testament to my mental, physical, and emotional exhaustion that I felt nothing more than that dulled sense of numbness as I followed him from the room. On my way out, I grabbed the note in the evidence baggy from Jimmy.

The chief sat behind his desk. He didn't exactly invite me to sit in the chair opposite him, but I was tired, so I sat anyway.

"I should apologize," I said. Even my words felt like they were slow coming out. Like they spilled out of me like thick molasses instead of taking on their normal brisk cadence.

"That's the worst apology I've ever heard, Rosetti."

"Sorry," I said, feeling like I was watching the exchange from a television somewhere.

It didn't feel like I was sitting in this office, facing the chief, saying these words. I also couldn't find it in me to muster up any excuses. I wasn't even sure I was all that sorry for what I'd said. My thoughts were a bit of a jumble.

"This note is from Ralphio?"

I gestured toward the evidence baggie. "I assume so. I found it on my door last night. I'm guessing you won't get any prints off it, but it hasn't been touched by anyone except the person who put it on my door."

"A message from your father?"

I nodded. "A follow-up from Ralphio's threat at the club, in my opinion. I don't have a lot of hard forensic evidence to back it up."

"I think it's a pretty safe assumption for the moment, though we'll explore all other avenues as well."

"What would you like me to do?"

"Go home."

"Excuse me?"

"Go home, Kate."

Again with the first-name use. The chief rarely called me anything but Rosetti. I was having a hard time knowing why the sudden shift. Gem had started it; the chief had continued it, and I had to wonder if it was something to do with feeling sorry for me. As if these people were finally seeing me as a human instead of a detective because my father was missing.

"With all due respect, sir, I can't go home right now. We're closer than ever to cracking this case wide open."

"Which case, exactly?"

"The—" I caught myself walking right into the chief's trap. "The murder of Gavin Harris."

The chief gave a knowing nod. We both knew I'd fallen for his little trick.

"You're tired. You would never have slipped up under normal circumstances."

"You're sending me home because I'm tired?"

"No. You know why I'm sending you home. I was hoping I wouldn't have to write it out on a report card for you."

I leaned back in the chair and tapped my knuckles against the desk. "You think Gavin's murder is connected to my father's disappearance."

"We're getting to the point where it's unreasonable *not* to make that leap."

"We don't know for sure."

"Ralphio blew up a club last night and killed two people. Immediately before, he had an altercation with you and mentioned your father who, ironically, not many people know is missing. There's been no press on it."

"Word travels in their circles."

"You mean criminal circles."

"I don't completely understand their circles, but sure," I said. "If that's what you want to call it."

"You're too close to the case, Rosetti."

"Not Gavin's case."

"I think you're losing sight of which case is which. I'm not sure there's a line anymore. Whatever line you've drawn in the sand between your business and personal lives has been washed away."

"Christmas is in three days," I said. "I promised my mother that I would have my father back by then. I can't break that promise to her."

"We're working on it."

"I know. I'm not saying you're doing a bad job."

"I heard what you said," the chief snapped. "You think we're on the case now that Ralphio's involved. I won't deny that's partially true."

I waved a hand to thank him for his honesty.

"But not for the reason you think."

I stared at the chief. "What do you mean?"

"I knew your father back in the day. He was older than me, but I worked with him for a bit."

"You did?"

"Back when I was a beat cop. Fresh out of the academy."

"I didn't know that."

"I don't make a habit of telling people every detail of my history. Unless it's relevant."

I nodded for him to go on.

"I always liked the guy. He made a mistake, a wrong choice, but he's not a bad guy."

"You have that weird loyalty code too, huh?"

"Everyone has a loyalty code," the chief said. "Yours is the strongest I've ever seen. It just veers more toward the black and white boundaries of the law. It's almost completely un-influenced by your feelings on a subject. It's what makes you a great cop."

Again with the somewhat backhanded compliment. At least what people thought of me was consistent. I wasn't sure what to make of it, but I wanted to hear more from the chief, so I kept my mouth shut.

"Your father helped me out of a scrape back in the day. The details are not important," he said before I could ask. "Ever since then, he's had my loyalty."

"Even when he went to prison?"

"I agreed with the conviction. I also agreed with his release when it was time. Angelo Rosetti took it like a stand-up guy. He served his time without complaint. He knew what he did was wrong. That's the difference between him and others."

"What, so you think he changed?"

"No."

The chief's answer surprised me. "If you don't think he's reformed, then why do you think he deserves to be out on the street?"

"I don't think he needed to reform who he was," the chief said. "He's always been a good guy at heart. Even when he made the wrong choice, his heart was in the right placc. He didn't need to change who he was, Kate. Trust me. He's not going to make the same mistake again."

I shrugged, not completely seeing the difference. What I did understand was that my chief felt like he owed my father something.

"We're going to find him. We're going to get Ralphio in the process," the chief said. "I'm not going to let you down."

"Thank you, sir."

"But if I let you talk to me the way you did in front of the other cops, I'd lose all respect." Chief Sturgeon rose. "You're off the case. Officially. You'll turn over all evidence you have to the team. We'll keep you apprised of our progress."

"Chief, you can't do that."

"I'm going to have Chloe step into your role for now. She'll work with Jimmy on the Gavin Harris case."

"But she's still new."

"Jimmy's not. They're capable of following up on leads together. Not to mention, we've got a half-dozen men and women working the Ralphio aspect along with your father's disappearance. I have a feeling we might find that the cases are even more intertwined than we think. We've got it covered."

"Sir, that's completely unfair."

"It doesn't matter what you think, Detective. You're off the case. Go home. Get some rest. After the holiday, I'll assign you to a new homicide, and you can start fresh."

I recognized the hard look on the chief's face as I stood. I gingerly made my way out of the room. I tossed the evidence baggie with the note onto Jimmy's desk as I strode past him. I didn't say another word. Didn't need to. It was clear by the look on Jimmy's face that he knew what had happened.

It was just as clear by the look on Chloe's face that she was completely clueless as to what had happened. I was sure Jimmy would fill her in before I got to my car. I had half a mind to think that Chloe was due on a plane sometime soon to visit her boyfriend, and I had half a mind to go back and let the chief know she couldn't take my spot. Then I realized that was no longer my job. Temporarily, I didn't have a job. I didn't know what to do with myself.

I debated calling Russo to get his advice before I realized I didn't have a boyfriend either. When it rained it poured.

As I made my way to my car, I was surprised to find a colorful car pulling in next to it. A few seconds later, the bright yellow car had parked and out climbed Gem. He looked as frazzled as I felt.

"Detective," he said brusquely, "do you have a minute?"

I looked over my shoulder at the precinct. "For now, it's just Kate. And yes, I have plenty of minutes."

Chapter 22

I was in Gem's car a few minutes later. He was driving somewhere, and I hadn't asked where we were going. He hadn't told me either. Frankly, I wasn't sure if he knew where he was taking me, and I didn't care.

"It's Mindy," he said finally. "She's gone."

"I'm getting a sense of déjà vu," I said. "She's gone? You mean, she's been kidnapped? Again?"

"I don't know."

"Where are we going, Gem?"

"I also don't know."

"Start from the beginning, and tell me what happened."

"The last time I talked to her was at your place. You heard how that went. She was upset with me. I didn't give her concerns adequate attention, and now she's gone."

"Gem, you were dealing with an explosion in your venue that left two people dead. You had every right to be a little distracted from your personal life."

"Even so, it doesn't change the fact that now she's gone."

"Any signs of a struggle? Have you reported this to the police?"

"I'm telling you now. You're the police."

"I'm not technically on duty anymore. I have to call this in officially."

"Give me a little time. Let them know when you get back to the precinct. I'm sorry to take you away from your caseload."

"No, I mean, I've been temporarily dismissed. I'm too close to the case," I said. "The chief thinks the murder case I was working is linked to my dad's disappearance."

"Do you think it is?"

"Very likely."

"So it was the right choice?"

"Maybe technically," I said. "But that doesn't change the fact that it still feels like the wrong choice to me."

"Of course. It's murky."

"I have to call this in, Gem."

"Just hear me out."

"Five minutes."

"Twenty minutes," he said. "I left her several messages. Maybe she'll get back to me."

"Fine."

Gem drove in silence for a while. "There were no signs of a struggle. I told you she was staying with her best friend."

"You mentioned it."

"I talked to her friend last night. Mindy left her place last night just after we talked."

"Did she make it home?"

Gem nodded. "Her keycard swipes show she made it back to the penthouse at Gem Industries. I saw the video footage myself. She made her way in and out. No signs of distress noted by my head of security. I don't believe she was under duress at all."

"You think she popped back to your place to grab some things?"

"Our place," Gem said. "It will be our place in two days."

"Right, sorry."

"It was not a hard assumption to make judging by the fact that she packed a suitcase and walked out of the building. She wasn't exactly held at gunpoint. I have video of her car leaving the parking lot shortly after. She was alone. Nobody followed her."

I was beginning to see the issue. The issue wasn't that Mindy was actually missing. It was that she'd left, and Gem wasn't quite sure how to handle it. I suspected he'd come to me for moral support more than my sleuthing skills.

"I'm sorry, Gem. Maybe she just needed some air. The footage coming out of Sapphire last night was pretty grisly. It's a lot for anyone, let alone someone getting married to the owner of the place."

"She's defended vicious murderers in court. A little bit of press footage of a fire isn't going to spook her. It was me. I screwed this up."

"You don't know that. Maybe—"

A minute later, Gem's phone beeped. He pulled over to the side of the road and looked at it. He expelled a breath. "It's her."

"Mindy?"

"She's at her aunt's house," he said. "She told me she's fine and she needs some space."

"That's great news."

"We're halfway there," Gem said. "Her aunt lives in this little cottage on the river. I need to swing by and just check on her, just see her, before we turn back."

"Are you sure that's a good idea?"

"No," Gem said. "But I've always fought for what I wanted, and I always apologize when I'm wrong. This time I need to do both. I need to show Mindy I'm willing to fight, and I need to express how sorry I am for causing her pain."

"I was wrong, you know," I said softly. "I'm sorry I doubted your relationship with Mindy. Moments like this show me how important the two of you are to one another. I shouldn't have been so negative when I heard the news of your wedding."

"You were just looking out for me. Everyone wondered if it was the right choice." Gem gave a faint smile. "Mindy and I included. You were the only one honest enough to say what you were thinking aloud. Maybe that's why I like you so much. Maybe it's why Mindy respects you so much, even if she pretends not to like you."

"Oh, I don't think she's pretending."

Gem turned us off a highway and led us down a long, winding road in silence. I was wondering how long we were going to be driving when eventually he stopped. "That's her car."

"I have a strange request," I said. "Can I go in first?"

He glanced at me. "She's not going to be armed. I don't need law enforcement protection."

"I don't mean for safety reasons. I'd like to go in first. Alone. I'd like the chance to talk to her."

"This is between me and Mindy."

"You brought me along," I said. "While I agree this is a matter between the two of you, I'd like the opportunity to talk to her. Please."

Gem seemed to hear something in my tone that convinced him. "Fine, but I hope you know you shouldn't feel obligated. In no way do I think any of this is your fault."

"It's just something I need to do."

Gem gave a nod that showed he respected my argument enough to oblige with my request. He sat back in his seat. "Her aunt's name is Marie."

I stepped out of the car and made my way to the front door. Gem had described this place as a little cottage on the river, and the description couldn't have been any more accurate. The tiny home was white on the outside with cute red shuttering. I could see remnants of a garden and terracotta pots sitting outside, covered in snow as I made my way up the shoveled path.

The outside of the house glimmered with Christmas lights despite the fact that it was morning. The sun was obscured by clouds, and the lights added a certain cheer to the gloomy day. I raised a hand to knock on a door covered by an enormous evergreen wreath.

A woman wearing a long robe tied at the waist answered. Her hair was a pretty silver color and was swept back in a low bun. She wore no makeup, and it looked like I'd interrupted her morning routine.

"Marie?" I asked. "My name is Kate Rosetti. I was hoping to talk to your niece. Is Mindy here?"

"She is," Marie said. "Does she want to talk to you?"

"Probably not," I answered. "But it's very important."

Marie's eyes seemed to go through a series of calculations. Eventually, she nodded and gestured for me to come inside. "I reckon it must be important judging by the state Mindy was in last night when she showed up here. She's on the porch. Can I grab you a cup of coffee? It's hot and black, and frankly, you look like you could use it."

"I sure could. Thanks for the hospitality."

Marie gestured to a three-season porch that'd been mostly converted to a four-season porch by a wood-burning fireplace in the corner. It looked old fashioned and perfectly cottage-like. The walls were mostly made of windows, and the room had the feel of a greenhouse. White wicker furniture lined the edges of the room, and a matching coffee table sat in the center. On the table was a tray with two coffees and some fresh chocolate chip cookies. I could smell the scent of baking still lingering in the house.

"Mindy," I said. "I'm sorry to interrupt. I was hoping we could talk."

The lawyer was seated on a love seat across the room. She was curled up with her legs tucked underneath her. She wore a soft-looking pink tracksuit and stared outside at the gentle snow that'd been falling all morning.

Mindy gave no sign of hearing me. Marie chose that moment to enter the porch. She handed me a cup of coffee, then quickly swooped her own off the table in the center of the room. Then she disappeared just as quicky as she'd arrived.

"I know I'm probably the last person you want to see," I said, "but I felt like I needed to talk to you. I hope you'll at least hear me out."

"I'm not going anywhere." Mindy turned to look at me. She reached for her coffee and cupped her hands around it. She raised her eyebrows. "What do you want? I assume Alastair pointed you here?"

"He's out front waiting in the car. He only allowed me to come in because I asked him to. He didn't ask me to talk to you."

"Of course. He'll do anything you ask him to do."

"It's not like that," I told her. "He called me because you disappeared on him in the middle of the night. After the last time that happened, he was concerned." I didn't want to dredge up old memories of her kidnapping. "Two people were killed in an explosion that targeted one of Gem's businesses last night. It was a threat to him. He was just worried about the person he loves more than anything."

When Mindy didn't respond, I took a sip of my coffee. Marie had been right. It was fresh, black, and strong. I felt an immediate jolt.

"You look like a wreck," she said. "You look even worse than me."

"Thanks."

Mindy gave a little smile. "Just telling it like it is."

"I am a wreck," I said, feeling like, at this point, honesty was the only way to go. "It's been a rough week."

"Right."

I sat down in a chair, taking a similar pose to Mindy and tucking my legs beneath me. There was something soothing about this place. The soft snowflakes flickering around us, safely outside the glass walls. The warmth of the fireplace, the fresh cookie scent, the hot coffee, the soft cushions. Marie's cottage had the ambiance of a lovely sort of haven, and I could see why Mindy had chosen here of all places to escape for a short while.

"It started with my father's disappearance," I said. "The next day, things escalated with a gruesome murder. A family man was shot up on the sidewalk outside of the grocery store."

"Sounds like an average day in the life of a homicide cop."

"Fair enough. Took a turn for the worse when I found out the victim's wife was pregnant with a second baby."

"Ouch."

"Last night, there was an explosion I felt responsible for. Barely an hour after I learned about that, my boyfriend broke up with me."

Mindy looked up. "Russo dumped you?"

"I guess that's one way to say it."

"Why?"

"I'm not entirely sure. We're still sorting through things. It's more of a break for now until we can figure things out."

"He didn't give you any sort of reason?"

"Mostly because I haven't been able to commit to more. Neither of us have," I said, unsure of why I was opening up to someone like Mindy before I'd told any of my closest friends about the breakup. Maybe it was the exhaustion. Maybe it was the comfort of Marie's home. Maybe it was because it felt therapeutic to just be honest with someone who wouldn't sugarcoat things. "Neither of us have been willing to let go of our jobs. We can't grow closer if we don't see one another."

"And neither of you saw that coming when you entered into a long-distance relationship?"

"You really don't mind kicking someone when they're down, do you?"

"I'm just being honest."

"I know." I waited a beat. "Thanks."

"Are you sure that's the real reason?"

"You said it yourself. We were both aware it was an issue from the very beginning. Our entire relationship was a ticking time bomb, just winding down until one of us couldn't take it anymore."

"Bad choice of words."

I registered what she said a beat too late. "That's part of what triggered it. Jack realizing that we were both putting our jobs before the other person. We just couldn't commit to making the changes that needed to happen to get to the next step in our relationship, so he wanted to take a step back. Give us some time to breathe. Surely you can understand. I know how you feel about your career."

"I was drunk the other night when we were talking."

"So was I. That doesn't mean the conversation we had wasn't somewhat honest."

She shrugged. "You *are* honest."

"So are you."

"I guess that's one thing we can agree on."

"Mindy, I didn't come here to unload my crappy week on you. I understand this hasn't been easy on you either, and I have some explaining to do."

"No, you don't. This situation is between me and my fiancé."

"While I agree, I'm here of my own accord because I feel the need to apologize."

"For what? Alastair makes his own decisions. You didn't force him to do anything."

"I asked him for a favor on behalf of the police department yesterday," I said. "I was desperate. I promised my mother that I'd have my dad back by Christmas. I was willing to do just about anything to make sure I didn't break that promise."

Mindy looked into her coffee.

"I should never have asked him for that favor." I swallowed hard. "However, because I did, two innocent people are dead. The woman's name was Gayle, and she was only twenty-two. The man was Freddie. Twenty-eight. Both of them dead because of my selfishness, and I'm going to have to live with that for the rest of my life."

"It's not your fault." Mindy's voice was dulled. "I've defended a lot of bad people in my life. They always rationalize what they've done, that it was someone else's fault, but the truth is, it's nobody's fault but their own." Mindy stared out the window. "Nobody put a gun to the guy's head who set the bomb. There were other ways to resolve whatever issue was occurring. It's his fault exclusively. I don't even like you, but I need you to believe that."

"Maybe, but if I hadn't been there—"

"What? If you hadn't been doing your job?" Mindy's eyes bored into mine. "That's what you were doing. You were looking for your father and hunting down a killer. Do you understand what I just said? The men behind this are killers. They deserve to be behind bars, and that's coming from the person paid lots of money to make sure that doesn't happen to some very bad people."

"Thank you for saying that."

"You'll find your father." Mindy sounded confident. "You're the best. I know it, Alastair knows it; everyone knows it. It's why people are drawn to you."

"I didn't come here to talk about me. I came here to apologize if I've made a difficult situation harder. I never intended to. You should know nothing has happened between me and Gem, and he has only been assisting me because I abused my role as a cop and asked him for a favor."

"You didn't abuse anything. Alastair doesn't do anything he doesn't want to do."

"Regardless, I'm sorry."

"Thanks, but I don't accept."

"I promise you—"

"I know nothing happened between the two of you. I trust Alastair, and you're so honest I'd be able to tell if you were lying." She shrugged. "There's nothing to apologize for. You are allowed to have friends and so is Alastair. You were friends before I came into the picture."

"Then why'd you run off last night?"

"I was overwhelmed. The bomb, the wedding, it's all a lot. Alastair was with you working on the case, so I knew he wouldn't be coming home. I didn't want to be alone. Plus, I needed some time to think."

"Think about what?"

"What I really want."

Mindy seemed to be on the verge of telling me something important. She hesitated, biting her lip.

"Why the hell is it always you who I'm talking to about this stuff?" Mindy asked. "I don't even really like you."

"So you've said," I mumbled. "Then again, I haven't told any of my friends about my breakup. I don't know the reason why I confided in you, but it should at least tell you I understand how you're feeling."

"The threat of mortality sort of puts things into perspective," Mindy said. "What if Alastair had been in the club when the bomb had gone off? What if I'd been there? What if..." She took a deep breath. "It's stupid to play the what-if game because we are both still here. But still, *what if*? It makes a girl think."

"Are you second-guessing your wedding?" I asked, surprised. "Because of the bomb? That shouldn't be a reason for you not to get married. It's a traumatic event, and it's understandable that you're shaken. Not to mention your nerves were probably already frayed, seeing as your wedding is in two days. And Christmas the day after."

"Do you think Jack broke up with you because of Gem?"

"What?" I was taken aback by the change of subject. "Jack knows there's nothing between me and Gem. Aside from this case, frankly, I haven't even seen your fiancé in months. Not to mention, I told Gem yesterday that I wouldn't be coming to the wedding."

"Why?"

"Because my presence seems to only cause problems at events related to your wedding," I said. "As a friend to Gem, I only want what's best for him. And right now, that's for his wedding to go off without a hitch."

"Huh. You really do care about him. As a friend."

"I care about all my friends."

"You mean it too. You only see him as a friend."

"Yes. I still love Jack."

She nodded, digesting. "You don't have to skip out on the wedding."

"I do," I said. "I told Gem I was declining the invitation. And I won't be bothering him with any more favors. It wasn't fair of me to drag him into cases like that. The two of you will be free of me. Well, after I get a ride home. Otherwise, I'd be sort of stranded here. But I guess I could always call a cab."

She gave a little smile. It was almost friendly. "You're not so bad, Rosetti."

"I hope you're not doubting your feelings for Gem."

"No, I have never doubted my feelings for Alastair," Mindy said. "I know I love him. I know he loves me. Our marriage will be a good one."

"Good." I stood. "Well, then, I guess this is goodbye. And congratulations."

"I hope you reconsider your invitation. I know it would break Gem's heart if you couldn't be at the wedding."

"I don't think so," I said. "I'm confident it's the right choice for everyone."

"Kate—"

Whatever Mindy had been about to say next never made it out of her mouth. At that moment, heavy footsteps sounded behind me. I whirled around just in time to see Gem rushing into the porch.

"I know where he is," Gem said in a rush. "Your father."

"What?" I asked, rising to my feet. "What do you mean?"

"Mindy, hi," Gem said, out of breath. "I'm so sorry, sweetheart—for everything. I don't know what Kate told you, but I'm sorry. For everything. I'm also sorry for this, but I can't stay. I need to get Kate back to the precinct. Her father's life is at stake."

Mindy's mouth parted in surprise.

Gem rushed across the room and planted a kiss on Mindy's lips. "I'm so glad you're okay. Please, please wait for me here. We'll talk about everything when I get back. Whatever you need, whatever you want, I'll give it to you. I love you."

I felt like I had whiplash watching Gem's movements. I'd never seen him so agitated before, so flustered. I couldn't imagine what had set him off. A text from a friend? A sudden revelation? I took one last look at Mindy, mumbled some sort of goodbye, then I followed Gem out of the cottage and to his car.

"What's going on?" I asked as we each took our seats. "What happened?"

"It's not what happened," Gem said. "It's what I realized. Something that might be important."

"What could you have possibly realized that will tell us where my dad might be?"

Gem looked at me. "You know how I used to be friends with Ralphio? Or something like that."

"Yes."

"I happen to know about a place he keeps that's quite private. Special events only."

The way Gem was being purposefully vague, I got the idea he didn't want to share details with me. He glanced my way.

"I like you Rosetti, but you're still a cop," Gem said. "I'd prefer to keep a few things about my past on a need-to-know basis."

"Okay. What about this place?"

"It's remote. No internet or Wi-Fi. Forty minutes outside of the Cities—from here, it's only about a ten-minute drive. The location is what made me think of it."

"But if people know about this place, why would he use it to hide my father?" I asked. "Don't you think he'd choose a place that everyone on his friend's list doesn't know about?"

"I wouldn't say everyone knows about this place," Gem said, edging toward being cryptic again. "I haven't been there in almost a decade. Last I heard, he retired this place a few years ago and moved locations. He does that every now and again. I think most people assumed he'd sold it—I know I had—but I am wondering if that's not true."

"So Ralphio's got a secret place that's off the grid. Only a few people know about it, and most of those people are probably criminals. The house is probably under some assumed name or shell corporation, which is why Asha hasn't found it."

"That's about the extent of it."

"I've got to call this in," I said. "If my dad's being kept there, I doubt he's being held alone. There will be guards. We need backup."

"I already called the chief." Gem cast me a sideways glance. "Sorry for going behind your back, but I thought the news might get you feeling like committing vigilantism. I couldn't take that risk."

"Gem, I'm not stupid."

"No, but it takes a lot longer to get here from the precinct. Jimmy's on his way with a team."

"If you're right, I'll owe you everything."

"You don't owe me a thing."

My phone ringing interrupted the moment. Russo's name flashed across the screen. I hesitated, but eventually I hit answer. A part of me was wondering why Russo was calling so soon. My gut told me it was worth the two seconds of conversation it would take to find out.

"Hey," he said on the other end of the phone, "I hate to skip right over the conversation we had last night, but I've got some important news for you."

"Okay, go ahead," I said. "You're on speaker."

"Hey, Jones."

Gem cleared his throat. "It's Alastair Gem."

There was a beat on the other end of the line. "Of course. Kate?"

"You can talk in front of him."

"I'd prefer not to comment on an active investigation in front of a citizen."

"That's too bad seeing as I'm a citizen right now," I said. "I was taken off all my current cases."

Russo cursed. "I'm sorry, Kate."

"Gem might have discovered the location of my father. We're on our way to check it out right now," I said. "Anything you want to tell me you can say in front of him."

I could sense that every rule-following bone in Russo's body was telling him to hang up the phone. But something stronger won that battle, and finally, Russo gave a cough, and I could imagine him steeling himself to do what he thought was right.

"Gavin Harris was in witness protection. Your assumptions were correct. The identity they set up for him was under Charles Marlo."

"That's the name we found on him," I said. "We assumed as much. It's my belief he made a few additional identities on the side because he was exceptionally paranoid of being found out."

"Yeah, for good reason."

"Did they give you the file?"

"Nothing so generous," Russo said. "They gave me enough. Your victim testified in a trial against Howard Donovan."

It took me a long moment to place the name. "Hold on a second: is that the guy who was arrested a lifetime ago?"

"Almost thirty years ago," Russo said. "One of the worst contract killers for the mob this country has ever seen. Last I read, his body count was in the seventies."

Even Gem reacted to that number. But he kept silent, listening. The only sign he'd heard was the flicker of an expression that crossed his face.

"I don't understand," I said. "How could Gavin Harris have testified against him? I don't know Gavin's real age, but I'd put him in his mid to late forties. That would make him a teenager, at most early twenties, when the case went to court."

"Correct," Russo said. "He was only a kid. It was part of the reason the courts cut him such a good deal. And get this. Howard Donovan had a signature style of killing."

"I'm not going to like this, am I?"

"He sprayed people down with bullets in public places. Always a drive-by. Rarely any witnesses. Never a spec of DNA at the scene of the crime."

"That's just how Gavin was killed. They were sending a message. I should've seen it."

"The case was thirty years ago. I doubt anyone was combing that far back."

"How'd they eventually catch Howard Donovan if he was so careful?"

"One botched job was all it took. Donovan shot a guy outside a liquor store that had just installed security cameras the night before. Pure bad luck for Donovan. Pure good luck for the cops. It hadn't been there when he scouted the place out the day before."

"And Gavin?" I asked. "How does he play into this?"

"Howard Donovan was in the process of teaching a new guy the ropes."

"Gavin Harris—or whatever his name was then—was Donovan's apprentice. A contract killer in the making."

"Bingo." Russo sighed. "Gavin was in the foster system when Donovan recruited him. The kid had been left to fend for himself when he was thirteen years old and his mom died of an overdose—Gavin found her."

"That's terrible."

"Donovan scooped him up at eighteen, took him in, fed and clothed the kid. Gave him a taste of the good life."

"All while teaching him the 'family' trade."

"Yep. Gavin had killed one person at the time of the court case. He was showing signs of wanting to get out of the business when Donovan was caught. The FBI didn't even have to put pressure on Gavin to spill the beans. He was looking for help."

"In exchange, he got a light sentence and was put in witness protection?"

"Bingo again."

"Well, this is starting to make sense. Parts of it," I said. "But does that mean my father's disappearance and Nick Ralphio's bomb really have nothing to do with Gavin Harris's murder?"

"I didn't say I was finished," Russo said. "I'm just getting to the good part."

I groaned.

"Guess who was one of the cops that brought Donovan down?"

My stomach started to sink. "Angelo Rosetti?"

"Your dad was young and hungry. It was his first big break, the Donovan case. He was the one who picked up the footage and made the arrest."

"Why would Ralphio kidnap him, though? He doesn't have a link to Donovan." I hesitated. "Or does he?"

"Gavin Harris wasn't Donovan's first apprentice."

"You're kidding me," I said. "Nick Ralphio was linked to Donovan?"

"Back then he didn't go by Ralphio. Nick Ralphio adopted his mother's maiden name later in life, sometime in his early twenties. Back in the day, he was known as Nick Steinbach. Or, if you were in the mob, you might know him as Little Nicky."

"Because he was young?"

"I think it was ironic," Russo said dryly. "Little Nicky carried a big gun. He's been linked to nine shootings during the time he ran with Donovan but was never convicted. Guess how all his shootings went down?"

"Drive-by, big gun, no witnesses?"

Russo confirmed. "Which means I think you might have a hit man who came out of retirement to go after Gavin Harris."

"This is worse than I thought," I said. "How has Nick Ralphio never been convicted for any of those shootings? That's insane."

"Don't forget Donovan racked up seventy bodies before he got caught. It's fortunate Ralphio decided to get out of that game and focus on the money before he could add to the tally. But that's not where it gets really interesting. The really interesting part is that someone admitted to all of the killings Ralphio was linked to in order to take the blame off his shoulders."

"Howard Donovan?" I asked. "I suppose if the guy had already been sentenced to a billion lifetimes in prison, what was a few more billion years?"

"Yep. Ralphio and Donovan were tight. Father-son-type relationship. Twisted though it was, I think they loved each other in a way, or at least had earned each other's loyalty."

I expelled a long breath. "Fast-forward to today. If Ralphio caught sight of Gavin Harris, he'd want revenge. After all, Harris is the one who put Ralphio's mentor in prison."

"Donovan took the fall for Ralphio. Ralphio was making things right in his own horrible way."

"I hate this criminal loyalty code," I said. "It's stupid."

"Sure can be," Russo agreed.

"What about my dad?"

"I don't know exactly why Ralphio chose now to go after him, but I have my theories," Russo said. "What do you think?"

I remembered my conversation with Patrick, how Patrick had mentioned Gavin and Ralphio's names together. How my father's eyes had lit up.

"Gavin Harris would've been essential in the case my dad and the team built against Howard Donovan," I said. "My dad might've felt protective over him, especially since Harris had been nothing but a kid at the time."

"That was my theory too. I'd go one step further and bet Ralphio was worried your father would try to warn Gavin. Why he kidnapped him instead of killing him, I'm not sure. Maybe he had a longer-term plan that hasn't been realized just yet."

"It's all speculation," I said, "but I think you might be onto something."

"Kate, if even a tiny thread of our theory is true, this is far more dangerous than I ever imagined. You need to be careful."

"We called for backup. We're on our way to a possible location where they might be hiding my father."

"You're essentially a civilian for now. Don't do anything until Detective Jones and the team arrives."

"Thanks for the information," I said, holding off on making any promises. "I appreciate it."

"Kate—"

"I'll talk to you later, Jack," I said. "I have to go."

"Good luck. And Gem?"

"Yes?" Gem responded, surprised.

"Don't let her get hurt."

Gem's face was grim. "I'll do my best."

Chapter 23

"This is the place?"

Gem nodded. "This is the place."

Alastair Gem had pulled off to the side of the road before we reached the house in question. Up ahead, about a hundred yards or so away, was the house in question. Ralphio's old place didn't look abandoned—in fact, it looked quite well kept. The home was perched on a lot with sweeping views of the St. Croix, and I was certain the land itself was probably worth a big chunk of change. The home was blocky and modern with big windows and sharp, clean lines along the exterior. The lawn was well maintained if not flashy. It looked like some rich person's lake house.

When I told Gem as much, he shrugged. "A boarded-up house in this neighborhood would draw attention. Ralphio probably hasn't set foot in the house in years, but that doesn't mean he lets it go to crap. It doesn't take much for him to hire a cleaning crew and a landscape company to keep up appearances."

"I suppose." I squinted and glanced out the window. "You think my father's in there?"

"I think he's probably in the boathouse."

"There's a boathouse? Of course there's a boathouse."

"It's around back, down by the lake. It's not visible from the road. In fact, there's a sharp drop to get down there. Nobody would see anything. Nobody would hear anything. Ralphio's lot extends for acres. The nearest neighbor is several miles away."

"How far away is Jimmy?"

Gem looked at the clock on the dash. "If he left when I called him, they can't be more than ten minutes behind us. Twenty if they needed a few minutes to gather some resources."

"We'll wait here, then," I said. "Your car's not exactly inconspicuous."

"That sounds reasonable—"

Gem's sentence was abruptly cut off as the glass behind us shattered. I ducked and pulled Gem down with me. I was acutely aware of a warm liquid on my hands, but when I looked into Gem's eyes, he seemed alert.

"I've got my gun," I said. "I'm going to go out the door. Stay here."

Gem nodded, his face going steadily paler. When I reached for the door handle, I saw blood on my hands. Gem's white shirt was soaked through with red.

"Gem, you're hit."

"Just a flesh wound," he said. "I'm fine. Where's my phone? Call Jimmy."

"They can't get here any faster than they already are," I said. "I'm going out. We're sitting ducks in the car—keep your head down."

Gem tried to argue, but I'd already pushed the car door open and was in a crouch on the ground next to the vehicle. I moved quickly around the front of the vehicle, trying to put Gem's car between me and the shooter. I hadn't seen where the shot had come from exactly, but it must have come from the wooded area of land that spread away from Ralphio's house.

I wondered if Ralphio had been the shooter. If he was as good at killing people as Russo had said, it was a miracle Gem and I were both still alive. For now.

I could hear Gem making a call on his phone, warning Jimmy that we were under fire from an active shooter. I couldn't make out anything else, and I had no clue how long it would be until backup arrived.

I continued moving in a crouch until I reached the driver's side door. Pulling it open, I reached a hand up and touched Gem gently on the shoulder.

"Gem? Are you okay? Where are you hit?"

"I'm fine," he muttered. "Stay down, Detective. Jimmy's five minutes out."

Five minutes didn't sound like a long time, but in a situation like this, it might as well have been five years. If we were dealing with Nick Ralphio, then we were dealing with an experienced killer. If we were dealing with one of his security guards, we were also probably dealing with a trained killer. Whoever it was knew the lay of the land better than us. This was their home turf, and they held every advantage in the book over us.

Gem fumbled for something under the seat. A moment later, he pulled out a gun that he held in his hand with suspicious comfort.

"Gem—"

"It's legal and registered to me," he grunted. "Now's not the time for reprimands, Detective."

"Just stay in the car, then. Don't shoot if at all possible."

"I'm not leaving you out there alone."

Gem slid out of the car, gently pushing me aside. His left arm seemed like it wasn't quite functioning correctly. He held the gun loosely in his right hand. Together, we crouched on the driver's side of the vehicle, keeping the car between us and Ralphio's property.

The minutes clicked by like molasses. The air around us was still. A thin layer of snow dusted the grass. Our breath puffed before our bodies. There was no sign of movement anywhere. The trees were too thick around the driveway for us to see anything. The Ralphio home remained completely still.

Then came the scream. It was a male voice, distant but distinct.

"Dad," I gasped. I turned to Gem. "I've got to go. Wait here."

"I'm coming with you."

"Wait here," I repeated. "You need to send backup after me."

I couldn't waste any more time, so I had to hope my explanation was good enough. I burst out from the side of the car and zigzagged toward the tree line, immersing myself in the thick foliage where I could. It was hard to blend in when the world around me was turning into a winter wonderland, but if the killer could do it, so could I. The breeze around us was picking up, whipping snow in every direction. Visibility was decreasing by the second.

I didn't see Gem anywhere and said a little prayer that he'd actually listened to me and stayed behind the car. I had to push onward. The new developments had made me suspect there was only one person here watching my father—the shooter.

I began sprinting in a wide arc around the house, keeping my head low and dodging between the evergreen trees. I made it to the rear of the house a minute later. I could see the boathouse below, down a steep cliff, just like Gem had said. The situation was even more precarious seeing that it was winter, and the incline leading down to the water's edge was sure to be slick with ice.

I started skidding my way down the hill at the sound of a second scream. I hit a particularly slippery patch and took a tumble, just barely righting myself before I reached the boathouse. By the time I pulled myself to my feet, the door to the boathouse had swung wide open. There stood Ralphio himself. He had a gun to my father's head. My father's nose was bleeding, and his eye was black and blue.

"Just in time," Ralphio said. "Good to see you again, Detective."

"Kate, you shouldn't be here." A drop of blood dripped from the corner of my father's mouth as he spoke. "Get out of here while you can. I'm already a dead man."

"Dad. Are you okay?" I asked. "What's he done to you?"

"Tell her," Ralphio said. "Tell her how kind I've been to you. Especially once I realized it wasn't really you I wanted."

"What are you talking about?" I asked. "I thought you went after my dad because he helped put your buddy Howard Donovan away."

"I told you she'd figure it out." My father glanced at Ralphio. Despite his blood-smeared face, the pride was evident in his eyes. "You messed with the wrong detective. She'll get you this time."

"Was it worth it?" I asked, interrupting their banter. "All of this?"

Nick Ralphio looked confused for a beat. "Worth what?"

"You're doing this for Howard Donovan, right? He's like a dad to you, your dark guardian angel. But he'll also be the reason you lose it all. You're going down, Ralphio. If you had just let Gavin Harris go on living his life, none of us would be here."

"You don't understand anything about my world," Ralphio said. "There are codes to be followed, and there are consequences for people who break those codes. Especially for snitches."

Ralphio spit on the ground. It landed next to the droplets of blood from my father.

"You're right," I said. "I don't understand your world. I think your honor codes are stupid. Killing people is never the answer."

"You don't have to understand my world, but you'll play by my rules." Ralphio winked at me. "In fact, I think you understand loyalty better than you let on. See, you and I, we're not so different."

"Everything about us is different."

"No, we just have different goals. You want to save the world, which is boring. I want to enjoy it."

"By killing people?"

"Here's the deal, Rosetti. You have a choice. I put a bullet in your father's head right now, or you trade places with him."

"No," my father said. "Don't do it. I'm a dead man either way."

"You understand me, don't you, Kate?" Ralphio looked me in the eyes. "You know I'm a man of my word. A man of honor, even if you don't agree with my rules."

I hesitated. A part of me did believe him. I'd seen enough of his world to understand the way things worked. I trusted that he'd make good on his awful promises.

"Why?" I asked.

"I could kill your father, but it wouldn't do much for me," Ralphio said. "It would upset you and your family, sure. But what else would it accomplish? I already killed the man responsible for putting Donovan away. Now it's my turn to prove a point."

"You're trying to tick off Gem."

"I'm not trying to tick him off," Ralphio said softly. "I'm going to break him. See, he didn't follow our little code—the one you loathe so much. He needs to understand why what he did was wrong. Now, come with me, Detective, or your father's dead in five seconds."

"I'll do it." I set my gun in the snow and raised my hands. There was no way I could get a shot off before he ended my father's life. I wasn't going to risk it. "I'll do it."

"Kate, no." My father tried to wriggle out from Ralphio's grasp, but it was obvious he was undernourished, exhausted, and injured. His efforts didn't amount to much.

Ralphio smiled. "Good."

Then Ralphio raised a foot and booted my father near the waist, hard enough that he fell over and lost his balance. My dad rolled down the embankment a few more feet before he slid to a crumpled stop.

"Reach for your weapon and you're dead," Ralphio said. "I'm going to get your gun, and you're going to come with me. Any funny business and your father's dead. I've got guys who'll make that happen on Christmas morning as a little present to your mother. Understand?"

I nodded, numb. The hardness in Ralphio's eyes was unlike almost anything I'd ever seen before, and I'd seen a lot. He was a true psychopath. I could feel it in my bones, and he wouldn't hesitate to pull the trigger—any trigger—if he deemed it necessary.

Ralphio took a step forward, and as he reached for my gun, there was the crack of a shot in the chill of the air. I hesitated, unsure where it'd come from. I glanced at my father, noting his face registered surprise as well. Then I glanced at my feet where Ralphio had stilled.

Slowly, he tipped over, a pool of blood blooming beneath him. It colored the snow as I kneeled next to him. I quickly retrieved my weapon and stripped him of his. Then I patted him down to feel for more weapons. I removed a knife from his waist, but that was all I could find. Then I began to apply pressure to his wound to stop the bleeding.

Only once that was underway did I glance up the hill. There, I saw Chloe Marks, completely frozen in place, her face as white as the snow around her. She still held her weapon before her as her face registered shock and horror.

I looked into Chloe's eyes, and I felt a wave of sadness for her. She had acted on instinct and training, and now it was all sinking in. She was wondering if she'd killed her first man. Then I turned back to Ralphio and continued my efforts to save his life.

Chapter 24

An hour later, the paramedics were loading Ralphio into the back of an ambulance. He'd regained consciousness, though he was in critical condition. The paramedics assured Chloe that Ralphio would likely survive, but it would be touch and go for a while. I had no doubt Nick Ralphio would survive—a man like him wouldn't give up easily.

My father was located in a second ambulance, fighting off a checkup of his own. They'd mostly determined that he was fine aside from severe dehydration, a few cuts and bruises, and a broken rib. He'd spent the last hour thanking Chloe profusely for saving my life.

Chloe was just finishing up giving her statement to another officer on scene. Ralphio's property was swarming with cops now. The chief himself had arrived not long after the paramedics had pulled up. Jimmy, Melinda, and Asha were all around despite the fact there were no dead bodies to deal with.

The second Chloe was released from her interview, I swooped in and grabbed her arm. I pulled her off to the side of the road and carved out a small bubble of privacy so we could talk.

"Hey," I said softly, "are you okay?"

Chloe nodded, but it was shaky. "I think so."

"He's not dead," I said. "You didn't kill anyone."

"I almost did. I missed the kill shot by an inch."

"Even if you had killed him, it would've been an easily justified shooting," I said. "He had a gun to my father's head.

He was in the process of kidnapping a cop. We have him linked to several murders."

I glanced over at Gem, who was calmly getting bandaged up. He was quiet. He'd barely said a word since backup arrived. I did notice the gun in his hand had suspiciously disappeared, and I suspected that if I checked his secret little compartment beneath his seat, I might find it. Of course, I wouldn't be checking any such thing after all he'd done for me.

"I could've killed someone today, Kate."

"But you didn't. And you saved my life."

She looked down. "I'm going to resign."

"What are you talking about? If it's because I've been calling you an intern, I'm sorry. I'll talk to the chief about getting you promoted to detective. You've certainly proven yourself worthy of the title."

She gave me a thin smile. "I was already thinking about quitting before today. This just confirms my choice was correct."

"But you're very competent at your job."

"Thanks," she said. "I know I could make a good detective. Lately, though, I've realized I like the thinking part of the job better than the shooting part. I'm just not cut out for it mentally or emotionally."

"But—"

"Yeah, yeah, I knew the job description when I went to school for it," she said. "But until you hold the gun and stare someone down. Until you pull the trigger..."

"I know." I squeezed her shoulder. "I understand. Nobody can prepare you for it."

"That's not all. I'm supposed to be in DC now with Agent Brody."

"Did you skip your flight?"

"I couldn't leave you alone out there." She gave a small smile. "I rescheduled for tomorrow. No big deal."

"I'd say sorry, but I'm not actually sorry," I said. "I'm relieved because who knows where I'd be right now without you. How'd you get to the boathouse first, by the way?"

"I don't know," she said. "It's like my brain shut down, and I just acted. When I arrived at the scene with Jimmy, Gem was waiting to direct us down the embankment. When I saw the blood on him, I just knew."

"Your instincts were correct."

"No offense to Jimmy," she said softly, "but I'm faster than him, and that's the real reason I made it back there first."

I couldn't help but crack a smile. "I think he'd agree. Let's just blame it on the chicken wings and not his age."

She laughed, though it was dry. "I knew I had to act or it might be too late. I just ran until I saw what was happening. I took the first shot I could get. Probably my only chance."

"It was a good shot. The timing was perfect."

"Luck."

"Some of this job is luck," I said, thinking of the Howard Donovan case and the lucky break that had finally ended his long career. "Sometimes it's on our side; sometimes it's not."

"Anyway, I wasn't supposed to be here because I was supposed to be with Maxwell. Did you know he asked me to move in with him? He wants to marry me."

"That's great, Chloe. Really great."

"I know it's fast, and I'm not totally ready to be engaged yet," she said, "but I think that is where I see this relationship going. If I want to fully invest in my life with Agent Brody, then I need to make a choice. I either stay here and work with you, or I move out there and find a new job."

"I understand."

"I'm sorry. I just can't find a way to rationalize choosing a job over potentially losing the man I love more than anything. It's just not a risk I'm willing to take. I can't fathom the idea of missing out on something so beautiful in exchange for a career that can be so devastating. Yes, this job can be rewarding, but it's not all I want out of life. I want a family and kids, and today, I just realized the sacrifices I might have to make to ensure that happens."

"I understand," I whispered again. "For what it's worth, Chloe, I think you're making the right choice."

"You do?" She looked confused. "But you and Jack..."

I knew what she was getting at, but she was hesitant to say it.

"Russo and I broke up last night," I said. "It wasn't working because we've both chosen our jobs over one another. If you really love Agent Brody and see a life with him, you should pursue it."

"Does that mean you and Russo are giving it another go?"

"Not yet," I said, the words tasting sad as they came out. But I also knew it was the only option for now. "We're different people than you and Agent Brody. I'm different than you, Chloe. Your right choice and my right choice might be two very different choices."

"Thank you for understanding," she said. "I wish things were different. I've loved working with you."

"You've been the second-best partner I've ever had." I winked at her, and she laughed. "Seriously, you will have a wonderful career whatever you decide to do."

"Actually, there's one thing I was hoping to ask you. A favor."

"Sure. A recommendation? You could try applying to the FBI. They'd be lucky to have you."

"Nah. I'm not ready to leave you guys yet," Chloe said. "Asha mentioned something about maybe contracting out some tech work to me. All stuff I can do on the computer remotely. We can start small, on a case-by-case basis to see how it goes. I already know how she works, her processes, and the systems. All I'd need is a computer and a WiFi connection."

I caught myself grinning broadly. "I think that's a great idea."

"Really?"

"Plus, you could expense business trips back to the Cities," I said. "You'll need to pop back now and again to check in with the team, won't you?"

Chloe reached up and threw her arms around me. "Thank you so much, Detective."

"It's Kate," I told her. "I'm basically a civilian for now, remember?"

Still grinning, Chloe nodded over my shoulder. "I think someone else is waiting to talk to you.

Turning, I found Gem standing a few feet away. His arm was wrapped in a sling. His shirt was stained with blood. The snow continued to swirl down around him as Chloe backed away.

"Gem," I said, "I'm so sorry."

"Sorry?"

"I got you shot two days before your wedding," I said. "I don't know if they'll be able to alter your tux in time to accommodate a sling."

"What, this?" He gestured to his arm. "It's just for looks. I'm fine, really. I mean it when I say it's a flesh wound."

"I'll ask the paramedics about that later," I said, letting the humor fade from my words as silence fell over us. Our banter had come to an end, and now it seemed like neither of us knew what to say.

"I really am sorry," I said. "I shouldn't have brought you out here alone, but—"

"It was your father. Nothing else needs to be said."

"I still wish I hadn't involved you in any of this."

"I'm glad you did. It's the most I've felt alive in a long time."

"Don't get used to it," I said. "Getting shot is no way to get your thrills."

Gem smiled. "I think I'm good for a long time now."

"Glad to hear it."

"Well, I should get back to Mindy." Gem waved to his injured arm. "When I walk in looking like this, I'm going to have some real explaining to do. Not to mention apologizing."

"Thank you for everything."

"Same to you, Detective."

"And, hey, congratulations," I said. "You deserve a nice, long, uneventful life together with Mindy. I mean that in the nicest way possible."

"I know you do."

I nodded as he took a step back. Before he turned to go, he looked over his shoulder.

"Merry Christmas, Detective."

"Merry Christmas, Gem."

Chapter 25

"Hey." I pulled my door open to find Russo standing on the other side. "I'm glad you came."

Jack Russo stood on my front steps. He wore jeans and a jacket that wasn't heavy enough for Minnesota winters. He didn't have a hat or mittens on. He also didn't have a suitcase with him.

"You showed up," I said. "Do you want to come inside?"

"Actually, I told the cab to wait for me."

I glanced behind Jack and saw an Uber driver putzing on his phone across the street from my house. "You didn't have to come all this way in person if you weren't planning on staying. Whatever you wanted to tell me you could've been done over the phone."

"That wouldn't have been right." Jack gave me a half smile. He looked sad, reserved, but still as handsome as ever. "We deserve better than that."

I nodded but didn't speak. My mouth felt dry.

"You decided not to go to the wedding?" Jack asked. "I mean, I assume not, seeing as it's Christmas Eve and you're at home, not at the ceremony."

"Yeah. It felt like the right choice." I glanced down at the clock on my phone. "They should be walking down the aisle right now as a matter of fact."

"So why *are* you home alone on Christmas Eve?" Jack asked. "I thought you'd be with your parents."

"I wasn't sure if you'd gotten on your flight or not. I'm heading over there later," I said. "But just in case, I wanted to be here."

"I'm sorry for the vagueness. We didn't wrap up our case until this morning," Jack said. "I hopped on the first flight out afterward. I didn't text you in case you'd decided to go to the wedding. I didn't want to change your mind."

"What would you have done if I wasn't here when you got here?"

Jack shrugged. "I hadn't thought that far ahead, to be honest."

"Fair enough."

"So, are you okay?" Jack asked. "I heard about what happened the other day."

"Thanks to you, we got to my dad in time, and he's fine. Everyone's okay. Even Ralphio will live."

"I didn't do anything," Jack said. "It was Gem who figured things out. Maybe if I'd tried a little harder earlier on, your case wouldn't have gone so far south."

"Jack, that wasn't your job."

"No, but you were my girlfriend."

"Past tense," I said quietly. "Sounds weird, doesn't it?"

Jack nodded. "I don't love it."

"But you didn't come here to get back together, did you?"

He watched me carefully. "No. I think you know that too. I don't think you're ready to get back with me either."

I swallowed. I didn't want to agree, but I also couldn't disagree. We were in an awkward sort of stalemate that neither of us was really happy about.

"I just wanted to tell you how much you mean to me, Kate," Jack said quietly. "Even if it's not the right time for us to be together right now, that doesn't mean it won't ever be right. At least, I hope not."

"That would be nice."

"You don't sound optimistic."

"I don't know," I said. "It's hard to picture things changing."

"I don't know," Jack echoed with a little smile. He raised a hand and ran his thumb along my cheek. "A little birdie told me that Maxwell Brody is clearing out half of his closet to make room for his new roommate."

I smiled. "I'm happy for him and Chloe. They make a great couple."

"I can't agree more. We'll be happy to have Officer Marks out in DC. I know Brody is thrilled, even if he won't say it aloud to me."

"Yeah, I can't picture him as the sappy type."

"Nah, but he's smitten. They'll be married within the year, mark my words."

"Well, then, I guess if I'm invited, I can wear the dress I should be wearing tonight. I stupidly took the tags off and can't return it. I blame my mother."

Jack grinned. "I look forward to seeing you there."

Another moment of silence passed between us.

"I love you, Kate. I really do." Jack stepped closer. "I'm going to miss you."

"Yeah," I murmured, feeling my eyes smart with tears. "I'm going to miss you too."

"Don't be a stranger," Jack said. "Anytime you need a hand with a case, or you just need to talk, you know my number."

"You think we can do that? Be friends?"

"It would break my heart if we couldn't be," Jack said. "I don't blame you for the breakup. I don't blame myself either. It's purely circumstantial. Timing. Maybe someday, we'll have better luck."

Jack pressed his arms around me. I sagged against him, feeling worn and exhausted. It was awful how a decision we both knew was right could feel so wrong. I wiped away the tears that were on my cheek.

When we parted, Jack held my face in his hands and gave me a long, lingering kiss. "I'll see you around, Kate."

"Merry Christmas, Jack."

EPILOGUE

"Come on, Kate. Put it on!" Jane laughed and threw a bow at me from one of the presents she'd ripped open a few minutes before. "We're all going to match."

"It's weird," I said. "We're five adults. We don't need to match our pajamas anymore."

"Even Wes is going to do it, aren't you, sweetie?" Jane nudged her boyfriend. "Come on, be a doll."

Wes sighed as he pushed himself to his feet. "You're lucky you're cute. Because I'm not going to be looking cute in these."

I sat back and smiled, watching the adorable exchange between my sister and her boyfriend. I thought it might sting to be surrounded by couples this Christmas when I'd so recently broken up with the man I loved, but I'd been wrong.

Russo had left a couple of hours ago, and after a good, long cry in the shower, I'd changed into some fresh clothes and headed over to my mother's house. There, I'd found my mother and father cooking next to one another in the kitchen. Mostly my mother was doing the cooking and my father was getting in the way. Every once in a while, she'd swat him with a spatula or stick a wooden spoon in his mouth and ask him to taste the pasta sauce for the seventeenth time.

My sister and Wes were already there when I'd arrived. My sister had been sorting presents underneath the Christmas tree. Wes had been lounging with a beer on the couch being a great sport with the over-the-top Rosetti family spirit this holiday season.

It was strange, a blast from the past. I could almost picture us just like this, a family back when I'd been five years old. Sorting presents with my sister, running upstairs to wake our parents the moment the clock struck 6:00 a.m. I could imagine the half-nibbled cookies that Santa had left behind, the half-drunk glass of milk. The warmth of the kitchen and the smell of freshly baked goods. There'd been so many cookies made in that kitchen that my teeth hurt thinking about it.

"Kate"—my sister threw the matching pants at my head—"put them on."

I rolled my eyes, but I was outnumbered. My mom and dad were sitting on the couch, cozied up next to one another. My mother hadn't stopped giggling all evening. The way she touched my dad's arm every other second reminded me of a high schooler with her first crush. My dad seemed to welcome every second of it.

I grabbed the pajama set off the floor. In the hallway, I passed Wes, who was returning from the bathroom. He was dressed in a set of pajamas that said *Chillin' with my Gnomies* and had pictures of Christmas gnomes all over them. I snorted.

"Yeah, wait until you put it on," Wes said good-naturedly. "We'll see how you feel then."

I immediately stopped smiling. Then I disappeared into the bathroom and slipped into my matching outfit. I returned to the living room to a round of applause.

"It's a real-life family Christmas." My mother's statement was followed by a burst of tears. She sobbed into my father's shoulder. "I'm so happy. Thank you, Kate, for bringing your father back."

I shifted, uncomfortable—both in my new pajamas and from my mother's attention. I shrugged.

"I was doing my job," I said. "I'm just glad we got there in time. It's not even me you should really be thanking. It's Gem."

"Yes, well, he gets free coffee for life," my mother said. "You tell him that. Tell him to stop by the next time you see him, okay? I want to thank him myself."

A moment of awkward silence followed. Jane and Wes had attended the wedding earlier in the day. They hadn't said a peep about it. I didn't ask why they'd left the reception early to spend Christmas Eve with my family, and they hadn't offered any explanation. I'd just assumed it'd been at the request of my mother. Jane still had on her heavy wedding makeup. Wes seemed indifferent about the whole thing.

What was clear was that neither Jane nor Wes wanted to talk about the ceremony in front of me. It was almost creepy how intensely they were avoiding the subject. I was sure it was out of respect for me and my choice not to attend. After Jack had left earlier this afternoon, I'd turned off my phone. I hadn't wanted to hear any news or see any photos of the happy couple—I had just wanted to celebrate Christmas Eve with my family.

"Maybe I can kick off the evening with my present," Wes said, breaking the uncomfortable silence. "Since you sorted all the presents there, Jane, you'll have probably found the one from me."

"This one?" Jane held up a shoebox-sized gift with a grin. "I was counting down until I could open it."

"Go on," Wes said, "as long as that's okay with everyone."

We all gave nods of encouragement. Jane ripped open the package with the fervor of a five-year-old. She stopped when she found a much smaller box inside. Then, carefully, she flipped open the lid of the smaller box and gasped when she saw what was inside.

Attention quickly turned to Wes. He had quickly lowered to one knee before Jane.

"Jane Rosetti, I've loved you since the day I met you," Wes said. "I never used to believe in love at first sight. I didn't even believe in marriage until I met you. But I can't imagine my life without you. You have been the best thing to ever happen to me, and I'd be honored if you'd be my wife."

Jane burst into tears and threw her arms around Wes.

"Is that a yes?" he asked, bewildered. "Are you saying yes?"

"Of course it's a yes!" she exclaimed. "I love you, Wes. Can you put the ring on my finger? It's so beautiful! How did you know? I had no clue this was coming."

"He asked my permission," my mother chirped, obviously eager to get in on the action. "I could hardly wait. I was bursting with the news."

"I, uh, would've asked you too, sir," Wes said to my father, "but you were indisposed this week."

My father grinned. "You know my wife's word is what goes around here anyway. Congratulations, you two. I couldn't be happier for you. Any man who makes my daughter this happy is fine by me. Welcome to the family, Wes."

I stood and drew both my sister and Wes into my arms for a hug. I echoed the sentiments of congratulations and felt a warmth in the pit of my stomach for my sister. She truly deserved a good man, and Wes had proven himself to be genuinely perfect for her. If I hadn't already cried for the better part of an hour today, I might've even shed a few tears myself.

"Sort of ruins my present, though," my father said. "Annie, I feel a little stupid asking you in the wake of such a heartfelt proposal, but..."

My father hesitated. He slid off the couch and went to one knee. The same pose Wes had just vacated.

"I know I shouldn't steal their thunder, but I've had this ring for weeks, and I can't possibly wait a day longer." My dad paused and took a deep breath as he cracked open a box. "I have never stopped loving you. I'm sorry for all the mistakes I made that took me away from you. This past week, when I was forced to be away from you, was the worst week of my life."

"I know," my mother said, choked. "I felt the same way."

"Will you be my wife?" he asked. "Again?"

"Oh, of course, Angelo," my mother said. "I've always been your wife. I love you."

My parents kissed as the next generation applauded. After another round of hugs, we all took our seats and began calming down from the exciting turn of events.

"This does not mean we are having a double wedding," Jane said. "I'm just saying, Mom, you already had your shot. I love you, but I get the big, white, poufy dress, okay?"

"I've got a small ceremony planned in Hawaii next month," my dad said. "Those are the only calls I've been hiding from you, Annie. It'll be just family. A sort of informal renewal of vows. Then we can go down to the courthouse and sign documents. Okay with everyone? That leaves plenty of time for you two to plan your ceremony. Everyone will have forgotten about us by then."

What followed was a cacophony of agreement and questions and excitement about the upcoming nuptials, and my parents' re-nuptials. Jane couldn't stop staring at her ring. Wes looked like he'd sweated out most of his Christmas dinner. My mother and father huddled next to one another under a blanket as if they'd never let go. I was pretty sure I was the only one who heard the knock on the front door.

I rose from the couch. Everyone else was wrapped up in the joyous festivities, so they didn't notice me disappearing from the room. If anything, they probably assumed I needed a minute to myself. Or another sugar cookie. Or five.

I headed to the front door, wondering who was out and about on Christmas Eve. Pulling the door open, I felt my breath catch my throat at the man standing on the other side.

"Gem?"

***

It took a long moment for it to sink in that Alastair Gem was standing before me. I stared at him for a minute confused by his presence. Then it hit me that today was his wedding day, and he should be pretty much anywhere but here. With Mindy.

"Do you want to come in?" I stammered. "What are you doing here?"

"Maybe you can come outside for a minute," Gem said. "I won't keep you long. I just wanted to talk to you."

"Um, okay." I grabbed my jacket off a hook and wrapped it around me. I closed the door behind me to give us some privacy. "Why?"

He gave a laugh. "Beats me. Seems like I call you anytime I have a problem. I'm not sure I even think about it anymore—I just dial your number."

"Well, people do tend to call the police when they need assistance."

"It's not that sort of problem."

"I see."

The snow fell in light gusts. Unlike the other day at Ralphio's place where it had felt like a blizzard, tonight the wind was calm, and the snowfall was settling, merry, peaceful. The world around us was quiet. Lights twinkled in almost every window. The faint sound of Christmas music came from someone's home nearby.

"Mindy didn't show up."

"I'm sorry?" I looked up. "Show up where?"

"To the wedding."

"You mean she left you at the altar?" I asked, feeling my lips part in surprise. "Are you serious?"

"Technically it wasn't at the altar. I mean, when she didn't show up, I didn't bother walking down the aisle. I felt like enough of an idiot without doing that." Gem gave me a hollow smile. Pain pierced his eyes. "There was no wedding today."

"Is that why you're here? Because you think she's kidnapped?"

"No. She gave me a note," Gem said. "The gist of it was that she decided she wasn't ready to get married. Nothing to do with me. She explained that she loves me, but she was pushing us to get married for the wrong reasons. I talked to her briefly on the phone. She's on a plane tonight to somewhere in Japan. She doesn't have a return ticket."

"She couldn't have figured that out months ago?" I asked. "Or at least weeks ago?"

"It's not her fault. Our situation was complicated."

"It's a little her fault," I said. "She knew she was having doubts. She could've talked to you about them a few weeks ago—heck, even a few days ago. There was no need to leave you at the altar."

"I wasn't—"

"Yeah, yeah, I know," I said. "You weren't at the altar. I had no clue that the wedding didn't happen. My sister didn't say a word to me."

"I asked her and Wes not to. I told them I wanted to have a conversation with you personally."

"No wonder they were dodgy when I asked how things went."

"I needed a little time to get my bearings this afternoon. Then I came here."

"That sucks," I said. "I'm sorry. That's not the most eloquent way to say what I mean, but you know I'm not great at expressing myself. I do know that you really loved Mindy."

"I did."

"I believe she loved you too. If that gives you any odd sense of consolation."

"I have no doubt about it. We still love each other, but I think we both knew we were forcing a marriage for the wrong reasons."

"I thought you were all in on this wedding business."

"I *was* all in. I think we could have made it work. We would have been happy enough."

"Happy enough."

Gem kicked at some snow. "Not what you're supposed to say on your wedding day, is it?"

"It's okay to be bummed."

"I am disappointed. Heartbroken, even. But I'm not sure if it's because of the loss of Mindy or because of the loss of the life I imagined we would lead together. Of course, maybe that was all a fantasy. Maybe things never would have gotten better."

"I understand. I understand more than you know how two people can be in love with one another but can't be together."

"Is that right?"

"Russo flew in today."

"Ah."

"He didn't bring a suitcase."

"And where is he now?"

"On a flight home," I said. "It's over for now."

"I'm sorry, Detective."

"It's the right choice. It just sucks."

"Sure does." Gem nodded and shoved his hands into his pockets. "Makes me feel a little better to be here with you."

"It's good to see you. Plus, it's nice not to be the only un-attached person here." I paused, then wrinkled my nose. "I'm sorry, too soon. That was uncalled for."

"You got broken up with today too."

"Touché." I gestured toward the window behind me. "Heads-up, there are two happy couples in there. A couple of engagement rings. There's a lot of love in the air."

"I'm not against love." Gem's eyes landed on mine. "I be-lieve in it more than ever. Just a different sort of love."

"What sort?" I whispered.

"The sort that you can't walk away from," Gem mur-mured, "no matter what."

"Do you really believe that sort of love actually exists?"

"Absolutely."

"It's frustrating it's so hard to find."

"Maybe it's not meant to be so hard," Gem said. "Maybe it'll find us when we're ready."

"I hope you're right."

We stood next to one another, both of our hands shoved in our pockets, both of our hearts battered. Gem's sling was off, and though he moved his arm tenderly, it seemed like his wound wasn't as serious as it had first looked.

"What are your Christmas plans?" I asked finally. "I guess your Christmas Eve was a little jilted."

"Seeing as I'm not getting on a plane to Fiji, I guess I'll be playing it by ear," Gem said. "There's a little Chinese food place down the street from my place that's open late for take-out. A guilty pleasure of mine."

"Come inside," I said. "You should celebrate with us."

"No, Kate. I couldn't do that. It's your first family Christmas all together in decades."

"Well, since Wes is practically your brother," I said, "and he's now engaged to my sister, you're sort of family-adjacent."

He gave a short laugh. "Convoluted, but not bad."

"If that's not enough, then how about the tiny fact that you're the reason we're all here together in the first place?" I raised one shoulder to prove a point. "If you hadn't figured out that little nugget of information on Ralphio's old place, my dad wouldn't be here. My parents wouldn't be reengaged. I probably wouldn't be here either because I'd be hunting Ralphio."

"When you put it like that, I guess I could stay for one mug of hot cocoa."

"Extra marshmallows?" I asked. "A blop of whipped cream?"

"I couldn't say no to that."

I turned and opened the front door, letting the warm air mix with the cold. "I should warn you though; the way we serve hot cocoa at the Rosetti house is one of those cheap Swiss Mix packets with the little marshmallows already inside. None of this flown-in-from-Mexico cacao beans business that I'm sure they serve at your office."

Alastair Gem grinned as he stepped into my family home. "Detective, I'd be honored to celebrate Christmas the Rosetti way."

THE END

Author's Note

Thank you for reading! I hope you enjoyed another adventure with Detective Kate Rosetti and team. The next book in the series is already available for pre-order on Amazon and will be launching soon!

For additional information on book releases, please sign up for my newsletter at ginalamanna.com to be kept in the loop. And, if you enjoyed the book, please consider taking the time to leave a review at your retailer of choice. It is much appreciated and helps other readers find books they love!

Thank you for reading!

Gina

List of Gina's Books![1]

** **

Gina LaManna is the USA TODAY bestselling author of the Magic & Mixology series, the Lacey Luzzi Mafia Mysteries, The Little Things romantic suspense series, and the Misty Newman books.

List of Gina LaManna's other books:

Women's Fiction:
Pretty Guilty Women
Three Single Wives
Detective Kate Rosetti Mysteries:
Shoot the Breeze
Riddle Me This
Follow the Money
Riddle Me This
Nail on the Head
Sleigh All Day
Time is Money

Murder in Style:
Secrets and Stilettos
Lipstick and Lies
Mascara and Murder
The Hex Files:
Wicked Never Sleeps
Wicked Long Nights
Wicked State of Mind
Wicked Moon Rising
Wicked All The Way

1. http://www.amazon.com/Gina-LaManna/e/
B00RPQDNPG/?tag=ginlamaut-20

Wicked Twist of Fate
Wicked Ever After
Lola Pink Mystery Series:
Shades of Pink
Shades of Stars
Shades of Sunshine
Magic & Mixology Mysteries:
Hex on the Beach
Witchy Sour
Jinx & Tonic
Long Isle Iced Tea
Amuletto Kiss
Spelldriver
Mint Julep
Mermaid Mimosa
MAGIC, Inc. Mysteries:
The Undercover Witch
Spellbooks & Spies (short story)
Reading Order for Lacey Luzzi:
Lacey Luzzi: Scooped
Lacey Luzzi: Sprinkled
Lacey Luzzi: Sparkled
Lacey Luzzi: Salted
Lacey Luzzi: Sauced
Lacey Luzzi: S'mored
Lacey Luzzi: Spooked
Lacey Luzzi: Seasoned
Lacey Luzzi: Spiced
Lacey Luzzi: Suckered
Lacey Luzzi: Sprouted
Lacey Luzzi: Shaved
The Little Things Mystery Series:
One Little Wish
Two Little Lies
Misty Newman:
Teased to Death

Short Story in Killer Beach Reads
Chick Lit:
Girl Tripping
Gina also writes books for kids under the Pen Name Libby LaManna:
Mini Pie the Spy!

Made in United States
North Haven, CT
21 April 2023

35721491R00200